D1796181

Crossroads

By

Mary Ting

World Castle Publishing

http://www.worldcastlepublishing.com

This is a work of fiction. Names, characters, places, and incidents are products of the author's imagination or are used fictitiously and are not to be construed as real. Any resemblance to actual events, locations, organizations, or person, living or dead, is entirely coincidental.

World Castle Publishing
Pensacola, Florida

Copyright © Mary Ting 2011
ISBN: 9781937085759
Library of Congress Catalogue Number 2011931988

First Edition April 2011
Second Edition World Castle Publishing August 2011
http://www.worldcastlepublishing.com

Licensing Notes
All rights reserved. No part of this book may be used or reproduced in any manner whatsoever without written permission, except in the case of brief quotations embodied in articles and reviews.

Editor: Maxine Bringenberg

"*Crossroads by Mary Ting has it all: danger, romance, suspense, incredible characters and an original plot that is sure to thrill. The action never stops as good and evil battle to the death. This well written and fascinating love story will keep readers entranced.*" ReadersFavorite.com

Crossroads is a lovely, heartwarming story about young love and hope. It is a wonderful escape into the world of an ordinary girl, an extraordinary love, and the forces of evil that try to keep them apart. We loved it! **Michelle De La Vara**, Owner of www.InspiredByTwilight.com

"*Crossroads is an exciting debut book with a rich paranormal mythology, unique angel-lore, forbidden romance, action, suspense and plot twists. With her detailed writing and a plot that flow wells, Mary created a world I enjoyed visiting, and a story that was hard to put down.*" **Katie with Mundie Moms**

"*Watch out Edward Cullen! The angel Michael has officially given you a run for your money! Teens everywhere will add a new fictional boyfriend to their ever growing lists! OMWings! An amazing paranormal angel romance that stays with you long after the last page has turned. I need more!*" **Jennifer Howell with LateBloomerOnline.com**

"*Crossroads has it all: forbidden love, angels, and suspense. Ting characters are vibrant, vivid, gorgeously drawn, and told with sheer honesty. I really enjoyed it, I'm anxious to see what happens in book 2!*"**Faye with Rambling of a Teenage Bookworm**

"*Crossroads is mysterious with a fantastic plot. Not to mention handsome guys, a sweet young girl, and a Fallen that could threaten everything. Crossroads will keep you up into the wee hours of the night, and you will be begging for more!*" **Andrea Newkirk with Dark Readers**

"*With easy-to-love characters, a fantastical and unique story line, and a delightful romance, Crossroads will captivate readers of all ages. A heavenly debut!*" **Shari Bergquist at My Neurotic Book Affair**

"Crossroads is a beautifully written debut novel that has everything you need for a outstanding read. Forbidden love, danger, angels and demons. What's not to love?" **Siobhan Phinn with lovefantasyscifinovels blog**

Dedication

For my grandmother, Lucy Rhee, the reason this book was written. I know you are in heaven watching over me.

My husband, Richard, and kids, Joshua and Kaitlin, you are my life and the reason for my happiness.

Enormous thanks to Kristina, Linda and Jennie. They have dedicated countless hours in making this book possible. Kristina, the most creative person I know, who has been there for me from the start. For your motivation, enthusiasm and love of the characters that got us excited to move forward with the book. Linda, for constantly challenging me to improve the story and for your critical feedback regarding characters and plot. Jennie, for your vital editorial guidance and wonderful suggestions that were essential to the story's development.

Michelle, who has inspired me that dreams can come true and for all your support.

For my parents-for the person I am today. Roy, Maggie, Nancy, Lily, Jane, Jenny, Patricia, Hung, Gracie, Holly, Barbara and Ai for your support in everything I do.

For my little cheerleader, Sylvie, my number one fan.

To Karen, my publisher, thank you for taking a chance on Crossroads and for being such a wonderful person. Maxine, thank you for your professional editorial feedback and for being easy to work with. Clarrissa Moon, you have a big heart. Thank you for all your help.

For the readers of this book, fly with me through this incredible journey. Fall in love with the characters as much as I did and make Crossroads your place to be. Thank you for your support.

Our destiny can be examined, but it cannot be justified or totally explained. We are simply here.

Every man has his own destiny; the only imperative is to follow it, to accept it, no matter where it leads him.

— Henry Miller

Prologue

There was something different about her this time. He didn't know how long it had been since her last visit, only that she had blossomed beautifully, and he knew that it had been too long. His eyes were immediately drawn to hers; radiant like the sun. Instantly, he was mesmerized by her. He saw her now in a way that he hadn't before—almost forbidden.

Her long and lustrous auburn hair shimmered in the sunlight, tousled from the gentle breeze and brushing softly against her delicate face. She was striking in her simplicity, yet she took his breath away. A flawless painting was what he saw, and he couldn't believe she was here again—all grown up. In his eyes, she was perfect in every way.

He had always watched her from a distance, like a guardian protecting her so she wouldn't be found as a child. And just like the past times, she always looked lost, as if visiting for the first time, though she had been there many times before. What tortured him the most was knowing that he was unable to comfort her.

She was unaware of his presence, and there wasn't a glimmer of a chance that she knew he was just beyond her reach. An endless field of tall, thick grass was the only thing separating them, but would she ever be able to cross over? It was nearly impossible. He watched as she pushed and shoved, trying to pass through. But there was only one way in, and she would never know. He reached out his hand to help her and then stopped. It took every ounce of energy to refrain from letting her in. His fist tightened and shivered as he fought against what he wanted most—her.

Suddenly, she looked straight at him, her eyes sparkling like the most perfect luminous stars. He didn't twitch, but inhaled the moment as if she really did see him, for he knew instead that her eyes were focused elsewhere. Although she seemed a world away, he imagined feeling her sweet breath on his lips. He gasped at the thought, wondering why he was feeling this way. The heat that infused throughout his body wasn't anything that he had felt or remembered before, whatever was left of his memory. He was trained not to have these types of human emotions, and yet it confounded him how she appeared to have taken him over. He didn't mind at all. He liked the way she made him feel. After all, she didn't even know he existed, although a part of him wished she did.

He watched as a butterfly landed on the tip of her finger, and she let out a huge, heartwarming smile. The innocence of her smile sent desire to every part of him. He knew he was completely spellbound by this human being. If only he could breathe in her scent, embrace her in his arms, and feel her warmth just once, even if that was all it could be. In the end, he knew it was hopeless.

Gradually she started to become translucent, as if he had made her up in a dream. As always, she never stayed long, just long enough for him to want her even more. Where did she come from? When would he see her again? With these thoughts, he desperately tried to memorize every detail of her before she vanished.

"Claudia, don't go!" Michael whispered, knowing his pleas would make no difference.

Now he could see right through her as the brilliant sun framed the outer lines of her body, blinding him. He took a deep breath and let out a heavy sigh, knowing she would disappear. At that very moment, she vanished completely, leaving him utterly empty.

"Michael!" a voice called out from a distance. "What are you doing?"

Michael ignored the voice as he continued to gaze into the empty space, trying to figure out what he was feeling.

"Michael," the voice called out again.

Michael broke away from his thoughts. "I'm coming," he responded, annoyed by the unexpected interruption. He walked away from where he had stood, with tangled emotions he had never felt before.

Chapter 1

A Year Later...

I was swallowed up by darkness. I could feel my body begin to levitate off my bed. Slowly, I floated higher and higher. I had no control. Was this a dream? Then suddenly, I was running. Running toward something or someone; but why? As my feet made contact with the naked road, the grinding of pebbles was all I could hear. Clearly it was a hot and sunny day, yet not a drop of sweat developed on my brows. Nothing seemed familiar, so I stopped.

I began to feel anxious. Where was I? Why was I here? Then I noticed that to my right stood a vast field of sweeping brown grass that stood at least twelve feet high. I had to bend my head way back to see the tips of the blades. As I lowered my head, I saw her. Her presence was like a magnet grabbing me to the point where I could not resist her pull. I knew then that she was the reason I was running, so I started to run again. Every fiber of my being told me to follow her, but I didn't know why.

She was a vision of pure splendor. Her flowing white dress reminded me of a Greek goddess. Her dark and silky brown hair was tied up in a ponytail, not a single strand out of place. Her body was slender, with all the right curves, and yet something about her was different. I realized then that I hadn't seen her face. She began to pick up speed as if she sensed me closing in. I ran faster, but no matter how fast I ran, I couldn't catch up to her. My legs began to feel as if a ton of concrete had cemented them to the ground. Every ounce of energy I had could not help me catch this "divine beauty."

Overwhelmed with frustration, all I could do was watch as she floated far ahead, turned right, and disappeared into the field. I kept my eyes rooted to the spot where I thought she had entered the tall grass, and when I reached it, I turned and stopped. With both hands, I reached out and parted the thick brown grass to enter.

What I saw was breathtaking. A sea of clouds was beneath me. These were not ordinary clouds, though...these were the clouds you only dreamt about. White, fluffy, foamy whipped cream was how I had imagined Heaven's clouds would look...the kind of magical clouds you could walk on without fear of falling through, like being in the most realistic fairy tale. I began to wonder, slightly panicked, as to where I was and why I was in this place. Was I dead? How beautiful this place was, but was this "life" for me now? Had my wonderment of Heaven finally been answered? Then I saw her again.

She spoke politely yet with a sense of urgency. "Claudia, you need to leave. It's not your turn." I was in complete shock. How did she know my name? In hearing the power of her words and the trepidation in her voice, my heart leapt. I stood there, frozen, and as the fear that pierced every bone in my body subsided, her words became insignificant as I stared at this fascinating vision standing before me.

As I continued to stare intently, I slowly began to feel hypnotized. The intensity of the light surrounding her was captivating. It was as if this brilliance was the inner depths of her soul radiating toward me—something I wasn't supposed to see, pulling me closer. The strangest part was that I still could not see her face. I desperately wanted to know what she looked like, so I just stood there ignoring her order, hoping that maybe the light would fade. But instead, the intensity of the light became too much to endure. I quickly covered my eyes with both of my hands.

"Please stop," I pleaded.

She spoke again, but this time her voice was unforgiving and commanding. "If you know what's best for you, you must leave now before it's too late!"

Before I could say another word, from a distance, I heard a male voice, "No, Margaret!"

Suddenly I was falling at the speed of light. It was so fast. Darkness was all I could see. My stomach felt like it did when I rode on roller coasters at amusement parks. My body never seemed to catch up with the ride, and my heart felt like it was going to be ripped out of my chest. When was this going to stop? All of a sudden, my whole body jolted for a split second and then became still. I was no longer falling, but rather, I had landed on something soft and familiar...my own bed. Had this all been a dream? There was dead silence. As I lay completely still, I managed to slowly peel my eyes open, one at a time.

Confirming I was where I thought I was, I closed my eyes again. I tried to remember the details of my dream before they faded. This was one dream I wanted to remember. I began pondering all that I had seen and analyzing every detail. Suddenly, I was startled by the sound of my cell phone. My heart began to thump, and my body felt like it had jumped twenty feet into the air.

"What the—" I placed my hand on my chest, only to feel my heart beating uncontrollably. I had to calm myself so I let the phone ring several more times. Feeling annoyed that I had forgotten to put it on silent mode and still lying on my bed with my eyes closed, I reached over to my nightstand to answer the phone. I didn't want to get up just yet; I wasn't ready to start the day.

"He...he...ello," I answered. Irritation crept through me as I wondered who would be rude enough to call so early in the morning. I could have looked at the caller ID, but I didn't want to bother to open my eyes just to close them again. This better be important!

"Claudia? Claudia Emerson? Is that you?" she asked, practically yelling with elation.

It was Patty, the sweetest social butterfly among my friends. Instantly the irritation disappeared, but I wondered why she was verifying who she was talking to. After all, she was the one who had called me.

Before I could even say a word, she shouted, "Oh my gosh! Oh my gosh! I'm so glad you're alive! I thought it was you! I'm so sorry I called so early, but I had to know!"

Patty was so loud that I had to move the phone away from my ear. "It's me. I'm fine. Why are you—"

"Claudia Emerson, you scared the life out of me!"

Even with the phone at a distance from my ear, I could still hear her loud and clear. I scared her? How? My eyes opened wide with curiosity. "It's me, but what did I—" I asked as I placed the phone closer to my ear.

Patty interrupted, shouting again, "It is you! Thank God! Thank God! I thought it was you! I thought you were dead! I don't know what I would do without you!"

Dead? Had something happened to me? Was she somehow connected to the bizarre dream I had? "What happened?" I asked, worried what her answer might be.

"What? Seriously, you don't know?"

"Know what?" I asked and sat up.

"Ohhh," she said softly. "You didn't hear? I can't believe you don't know. I thought you would have been the first person to find out."

"Hear what?"

"Well, that doesn't matter. I'm just glad it wasn't you."

"Patty," I said calmly.

"I mean, not that I'm glad she's gone, but as long as it's not you."

"Patty...Patty!" This time I said it with more intensity.

"Gosh! What a relief. I was about to faint. I—"

"Patty!" I stopped her in the middle of her sentence.

"Oh...sorry. I got carried away. You know how I get when I get too excited. What did you say?"

"What happened? I still don't know what you're talking about!" My tone was intense and urgent, needing an answer.

"Ohhh," I heard a big sigh. "Claudia Emerson died last night. You know, your friend who has the same name as you."

"What?" I asked in disbelief as my body stiffened, but it was more of a rhetorical question. I heard what she said, but I didn't want to believe it. "Are you sure? Are you sure you got the right Claudia? I mean, I just saw her last week. How could...I mean...I just saw her."

"I'm sooo sorry. I wouldn't have called if I wasn't sure."

"What happened?" I asked, still in disbelief.

Patty spoke slowly, providing me with all the details of the incident. Claudia had just been voted homecoming queen, and her date was the homecoming king. She was having the time of her life. They were going home after the homecoming dance and were driving through an intersection when a drunk driver ran a red light and collided with their car. Claudia was thrown head first through the front window. She died when her body hit the street below.

I sat completely still, unable to move or speak, as I tried to comprehend what Patty had just told me. It just didn't make any sense. It couldn't have happened. Claudia was not dead; surely it was a mistake. Patty's words brought me back to reality.

"Claudia, are you there?" Patty asked.

"I...I...what?" I replied, trying to come to terms with this gruesome truth.

Patty continued to tell me details of that tragic night. "I heard she wasn't wearing her seat belt because she didn't want to wrinkle her gorgeous dress. Oh my gosh! I just had a thought. I wonder if she would still be alive had she put on her seat belt."

"Uh...uh...," I replied.

"Claudia? Are you okay?"

"Um...what? Did her date survive?" I asked, ignoring her comment.

"I guess. I didn't bother to find out. Why? Do you know him?"

"No. I was just wondering," I said. I let out a heavy sigh as I played the images of what Claudia's accident would have looked like in my head.

"I won't be at church today. I'm scheduled to work all day. I can try to get out of work earlier."

"What? No...no. Don't worry, Patty. I'll be fine. Really, I'm fine," I tried to convince her as well as myself.

"Okay, but I'll come by after work. You may think you're fine, but I think you're in shock. I'll text you to let you know when I'm on my way."

"Sure, see you then," I said wearily.

Patty had started attending our church when we were both freshmen in high school. Her natural connection with people drew them to her, and instantly she became friends with everyone. She knew everybody and everything about them. I don't remember how it happened, but we immediately became best friends. It was an inexplicable bond that happened to two people without really having a reason.

Patty had delicate facial features, and her sweet voice was very pleasant, when she was not ear-piercing on the phone. Her tall slender body would make any girl envious, but that didn't bother me. She was my good friend; someone who I knew would be there for me through thick and thin.

After we hung up, all I could think of were "what if's." I just sat there, as stiff as a board, trying to make sense of what had just happened. Patty was right, I was in shock. You hear about things like this happening to other people, but situations like this never happen to someone you know. There was a quiet knock at my bedroom door.

"Are you all right, Claudia?" my mom asked. "I got a lot of phone calls wondering if it was you."

"I'm fine, Mom, I'll be right out," I replied.

That would explain why my mom's phone was ringing like crazy. I could imagine there would be a great deal of confusion and concern since Claudia Emerson, homecoming queen and now a drunk-driving victim, had the same name as me. What were the odds of having a good friend who had the same first and last name? It was strange and uncomfortable at first, but I had gotten used to it, since we had been friends and schoolmates since third grade.

There was another quiet tap on the door, and I heard Mom's voice again. "We need to pick up Gamma, and we should get to church a bit earlier."

As she spoke, I opened the door. We were face to face. As I nodded to respond, I was struck by the beauty of her face. I guess I had never realized it before, but she didn't look like she was in her late forties to me. In fact, she could probably have passed for my older sister. Her skin was as smooth as velvet, and there was not a wrinkle on her face. Her ebony hair reached just above her shoulders. At times I wondered what I would look like had I acquired her emerald green eyes. But instead, I inherited my father's brown eyes. I didn't know if I looked more like him than her, and I never would because we didn't have a picture of him. My parents had eloped, and shortly after, she was pregnant. Tragically, he passed away in a freak car accident before I was born. I hardly asked about him anymore since I knew that I was dredging up painful memories. It was already hard enough being a single mom, especially one working long hours as a nurse. Through it all, she was never a woman of complaints.

Fortunately for us, we had Gamma in our lives. Gamma was my grandmother's best friend and also my godmother. I was just a toddler when my grandmother passed away, and Gamma filled the void by visiting frequently. She never got married, so we became her family. She was a great help to Mom and took care of me, especially when she had to work the late shifts. Gamma pampered me, which was the best part. But at the same time, she sheltered me, perhaps too much.

Gamma and I sat in the back while Mom drove us to church. It was quiet in the car, and we hardly spoke a word, but Gamma held my hand the whole ride there as her way of comforting me. What was normally a short ride seemed twice as long as the anticipation of getting to the church settled in my stomach. Still feeling numb from Claudia's death, I walked to where my friends were standing. We hugged to say hello, but this morning it was a different kind of hug. I understood the meaning of these hugs...they were "I'm glad to see you alive" hugs. One by one, they got the physical confirmation they needed that I was alive. Then we all stood in a circle in dead silence. I guess no one knew what to say or how to react around me. They knew how close Claudia and I had been.

Receiving those hugs reminded me of how Claudia and I would hug every time we saw each other, with the exception of last week. I had seen her from a distance. We waved hello, but that was all. Claudia was missing a lot of church. She and I were starting to be more like acquaintances than friends. We had been best friends throughout junior high school, but our friendship drifted apart when we attended different high schools. It didn't matter, though, because the fact that we shared the same name bonded us forever.

As if having the exact first and last name wasn't odd enough, we also had the same hairstyle, and were even the same height. The differences were that she knew everything about boys and fashion, was more outgoing, and less sheltered than me. My thoughts began to reflect back to the last time I saw her. Why didn't I just go up to her and give her a hug? The more I thought about this, the more pain I felt deep in the pit of my stomach. Had I known that it was going to be the last hug, I surely would have held on tightly. Now it was too late, and there was nothing I could do.

Without warning, I felt an arm around me. It was John, dressed in his usual T-shirt and jeans. I looked up at him and noticed that his hair looked two-toned under the sun, brown with lighter highlights. He gave me a half smile, and I could feel his uncertainty through his body language. It was almost as if he wasn't sure whether his closeness was appropriate at this given time. After a few seconds, he finally spoke.

"Hey, Claudia, are you okay?"

"I think so. I'm not sure. I don't know how I feel right now. It's like a dream. Did it really happen?"

"Yeah," he said, as he tucked his hands into his pockets. I could tell he felt nervous because he changed the subject. "So where are we going for lunch?" He tried to sound cheerful.

"I don't feel like going today," I said in a monotone as I stared into space.

"Sure, I understand," he agreed, though he sounded disappointed.

There was an uncomfortable silence, which was unusual because John and I could talk about anything. None of us knew what to say as we stood next to each other. I was beginning to wonder how long we would just stand there when Marie broke the silence. "Come on, we're gonna be late for Mass," she said.

Inside, I felt overwhelmed with guilt and shame. I stared at the cross. I wasn't paying attention during Mass. In fact, I couldn't even recall if I placed an envelope into the donation basket. All I could think about was how I would never see Claudia again. I vaguely heard Father Roy speaking about the tragedy of Claudia's death, but all I could do was to dwell on the last hug I hadn't given or received. The strangest part was that I couldn't even cry. I felt no emotion. Wasn't I supposed to cry when someone I cared about passed away? Why wasn't I crying? I was always good at hiding my feelings, but this was impressive. Perhaps this numbness would carry over and get me through the funeral.

Chapter 2

It had been a week since my friend passed away. As much as I wanted her death to be just a dream, burying her was a reminder that it wasn't. Dreadfully, I looked inside my closet to look for something appropriate to wear. There wasn't much to choose from. My wardrobe consisted basically of jeans and T-shirts. Besides, it's not like I would have a funeral outfit just hanging there. It's something you don't expect to prepare for at such a young age, especially for a friend's funeral.

After fruitless searching, I finally found black slacks and a black button-down blouse. I couldn't remember when I bought these, but they were good enough. Maybe I should have gone out to buy something, but shopping for clothes to wear to a funeral seemed too morbid.

When we arrived at St. Thomas, Mom, Gamma, and I slowly walked down the aisle toward the front together. After we found a place to sit, I looked around. Looking out into an entire congregation of nothing but black attire overwhelmed me with sadness so I glanced upward. The sun's rays captured each color so vividly, illuminating a dazzling brilliance of light. Every color of the spectrum could be seen throughout the church. At the front, one could clearly see Jesus on the wooden cross. The cross was enormous and hung directly over the altar, which was made of light gray marble and stood as the focal point. I was mesmerized by the colorful stained-glass windows, The Stations of the Cross to be more accurate, portraying the stages of Jesus' life.

This was a special church. This was where all of our adventures began: the retreats, gatherings, and lifelong bonding between friends. It didn't matter if you were rich, poor, or had a different color skin. Anyone who attended St. Thomas found a way to make lasting friendships. I clearly remembered the first day Claudia and I became friends. It was an amusing moment for her and a dimwitted one for me. I smiled as I recalled the conversation that made us simultaneously laugh like silly schoolgirls. I had asked her what kind of jeans she was wearing because I thought they looked cute. She simply replied, "Guess."

So I did! I was a little bit scatterbrained since there were so many types of jeans, so I randomly picked a brand name. "Are they Gap?"

She responded back with a smile, "No, Guess."

I really didn't want to guess because I was not at all into that fashion stuff. Besides, I was a little annoyed that Claudia was finding this entertaining.

"Claudia, could you just tell me? I don't know too many brand names."

She replied, laughing hysterically, "You are so cute and naïve. Guess is a brand name."

I started laughing uncontrollably with her at this point; laughing at myself because all that time I thought she wanted me to "guess" the brand name of her jeans. That was all it took. Just like that, we became best friends.

My attention shifted to below the altar, and that's when I noticed a picture of my friend. It must have been her senior portrait. She was smiling, her hair flawless, and a look of contentment was on her face. This was the face I would never see again, one whose life was taken so abruptly by a drunk driver. Would I remember this face in years to come? How I wished that I could have exchanged some comforting words with her last week. I'm so sorry, I said to myself, as if she could hear me.

At that moment, the shock of her death disappeared, and reality settled in. My friend was gone forever, and I would never see her again. Tears started flowing down my cheeks, one after another. I had no control now. No matter how much I tried to hold back the tears and no matter how many deep breaths I took, tears were streaming down my face.

Stop crying. Stop crying, I commanded myself, but nothing seemed to work. I tried to fight back the tears, but that made the heartache heavier and more painful, as if I had been stabbed in my heart. The pain of her loss cut so deep, and I didn't know how I could say good-bye. It was worse than anything I had ever endured. Would I ever forget this pain?

What came next was a sight I had not prepared myself for — Claudia's mom. To be in the presence of a grieving mother was heart wrenching. Watching her mourn the daughter she loved, knowing she would never see her graduate high school or college, fall in love and get married, or have a child of her own to love the way she so loved her Claudia, made me cringe and tremble. Looking at the father who would never walk his daughter down the aisle and the sister who no longer had a confidant broke my heart, and I began to sob. My tears were no longer just for Claudia, but for the family she had left behind.

The pain had overtaken me, and I was gasping for air. My throat felt irritatingly dry, and my heart was beating too quickly for me to catch my breath. Just when I thought I was going to faint, I felt a warm body next to me. It was Patty. She had managed to slip in between Mom and me. As our eyes met, I saw her teary eyes. She simply took my hand and squeezed it to show me she was there for me. We didn't need to exchange a single word. Her sole presence made me feel better, and having Gamma, Mom, and Patty next to me gave me comfort beyond words.

After the funeral Mass, we all went to the burial site. Patty had to leave for work, so I stood next to Mom, Gamma, and my friends. I'd lost some of the comfort when Patty left, but I was thankful that she had even come at all. I knew she had come for one reason only, and that was to be there for me.

Saying good-bye to someone you love is hard enough to do. Having to watch them being lowered into the ground into what is basically a glorified box is excruciatingly painful. I couldn't say that I understood why some felt the need to witness this. A marker on the grass was all that was left of this dark and miserable day. Everyone was sobbing uncontrollably as we consoled each other. There was a brief moment of solace as we stood together united by grief, aching with agony. I didn't want to say good-bye, but I had no choice. Her family had no choice. Life would have to go on, and somehow they would find a way to cope with their loss.

Then I thought, if they had left for the dance just a little later or a little earlier, she would still be alive. I was raised through faith; believing in a higher power, knowing that all things happen for a reason beyond our control or ability to understand. Had they been at the wrong place at the wrong time? Or perhaps they were at the right place at the right time? I could only comfort myself by thinking that it was meant to be. It was her destiny to pass on to another world.

With these thoughts, I looked up to see the most perfect blue sky with beautiful fluffy white clouds. How I wanted to touch them. Then suddenly, I saw a hint of the sun's rays peeking out through the clouds. For a split second, it radiated down to where Claudia was buried, and then it was gone. Afterward, I saw the most vibrant butterflies fluttering around, disappearing almost as quickly as they had appeared. How odd. Had anyone else witnessed what I had just seen? I felt shivers running down my spine. I imagined her soul being carried away, the light acting as her guide. It was a beautiful sight in contrast to this sadness. In that instant, I knew Claudia's soul had gone to a peaceful place.

Claudia's death and the funeral took a toll on my body for the next couple of days. It was still difficult to come to terms with the fact that she was really gone and that I would never see her again. Did she suffer? What were her last thoughts? As these thoughts ran through my mind I fell asleep, only to dream again.

I was walking aimlessly and came across my elementary classroom. I hesitated to open the door, afraid to see what or who would appear in the classroom. Behind the door wasn't a classroom, but remarkably the biggest church I had ever seen. The strangest part was that I couldn't make out the back of the church. The rows of pews went as far as I could see, and there were no other doors.

As I looked around, I saw many children, ranging in ages, laughing and having fun. Either they didn't notice my presence, or they were simply ignoring me. Unexpectedly, I saw her from a distance, smiling at me. She motioned for me to come to her. I walked toward her, noting how her pale skin glistened from the sunlight that was projecting through the windows high above. How beautifully serene her face looked, like an angel, just the way I remembered it to be the last time I saw her. But Claudia was dead, and yet I could see her as plain as day. Was I dead too? This was the second time I questioned myself. How was this possible?

"Claudia, is it really you?" I asked, uncertain of what was going on.

"Yes, it's really me, and it's so good to see you. I wanted to see you one last time," she said, smiling.

As she placed her arms around me, I embraced her as tightly as I could. I don't know how long we stood there, but I didn't want to let her go. It felt as if I would be burying her all over again if I did. I was given this moment, and I knew that once we let go, she would disappear forever.

She whispered into my ear, "Good-bye, my friend."

Tears began gushing down my cheeks. She had known the burden I was carrying inside of me, how heavy my heart had been, not being able to give her that last hug before the accident. Please don't leave, was all that I could make out in my mind. Let me hold on to this moment a little bit longer, please! But just like that, she was gone.

I woke up bawling, with a tremendous ache in my chest. It was hard to open my eyes because the tears wouldn't stop. My whole face felt swollen. I knew it was a dream, but the pain was real. I finally managed to control my sobs so I could try to remember the full details of my dream, but the only part I was able to remember with any clarity was giving Claudia that final hug. A hug so real, it lifted the heavy brick from my chest. I wiped the last tears away, and with that came the realization that Claudia's hug had given me peace and comfort.

For the next several days, I replayed the dream over and over again in my head. I wanted to hang on to the memories of her being happy, rather than the memories of her tragic death. Thoughts rambled through my mind: Does such a place exist? Was it just a dream? Or did she visit me in her spiritual form? I vaguely recalled a conversation I had overheard that said if a person who passed on appears in your dreams; they were visiting you in some spiritual way. It was their only way to get in touch without frightening their loved ones. I knew dying was inevitable, part of the circle of life, but the big question was, what happens when you die? Do you float out and away from your body? Do you see lights? Is someone waiting for you to guide you in the right direction?

Some people believe in a place called Heaven, a home where your soul goes after life here on Earth ends. I often wondered what Heaven was like. Were our loved ones somewhere out there, looking down on us? What was the meaning of life, and did everyone feel the same way as me?

Besides Heaven, I was also captivated by the uncertain existence of angels, glorious, mysterious and powerful beings. As a young girl, with many years of Sunday school behind me, I learned that angels may appear as guardians, messengers, or avengers. By their own free will they had been divided—good angels and bad. The bad angels had cut themselves off from their Creator, consumed by jealousy and a desire to be powerful like Him, superior above all else.

That night, as I lay in bed thinking idly about angels, I thought about what they would look like. What was their purpose? Did they really exist? As I pondered these questions, I started singing, "Somewhere over the rainbow, way up high, there's a land that I heard of, once in a lullaby…" Unable to finish, I drifted off to sleep.

Chapter 3

I was back on the same dirt road, only this time I wasn't running. Oddly, everything looked familiar. Feeling a bit anxious, wondering if she would appear again, I began to walk cautiously. I was wondering why I was here again. Is it possible to dream about the same place? While contemplating this question, I tried to find an opening through the field. Using my hands as tools, I pushed and shoved every which way that would allow me to break through the blades of grass. No matter how much I pushed, all I could see was a vast wall of grassland. Feeling defeated, I thought I would try one last time. That's when he appeared.

"Don't you ever give up?" he said in the most hypnotic voice, appearing to be slightly amused by my efforts.

"Umm...," I said, stunned to see a face looking back at me. I stared at the most perfect, glorious face. I couldn't take my eyes off him. As his eyes pierced into mine, he stepped in my direction. I had no other choice but to walk backward, feeling intimidated, yet compliant of his authority. I wanted to look away, but I was deeply lost in his eyes. My heart was pounding, wondering what this guy could be doing in my dream.

He certainly fit the description of how I had envisioned the man of my dreams. He was at least six feet tall, with dark brown hair and deep warm brown eyes that were so inviting. He was lean and extraordinarily muscular, and his skin appeared to be made of satin. My heart was melting. It felt sinful admiring him this way. I wondered if he could hear my thoughts or feel my heart racing as he stared back at me. I began to feel my face become warm with embarrassment at the thought. Time seemed to stop as we stared into each other's eyes. No need for words, just alone in each other's thoughts. How I wondered what his were!

The tension broke when he spoke to me again. "What are you doing here? Do you want to be sent back like before?"

Hearing his velvety voice again gave me goose bumps all over my body. Send me back like before? I repeated his question in my head. I was confused. Then it dawned on me; it was his voice I had heard in my last dream. Although I felt frustrated and angered by his comments, I needed to stay calm.

"First of all, who are you? And what are you doing in my dream?" I tried to sound composed.

"Your dream? You think this is a dream? Think again," he said with a condescending tone.

Confusion began to fill my head, and I was angered again by his unfriendly remark. I wanted to yell at him for being so rude, but all I could do was stare at his stunning face. He was so attractive that I couldn't stop staring. Then he said, "Can't think fast enough? The answer is not on my face."

I looked away quickly and dropped my jaw. I couldn't believe he had just said that to me. My face flushed with embarrassment and anger. Was it that obvious that I was staring at him? I had to think fast and say something intelligent, but I was so infuriated that I couldn't think of anything to say. I calmed myself and looked at him again to speak, "I am dreaming, and you are not real."

"I'm real. There is no doubt about that. And you may think you are dreaming, but you are actually at the Crossroads, somewhere between Heaven and Earth, or between life and death, whichever you prefer."

He was so matter of fact, like he was telling somebody for the hundredth time. But his words were significant. I felt a chill run up my spine. Who was he trying to scare? How dare he lie to me!

"That's not true!" I began to argue. "There is no such thing, and this is my dream…perhaps a nightmare after meeting you!"

Apparently that was not the response he had anticipated. His cold stare was enough to make me wish I could take it back. "I see; perhaps I'll just disappear."

"No! Please! Wait! Don't go. I don't understand what is happening. Could you at least tell me how I got here?"

He arched his brows. "If you don't know, how am I supposed to know?"

"Well, I thought…I thought because you seem to live here?" I was hesitant to say those words because I wasn't sure.

"Don't assume anything!" he said sharply.

I was perplexed by his coldness. What a jerk! I didn't want to talk to him anymore, but I needed answers. "Is there anyone else I can talk to that may give me some answers? Perhaps someone…nicer?" Now I was being rude, but he had been rude to me first.

He hesitated to answer, looked away, and responded sternly, "No. There is no one else here."

"Really?" I fired back, vaguely remembering the lady I saw the last time I dreamt about this place. "You're telling me that you are the only one who lives here or…or whatever the reason…by yourself…absolutely alone." I was so furious that I mumbled my words. I didn't know if I made sense.

"I don't need to tell you anything, but if you must know, my answer is still the same." He paused a few seconds and spoke again with a smirk, "Labera lege."

"Excuse me?" I asked, wondering if I had heard correctly. Why was he speaking Latin? Was he playing games with me? I was boiling with rage.

He looked at me squarely in the eye. "Let me repeat what I said in simple language: read...my...lips," he said softly. "That's what I said."

So I did, thinking he was going to tell me something important.

"No, nobody else here," he said slowly and sarcastically.

I couldn't believe he just did that to me, but I didn't believe his answer. "You're unbelievable!" I shot back.

"I know I am," he said matter-of-factly.

"I didn't mean it in a good way!" I said coldly, wanting to burst his ego.

"I did," he said with his chin held up high.

Now he was just being egotistical, but all I could do was stare at his smooth kissable lips. Stop! I told myself. What was the matter with me? Why was I having these thoughts? I started pacing back and forth, and out of frustration, I yelled, "Ahhh! You are just...just...just..." I was lost for words again.

As I was having my little tantrum, he looked away. Then I thought, Maybe he is telling me the truth. Maybe there is no one else who can help me. Suddenly, a feeling of loneliness began to penetrate. I didn't know what I was doing here or what the significance of this guy in my dream could be.

I felt his stare from the corner of my eyes and as if he sensed my frustration, he asked in a calmer tone, "Do you have any idea why you are here?"

"No, I don't know why I'm here or how I got here...and you don't know why I'm here. So what do I do?" My voice trembled as fear set in. I became desperate for answers.

"Since I have no answers for you, perhaps you should go back." His tone was flat.

Had he not heard anything I said? Now I was beyond irritated with him. He wanted me to go back, and I didn't even know how I had gotten here in the first place. For a man who was so pleasing to the eyes, I began to think what a shame it was that he didn't have a friendlier disposition. Besides, this was my dream. I wasn't about to go back. In part, I couldn't go back. I didn't know how. He started walking through the field, and I had to make a choice. What would become of me if I stayed? What would happen if I followed? So I followed after him into the unknown.

Unexpectedly, he swiftly turned to me and said, "You shouldn't follow me, and you shouldn't be here. I don't care how you get back, but it's too dangerous here and humans are not allowed. You must go. Do you understand?"

I was about to give it to him with my words, but his warning had frightened me. If I was human, what was he? Reluctantly I nodded yes, but I really didn't understand. Who was this guy? Why was he here if not to help me? When he noticed that I stood motionless, he said, "You give me no choice." Then he shouted, "Davin, I know you're listening! Get her out now!"

Before I even had a chance to stop him, I woke up back in my bed. What the heck! The dream was so bizarre. I was extremely confused, and I didn't know if there was a rhyme or reason for any of it. It seemed so real, but clearly it had all been a dream.

A smile crossed my lips as I vividly recalled the man I saw. I couldn't forget his face. The curvature of his jaw, his smooth brown hair, and those eyes, so inviting—I could have stared at him forever. His voice was so intoxicating. It was distinct. I could hear it repeatedly telling me that I needed to leave. But why, I wondered. Then I thought about his lack of people skills, and I felt really annoyed with him. Oh, forget it, he's not even real. It was just a dream, I thought to myself as I looked at the clock.

"Oh, shoot." I dashed out of bed when I realized I would be late for school if I didn't hurry. Almost falling flat on my face putting on my jeans, I promised myself that this wouldn't happen again. I hated being late, especially for school.

As I entered my English class, the second bell rang. Everyone was already seated, and I noticed Kristina looking at me. Her seat was two rows to the right of me.

"Hi," I whispered, and collapsed on my hard wooden seat, letting out a heavy sigh.

"You okay?" she whispered.

"A long story, I'll tell you later," I whispered back. But there was nothing to tell because it was just a dream. How silly it would be for me to even repeat any of it. I reached into my backpack to take out my book. Then I realized I had forgotten to bring my lunch. Great! Now what? Forced to eat the nasty cafeteria food. That's just great! That's what I get for daydreaming about an imaginary guy. Without realizing it, I slid down further into my seat, but sat up quickly when Mr. Moore looked my way, giving me that "pay attention" look.

It was extremely difficult to concentrate in class. I kept thinking about my dream, even though I told myself that I wouldn't. Periodically, a blurred vision of his face would pop up. If only he had been nice, it would have been a perfect dream. Then out of the blue, I remembered his comment about me being a human. Wasn't he human too? It just didn't make any sense. My friend Kristina thought I was coming down with the flu from the way I looked. Not only was I exhausted, but also deep in thought, and I was walking around like a zombie.

"Are you okay, Claudia?" Kristina asked after school. "You look like you're half asleep."

"I'm just sooo pooped," I said as I lay my head on her shoulder for a second. "I don't understand." I yawned. "I slept last night, I think. Why do I feel like I didn't sleep a wink? Maybe I am coming down with something. Ahhhh…" I yawned again.

"Well, try not to get sick. Ryan's eighteenth birthday party is four weeks from Saturday."

"That's a month away. I have time to get sick," I said jokingly. "Counting down till the party?" I asked, nudging her on the shoulder.

"Heck, yeah! It's at the Grand View Hotel. Who has a birthday party at the Grand View Hotel? For a wedding, I would understand. It's a five-star hotel. I heard he invited practically the whole senior class. Can you imagine how much the whole thing would cost? I guess if my parents were rich like his, I would have it there too. But you already knew that.

"I only dated him for six months," I said, implying that I didn't know much about him.

"You got the Evite, didn't you? I mean, you did break his heart, and I didn't know if he would invite you," she said, her eyes uncertain.

"I got the Evite. Don't worry. Anyway, we're friends. Party at the Grand View Hotel…that's one party I wouldn't miss…though I really don't know how to dress cocktail," I said.

"Good. I'll tell Maggie you're going. We were debating whether you would go or not 'cause…you know," she said, with a raised eyebrow.

"Talking behind my back," I teased.

"Always," she said with a smile.

"No wonder my ears were burning," I said.

"Your ears will be more than burning if you back out," she said in a half serious, half teasing tone.

"Don't worry. I'll be there even if I'm sick," I said as I closed my eyes, hoping that it would be just enough for my eyes to rest before I opened them up again. Then I yawned.

"Okay then. Now that we got that straightened out, see ya tomorrow," she said as she yawned. "Stop yawning, you're making me yawn," she scolded playfully.

We both laughed. "Same time, same place," I said, waving good-bye and walking away.

"Don't forget to RSVP!" I heard her shout from a distance.

"It's a month away," I murmured under my breath, knowing it was pointless to say it out loud since I could no longer see her.

Ryan was my first boyfriend; the first guy I had held hands with and the first guy I had kissed. He was tall, good-looking, and mega-rich. Any girl would have loved to be in my shoes — except for Patty. She thought he wasn't good enough for me. I told her that she needed to get to know him better, and that being rich didn't automatically make him a snob. But I guess that wasn't the reason she disliked him, and I didn't see him the same way. She had more experience with boys than I did, so I figured she had her reasons. But I continued to date him anyway.

We started having problems when Ryan started getting more serious. Not only was I not ready to move forward, I had also realized that he didn't make me feel the way a girl should feel when she's in love. Like how the guy in my dream made me feel, I thought unexpectedly. I quivered from the sudden feeling I experienced, the fluttering butterflies everywhere, like when I first looked into his eyes. I had never believed in love at first sight; maybe I did now, even with his bad manners and all. I wasn't sure what it was that I felt, but I knew it was something I had never felt before. Regardless, it didn't matter because it was just a dream, after all. These feelings confirmed that breaking up with Ryan was the right thing to do. It was best for both of us.

After school, I headed straight for the refrigerator. I grabbed something to snack on, and sure enough, there it was. The note read, "Working late tonight, left dinner in the fridge." Mom never failed to leave me a note letting me know whether she'd be working late or not. Home alone, I thought. It never used to bother me, but for some reason, it did tonight. I couldn't quite put my finger on the reason why, but I was guessing it had something to do with the dream I had last night.

All was quiet in the house, until the sound of my cell phone made me jump. The caller ID read Lucy Reed. Lucy Reed was Gamma's real name, but as a toddler I was unable to say "Grandma", so she became Gamma to me.

"Hello, Gamma," I answered excitedly.

"Hello, Claudia. I haven't heard your voice in days, so I decided to call you and see how you are doing. Is it a good time to talk?" she asked.

"It's fine, Gamma. I'm fine. How are you?"

"I'm fine, honey. Don't worry about me. You will come and visit me on your birthday, won't you?"

"Yes, of course. I'll be there," I said.

"Okay, honey. I just called to say hello. I'll see you soon."

"Good night, Gamma," I said, and blew her a kiss through the phone.

After hanging up the phone, I completed my homework and ate dinner. I decided to head to bed a bit earlier than usual because I felt so drained. Just snuggling inside my bed was all I could think of. As exhausted as I was, though, I was fighting sleep. But no matter how hard I tried, I couldn't resist the need. I had no choice; my eyes were so heavy that I could no longer control them. One lid at a time, they slowly closed, and I felt my whole body relax. Please don't dream was my last thought before I drifted off to the unknown world once again.

Chapter 4

Back on the same road, I stood there alone. I decided to sit and just wait. Why did I keep dreaming about this place? There had to be a reason, seeing as this place was consuming my dream world. Yet, what was the point of being here when I couldn't get any answers? Would I see her, or him, again? Perhaps someone new? Not knowing what to expect was a bit frightening, but a sense of excitement began to seep through my bones as I saw someone walking in the distance. My heart was pounding rapidly; I had almost forgotten how good-looking he was.

All I could remember was this strange queasiness in my stomach, but as he got closer, I saw that it wasn't him. This man's features were very similar to the guy I had met before, sharing much of the same beauty. He had a similar body frame, but his hair was a lighter shade of brown, and his eyes were emerald green. I felt disappointed and saddened because he had lied to me. He had told me that he was the only one here, but seeing this new guy just confirmed that there were others. As the stranger approached, I prepared myself for rudeness, like the last guy. But instead, I was surprised by his amiable voice.

"Hello, my name is Davin," he said cheerfully. I was relieved by the sweetness in his voice, and as I tried to remember why that name sounded familiar, he spoke again. "So you're back."

Back? How did he know I was here before? I wasn't sure how to answer his question. "Honestly, I don't know how I ended up here. The last thing I remember is falling asleep, and now I'm here."

As I was talking, he started circling around me, eyeing me slowly and intently from head to toe. Did I say something wrong? I was starting to feel more and more uncomfortable; it seemed he was staring endlessly. Did he have to make it that obvious? He was totally checking me out. Oh my gosh! What a player. I should have known from his friendly approach. When he finally stopped, I expected him to say some stupid pick-up line, but instead, he just smiled.

I crossed my arms with irritation. "Excuse me, but are you looking for something?" I finally got the courage to ask this unnerving stranger.

His right hand was under his chin and his eyes were elsewhere in thought. He finally murmured something to himself, just loud enough that I could hear. "So you are a human after all. How is this possible?"

"Of course I'm human. What else would I be?" I snapped. "Do I have horns coming out of my head or wings behind my back?" I asked sarcastically.

His eyes fixed on me. "Ummm...," he said with a puzzled looked on his face, as if he was searching for words. Now he looked confused.

Our conversation was getting us nowhere. I had to be direct and to the point. "Let me get this straight. If you are calling me human, then what are you?" I asked, regretting my question almost instantly, out of fear of what his answer might be.

"I'm what you would call an angel," he said proudly, without any hesitation.

It was hard for me to take in what he had just said. Was this guy for real? Oh great, now I am stuck who knows where, and this guy thinks he's an angel. I guess it is possible. After all, if this is just a dream, then it can be whatever I want it to be, right? People have strange dreams all the time, and they don't necessarily have to have any meaning. Yeah, that's all it is. All of this rambling in my head was in an effort to convince myself that I wasn't going crazy.

"An angel?" I questioned, as if I had misheard his reply.

He just stood there, nodding arrogantly. Okay, I thought. I'll bite. Doesn't look like I have anywhere else to go, so why not? So I asked him the first question that popped in my head. "You have no wings. How can you be an angel?"

"You humans and your overactive imaginations," he smirked. I rolled my eyes and prepared to listen. "Imagine us with wings," he said. "We don't need wings to fly or get around. There are only a few angels among us who actually have wings. Those were the angels that came long before humans."

"Gabriel," I named quickly. "He is a messenger angel, correct?"

"Yes, very good. I see you did your homework, but then again, everybody knows about angel Gabriel."

I felt proud to know the name, but he just shot me down. The years of attending Sunday school did not pay off. Then I shot back with another question. "Tell me, what kind of angel are you? If memory serves me, there are three different types of angels: guardian, messenger, or avenger, right?" Confident that I had impressed him with my "angel knowledge," I smiled proudly and stared back at him, much the way he did when questioning me being human.

"If I had a choice, I would be an avenger, but I'm not any of those. I'm different. I'm…" he paused, as if searching for the most appropriate words. None of this was making sense. "It doesn't matter what kind of angel I am. An angel is an angel."

He was right, I suppose. An angel is an angel, but I didn't believe him. I quickly changed the subject as he entered my thoughts. I was hoping Davin had some insight as to who this person could be.

"Where is, ummm…?"

Cutting me off in midsentence, he said, "He is very upset that you're here again. You didn't take heed of his warning so he sent me. I'm the nice guy. After all, you did ask him if you could speak to a nice guy, and here I am," he said with a big grin, obviously knowing exactly who I was referring to.

There was a cuteness about him. Something about being "the good guy" made him likeable in a non-conceited way.

"He's mad at me?" I asked, feeling extremely disappointed.

I didn't know why I even bothered to care. I mean, who was he to me? I told myself, I'm the one who should be mad; he lied to me. He isn't the only one here. I wondered how many of them existed—wherever here was, as I vaguely recalled him mentioning something about a place between life and death. Why should I believe him when he had already lied to me? And again, WHY WAS I HERE?

Then that knot in the pit of my stomach started to creep back as a sense of helplessness set in. I was at a loss for words once more as I found myself questioning my presence in this foreign place. I sat down, uncomforted by Davin's words, and curled my knees into my chest. Alone and frustrated, my eyes began to tear. A good cry now seemed appropriate.

From the corner of my eyes, I saw Davin pacing back and forth at a distance, looking extremely uncomfortable with my emotional display. Then, suddenly, he was reaching down toward me, wiping every teardrop before they could fall from my cheeks. I was perplexed by the speed at which he came toward me. Humans don't move the way he just moved. Had he been telling me the truth all along? Was he truly an angel? It didn't matter what he was. I was just glad that I was not alone, and his touch was comforting.

"Don't want people down there to think it's sprinkling," he said in what appeared to be an effort to lighten the mood.

I looked up into his eyes, pondering his words in my mind.

"It's a joke," he chuckled, trying to make me laugh.

I wasn't laughing; I wanted to give him a piece of my mind. No amount of humor was going to help this situation. I stood up quickly to turn away from him, but began to feel dizzy and almost fainted. I saw three of him. As I reached out trying to catch my balance, Davin wrapped his arms around me from behind. His strong arms were locked, holding me tight. I felt uncomfortable by his embrace, but at the same time, in this moment of weakness, I was strangely comforted by his strength.

"I'm going to be in a whole lot of trouble for this," he whispered into my ear.

I felt a warm sensation run through my body, like when you step out into the sun from the cold. Instantly I was calmer, but confused about what was happening. I had no control over how I was feeling. Was this because of Davin, or was something wrong with me?

"Davin!" Out of nowhere, he appeared. It was him, the perfect being I had encountered in the field. "What have you done?" he demanded.

Davin dropped his arms, as if he was caught taking a cookie out of the cookie jar. He swiftly moved away from me, now keeping his distance.

"Michael, I was only trying to—"

"Silence!" he interrupted. Davin didn't have a chance to explain. We both stiffened by the sound of his command.

Michael, like the archangel. One who is good. He was strong and powerful; a protector. What a perfect name.

"It doesn't matter," Michael said. "Now there is no turning back, everyone will know!" He spoke through clenched jaws, eyes glaring. I became frightened. I stared at him and realized there was fear in his eyes. Behind his anger, I saw a man, a beautiful soul looking back at me.

"I was trying to console her, and I got carried away. It's been ages since I've touched a human, and I couldn't help myself," Davin said, shrugging his shoulders as if it was no big deal.

Human? Here we go again with the human thing. Michael glanced back my way. I blushed, turning my face away, in hopes that he didn't realize I had been staring so intently at him.

"You need to go back," he said softly, almost sorrowfully. He sounded very concerned.

Quickly gathering himself, he yelled, "Get her out, Davin. Now!"

"No. Why don't you do it?" Davin argued back.

Michael replied, "You know very well that I don't have that kind of power. I'm not a gatekeeper like you. I can't send her back. I would do it myself if I could."

Davin paused. He gave me a thoughtful look as he faced me with tenderness, "Do you want to go back?"

As soon as Davin asked me, Michael shook his head and rolled his eyes.

Did I have a choice? Did it matter what the choice would be? What did they mean by having power? And what was a gatekeeper? While focusing solely on Davin, afraid to look at Michael for fear of disapproval, I shook my head no. I did not want to leave. I was fascinated by their being. And frankly, at this point, I had Davin on my side. I didn't care what Michael thought.

Davin turned to Michael after I responded with the answer Davin wanted to hear. "Michael, aren't you a bit curious as to how a human found a way to cross over from Crossroads? Besides, you asked for my help. I think we should take her to Phillip."

Michael, looking quite upset, paused and responded carefully, "I don't understand it myself, but you know the risk we're putting her in. Do you realize what this means?"

"I know. I know," Davin replied, embarrassed at being scolded for doing something he knew very well he wasn't supposed to do. Looking at me, he said, "Now the fallen will be after her."

For a brief second, I felt my breath stop short as I replayed what Davin had said. Now the fallen will be after her. I gaped back and forth, from Michael and then to Davin, as I listened carefully to their conversation, contemplating what I should say. I already knew why Michael didn't want me to stay. All I could mutter was "fallen." I wondered who they were and why they would be after me. What did I do? Without warning, Michael and Davin placed their arms around me, and we were in the air.

"Ahhhhh! Oh my God!" I screamed at the top of my lungs. "You're flying. I'm flying! What's going on? How is this possible? Where are we going?"

"Sunday school sure didn't pay off for you. Don't you know your Ten Commandments? Thou shall not take the Lord's name in vain?" Davin replied with a smirk. "Are you human girls always this dramatic?"

"Are you serious? You're scolding me about the Ten Commandments? This isn't normal. What are you?"

"You don't listen very well, do you? I told you I am an angel," he said with a huge grin. "You believe me now?"

I didn't know what to believe. As far as I was concerned, I was dreaming. And if what they were telling was true, what kind of angels were they to be this rude? I thought all angels were kind and noble.

Michael, to my right, was silent while Davin, to my left, was thoroughly enjoying himself. This can't be happening, I thought. Dream or no dream, I needed answers.

"Where are we going?" I pleaded. "Why aren't you telling me anything?"

Michael turned swiftly with a cold stare and said, "I told you not to come back."

Chapter 5

We were gliding just above the clouds, the warm breeze gently brushing against my face. I was flying, and it was incredible. As their bodies protruded forward, we picked up speed. Soon we were at an angle, and all that was beneath me were the clouds—white and fluffy, soft, cottony clouds—oh, what fun it would be to bounce on them. I was overwhelmed by the magic of this moment. How I wished this was more than a dream.

We looked down upon a castle which looked like an ice sculpture, one that you might see at a black-tie affair. Or perhaps it was something grander, like crystals. With all that I had already seen, I didn't think it was possible that I could still be amazed. A bright ring resembling a force field encased the castle, protecting it. But from what? There were no windows, only a colossal door, as if meant for a giant. There was a simple elegance to it, yet it looked cold and empty from the outside. Certainly one could get lost inside this enormous castle.

As we approached the entrance the ring disappeared, leaving me to think it had been a figment of my imagination, but as we stood at the front door, it returned. The gigantic door opened, seemingly sensing our presence, and we walked in.

While I was making my observations, Davin spoke. "Welcome to Halo City, my human." He slowly knelt down on one knee, much like an old-fashioned gentleman.

Not knowing what to say, I simply gave him a smile. He linked my arm through his and led the way. Contrary to the coldness surrounding this place, it felt strangely warm and inviting inside. Although I had imagined it to be dark, it was surprisingly bright, even with the absence of windows. The light somehow penetrated the walls. I imagined this was what being in the center of a diamond would be like, thousands of brilliant facets sparkling through. There was no fancy furniture; just unadorned and elegant décor.

"What are we doing here?" I whispered as I unlinked Davin's arm. I had a slightly uneasy feeling, like we were sneaking into a stranger's home.

Michael turned slightly, purposely avoiding eye contact with me, and said flatly, "You are here to speak to Phillip. He will know what to do. He knows you're here, and he will ask you many questions, thanks to Davin." As soon as he finished speaking, he walked right past me, brushing my shoulder as if I wasn't there. As I moved forward, he turned to look at me with narrowed eyes, insinuating that I was the one at fault.

"Jerk," I mumbled to myself.

Davin looked at me and said, "Well, I, ummm…well…" He shrugged his shoulders and smiled, succumbing to the fact that we had no other choice. Then he realized I was more focused on Michael. "Don't worry about him. He's quite nice once you get to know him. He is somewhat of a grouch today, maybe because you're around."

"What?" I muttered under my breath in shock. Did I hear him correctly? It didn't matter. Being a grouch was an understatement.

Egotistical and rude was more like it, but I didn't say anything. For no apparent reason at all, I was getting annoyed with Davin, but that quickly subsided when I realized it was me who had wanted to stay. He was just being friendly. I was also anxious to meet Phillip, and was feeling uneasy about what he planned to ask. At this point all I wanted were answers. I would endure rudeness, annoyance, and just about anything to understand this mysterious world.

While waiting for Phillip, I began to become intrigued by these angels. How many were there? Were there male and female angels? This Philip must be powerful and wise if we were coming to speak to him. I had expected to see an old man with a long white beard, perhaps with a cane. I suppose it had been ingrained in my mind that age and gray hair implied great wisdom. But that wasn't the case. When Phillip arrived, I was surprised to see that he was quite handsome, and appeared only slightly older than Michael.

"Hello and welcome," he said with an authoritative tone.

He took several steps down and faced me directly. Excitement rose through me; my heart beat faster, simultaneously feeling joy and fear, knowing he was someone of great importance. I timidly held my head up and looked directly into his eyes. I saw that he had the same shade of brown eyes as Michael.

He continued, "I was wondering if you could tell me how you got here?"

I paused to figure out how I should answer his question. I couldn't believe he had just asked me that! Here I was, waiting patiently to get my answers, and I kept getting questioned the same way. Why was it that I had no answers, and everyone kept asking me, as if I knew? I felt frustrated by his inquiry, since I was hoping to finally receive the answers I had been searching for. Flushed with anger, I spoke with attitude. "To tell you the truth, I really don't know, and everyone keeps asking me the same question. How come you don't know—you had to have seen me coming. Aren't angels all-knowing?"

I couldn't believe I had blurted out like that, and I immediately regretted how I had said it. What was I thinking? I was appalled at myself for being so rude. I couldn't take it back even if I had wanted to. I wanted to apologize for my bad behavior, but what I feared more was how he might react. Surprisingly, he just smiled, and I instantly relaxed.

"You see, I might have some answers for you, but I wanted to know if you knew anything first."

"You know how I got here?" I asked in an apologetic tone, realizing what an idiot I had been for not being more patient.

"Perhaps we can figure it out together," he said with certainty. "Please, have a seat next to me."

He pointed to a chair beside him that I was certain hadn't been there before. I thought that was peculiar, but maybe I had missed seeing it. I hesitated to sit next to him, but I did as instructed. Philip sat down next to me and paused, appearing to be deep in thought. He glanced at Michael and Davin, who nodded, clearly agreeing to whatever task Philip was suggesting. I gathered they could communicate telepathically.

He inhaled deeply and began to speak. Whatever he was about to reveal seemed to be something I wasn't supposed to know. "Humans only know a fraction of our history, although they spend years and years of research trying to find concrete evidence of our existence on Earth. What I am about to tell you has never been disclosed to any human. Fair warning, if you decide to share this information with another human, they may think you have lost your mind. You understand what I'm trying to say, don't you?"

"Yes," I replied. In his own polite way, he was asking me to keep my mouth shut. There were tons of people I could share this information with, but Phillip was right. Who would believe me? I was so humbled and honored to be here in their presence that I would do just about anything they asked.

"Very well, let's start from the beginning. I will make it short and simple. A long time ago, angels roamed the Earth with the guidance of the Twelve Angels. We refer to them as Earth angels. They learned how to be human. Much time was spent studying their mannerisms, learning about their emotions and anything that would help make the task of blending with the humans easier. There were thousands of them. They could travel at immense speed and were exceptionally stronger than anything imaginable. They didn't look anything like the angels you are taught about in school or church. They didn't have wings or bright halos around their heads.

"The humans were completely unaware of their existence. Their sole purpose was to observe and guide humans away from temptation, poor judgment, and sometimes death. Just like humans have the Ten Commandments, angels had their Ten Divine Commandments. The second one proclaimed that they were forbidden to love a human or to procreate. The resistance proved to be far too difficult for some, though most were able to resist. For the others, the urge became unbearable the longer they stayed in the human world. They had forgotten who they were and their purpose, thus procreating life that was forbidden. For a long period of time, the 'forbidden children' remained hidden. Many were able to grow well into their teens, some making it to their twenties.

"You see, our kind is governed by a Royal Council. The Royal Council consists of God's first angels—Michael, Gabriel, Raphael, Raguel, Uriel, Zerachiel, Remiel and many others who were created before us. They make decisions based on what they agree to be in our best interest. When they found out about the children born into human society, all angels were immediately banned from having any physical or emotional contact with humans. However, permission was granted for a select few to stay behind and continue their duties. The agreement was that they could not procreate, and in return, they would be allowed to live and die as humans."

Angels lived among us, I thought to myself. It was hard to imagine, but I could have spoken to one. The thought of actually being that close to an angel was unbelievable. I broke out of my thoughts when Phillip spoke.

"I know this is difficult to take in, but do you understand?" he asked.

"What you are telling me is that there is a chain of command with angels?"

"Yes, first the Royal Council, then the Twelve, followed by Earth angels. These angels have no wings. They blend with the humans quite well, perhaps too well. Lastly, the forbidden children."

"What happened to these children?" I asked, afraid of what his answer might be.

"They were sent here, this place called the Crossroads, and you are standing in Halo City. Humans use the term, nephilim for these children, but we call them alkins. "Alkin" are the alpha — the first of its kind, half angel, half human. They are the first generation to be born into human society."

Michael and Davin came to my mind. I remembered Michael saying that we were at Crossroads, between life and death. Davin referred to himself as an angel with no wings. Alkins didn't have wings. Thoughts flooded my mind. Everything was coming at me hard and fast. Out of impulse, I turned to look at Michael and Davin. I felt ashamed that I was the reason a secret so profound had been revealed. A secret that had been concealed for who knows how long. And I, a mere human, was responsible for its exposure. I wanted to tell them how sorry I was, how ashamed I felt, but they didn't even look up at me. Their heads remained low, almost as if they were embarrassed about who they were. I quickly turned back so they wouldn't notice me.

"Are you an alkin?" I asked Philip.

"No. I am one of the Twelve." There was a note of arrogance to his tone. "When the alkins were found, a few of the Twelve Angels were reassigned to Halo City with them. It became our responsibility to guide and mentor the alkins to be more like angels rather than humans. That was the day the Twelve Angels were divided. Margaret, Agnes, and I were chosen to become their mentors. The rest stayed behind to continue their assignments. Like humans, angels were not created perfectly. There is one particular angel who has rebelled and has taken many alkins with him. We call them the fallen. We don't know where they are."

He suddenly and gracefully stood up and spread his wings. It was a vision of elegance and poise, majestic and holy; a miraculous moment that I knew I would never forget. I was overwhelmed by the beauty and reality of what was happening. Part of me wanted to touch him, to be sure that this was real. Was I truly witnessing an angel? Was I really having this conversation? I was completely unaware of the fact that my eyes were wide and my bottom lip might as well have been on the floor, until Philip cleared his throat.

Embarrassed by my actions, I quickly diverted attention by asking another question, "What do the fallen look like?" I was relieved to finally get to this question, seeing as they would be the ones coming after me.

"You ask many questions. You already know too much," he said softly. I thought that was the end of our conversation, but he continued to speak. "Humans would imagine them to look like monsters, but in fact, they look like us."

I was in shock. I had expected him to tell me otherwise. "Then how can you tell the difference between a fallen and an angel?" I asked with a worried expression.

"By appearances, you can't tell us apart."

A part of me was glad that they didn't look like hideous creatures, but knowing the possibility they might be after me sent a painful chill through every bone in my body. Now that I had that information, I wanted to know more about the alkins.

"How many alkins exist here?" I asked, eagerly thinking that I'd finally get the answer that Michael wouldn't reveal. Then I worried that maybe he wouldn't tell me since he thought I knew too much.

"There are thousands of alkins who reside here. I would like you to meet the officers who already know you are here. The other alkins are not aware of your presence, and I would like to keep it that way."

Wow! Thousands, I repeated Phillip's words in my head. My whole body seemed to explode with excitement and I could barely contain myself.

"I would like to introduce you to..." motioning his hands, they entered one by one. "Vivian, Caleb, Ruth, Paul. And you've already met Michael and Davin." Each was flawless. Their beauty was breathtaking, a vision of royalty at its finest, and they all possessed a soothing glow in their eyes. I had pictured them in white gowns, but they were wearing jeans and T-shirts just like Michael and Davin. They were dressed just like human beings. It was true...you couldn't tell the difference between humans and the alkins.

Nobody said a word. There was an uncomfortable silence. I became their subject, and they stared at me with confused and curious eyes.

Phillip broke the silence, "You have to excuse their demeanor. It has been quite some time since they've seen a human. We are going to have to monitor you from here on. It is important that we keep an eye on you, just in case the fallen find out about your involvement with us. They are not so friendly. You are an easy target since they can sense your presence now. Once you have entered our world, your aura will stand out from the rest of the humans on Earth. There is a possibility they may think you are an alkin."

Fallen may think I'm an alkin echoed inside my head. I couldn't believe what he was saying. What kind of mess did I get myself into? I thought I was only dreaming, and it was turning out to be a nightmare.

"Do you think it would be safer for her to stay here?" Davin asked hopefully.

"She can't stay here. She is not an alkin," Caleb replied.

"However, it would give us the opportunity to be educated about her world," Vivian said, enthusiastically. "Her world has advanced so much since we came here."

Michael shot her a disapproving look. I could tell that he didn't like her response at all. I knew the reason. He didn't want me around.

Phillip interrupted, "I don't think that would be a good idea. You don't need Claudia in order to learn about her world. You can research on your own."

"True. But hearing it from Claudia would be much faster. And why wouldn't it be a good idea?" Vivian spoke out. "Divine Commandments can be altered to fit the situation."

"She is not one of us. Need I remind you of the obvious again? She is human, not an alkin," Caleb said with slight irritation, and then paused to think. "What if the fallen come here?"

Phillip was about to answer Caleb's question when Agnes and Margaret entered the room, and everyone became silent. It was the first time I was able to see Margaret's face. She was stunning, just like the goddess I remembered. This time, she wore her hair straight down, as smooth as silk. She looked at me, nodding her head to acknowledge my presence. She began to speak, her hypnotic voice exactly the way I remembered from before.

"The fallen can only enter our world if they take an alkin who has the soul of the Holy Spirit. Only Royal Council angels have the soul of the Holy Spirit. Isaiah was one of the Royal Council. He fell in love with a human many lifetimes ago. His descendants are now with the Royal Council. I doubt any of them are left on Earth. If there is a possibility that the one still exists, the chances are very slim to none. We do not make mistakes. So you need not worry. Hypothetically, if one does exist, then it is out of our hands. And if the fallen finds the one, there will be war."

"Let the danger come!" Davin shouted passionately, raising his fist in the air, as if already victorious.

I was startled by his sudden outburst. A multitude of arguments began. They were speaking in Latin, and I could not understand. Realizing instantly that this was all because of me, I began to feel horror in my body. I was plagued by thoughts of this mysterious, beautiful, unknown existence, possibly on the verge of destruction, all because I couldn't, or rather didn't want to, go back. I was desperate to make this right.

"Can you please stop? I'll leave! Just please don't fight. I'm so sorry." My voice became softer as I saw them glaring down on me. Maybe it was not my place to have an opinion. I was sure my sudden outburst didn't help matters. All I wanted to do was hide. Nobody wanted me here, and I had nowhere to go.

Vivian interrupted, "Why not ask the human?"

Ask me what? I didn't even know what they were arguing about.

"She has a name," Michael said.

I was surprised to hear him respond in that way. It was as if I mattered to him, like he was defending me. Could he care a little? Could it be possible that he wasn't mad at me anymore? But then I thought What does it matter, and why do I care so much about what he thinks of me anyway?

Phillip looked at me tenderly and said, "I'm sorry, but it's time for you to leave. We will be keeping an eye on you as promised, to make sure you stay safe. However, this is an unprecedented incident. I can only hope that my judgments are correct. Michael, I think it would be best that you be appointed as her guardian angel."

"What!" Michael and Davin exclaimed simultaneously.

"Why?" shouted Davin. "He doesn't even like her."

In the midst of Davin's opposition, I tried to wrap my head around his words—he doesn't even like her. I was disappointed at this thought, and admittedly, a bit sad too. Why did he think so little of me? I felt cursed, like being human was dirty and not worthy of this angelic being. How could someone who disliked me be the right guardian angel to protect me? I guess maybe I did care what he thought.

"Like has nothing to do with this, Davin," replied Philip. "Michael is trained to be a guardian angel. And you are one of our gatekeepers. I need you here for now."

"I see your point," Davin replied, looking disappointed.

Michael glanced at me and then turned to Phillip. "I don't think I'm ready to be a guardian angel."

"Nothing can prepare you for what you are about to do. One can never be ready enough," Phillip countered. "I believe you will be fine. Just listen to your heart and stick to the Divine angel rules."

"You don't understand. I...," Michael said as he was about to protest again.

Phillip interrupted him. "Nothing you say will change my mind. I've appointed you as Claudia's guardian angel, and that is final."

Michael just stood there, looking down, impassive. From his body language, I could tell he wasn't happy with Phillip's decision. Great! I might as well be dead. The way he felt about me, he probably wouldn't lift a finger to save me. I was just about to tell Phillip that I didn't need a guardian angel and that I could take care of myself when Michael looked up. I waited to see what he would do.

Michael looked at Davin and then looked at me blankly. How I wished I could read his thoughts. He must be cursing inside, wondering how he could get out of being my guardian angel. He started walking toward me.

"Michael, wait." A soft-spoken, gentle voice came from a distance.

It took me a second to even see where this voice was coming from. As she appeared, she jumped up eagerly and wrapped her whole body around Michael, like a child hugging her daddy. Michael held her tightly but tenderly and pulled her face away to give her a kiss on the cheek. I was taken aback by the sight of a child and by seeing a different side of him, affectionate and caring. Part of my anger toward him subsided, but not completely. My heart softened to see their interaction. I estimated that she was about seven years old. She had long blonde curls, reminding me of Goldilocks. It wasn't hard to stare back when she gazed at me with those irresistible baby blue eyes. Where did she come from? Was she the only child here?

"No need to worry, Alexa Rose, I'll be back soon. I need to take Claudia home, then I'll be right back," Michael said sweetly, a tone he had never used to speak to me.

"Promise?" she pouted.

"I promise," he said as he placed her down slowly. Before he stood up, he whispered something into her ear, making her giggle.

"Okay. I will," she responded cheerfully.

As she walked away, she acknowledged my presence with a cute little smile.

After Alexa Rose left, Agnes turned to me and said, "It's time to send you back. Meanwhile, try to stay calm."

As she said those words, I felt my body slowly droop. I heard a faint voice from a distance, "Davin, send them back safely. Michael, be on your guard!"

Chapter 6

My alarm clock buzzed with excitement, and without looking at it, I slammed it to snooze. Had I dreamt last night? I couldn't remember. I strained my thoughts as if I could squeeze it out of my head, but it was no use. I guess I didn't dream at all. No wonder I felt refreshed. What I knew was that it had been about five days since I last dreamt about Michael and the alkins, but it seemed so long ago.

It was Saturday, and today would be my first day of work on my first job. It was at Fashion Wear, which was located in a small shopping plaza adjacent to a pizza store and an ice cream store. I applied there as a cashier because of Patty. She thought it would be fun to work together.

I can still remember our conversation when she tried to convince me to work there. "This would be a great opportunity to see each other more often. You can work on weekends. You also get 20 percent off your entire purchase. What more could we ask for?"

I quickly agreed and got hired the same day I applied. She must have put in a few good words for me; I always earned excellent grades, but I didn't have any employment references since I had never worked before. I better stop thinking in bed, I thought to myself as I looked at the clock.

"Oh, shoot!" I said out loud. "Not again!" It was close to noon. Had I pushed the snooze button that many times? I couldn't remember if I had or if I had accidently set the wrong time. Regardless, I couldn't believe Mom let me sleep in this late; but then again, it was Saturday. I couldn't blame her. I didn't let her know what time I was starting my new job. I had no time to waste. Quickly I got ready, kissed my mom, and ran out the door, hoping she wouldn't say anything about me sleeping in this late.

"You should at least take something to go!" my mom yelled through the front door.

I didn't want to upset her, and my stomach was rumbling like crazy from hunger. I ran back in and grabbed a banana, a granola bar, and a bottle of water, then ran back out the door. I didn't realize she was following me outside so I practically slammed the door in her face.

"Mom!" I yelled, reaching for the door, nearly having a heart attack. "Your steps are too quiet. Please don't follow behind me like that."

"Sorry, but you need to slow down."

I paused for a second to show her I was slowing down and hopped on my bike.

"Have a good first day, Claudia. Please be careful, especially since you're working late. Make sure you call me when you get there and from time to time."

"Mom!" I retorted as I kicked the stand from my bike.

"Okay! At least text me then." She was standing in front of me with her hands on the handlebar so I couldn't leave.

"I gotta go. I'm gonna be late on my first day," I said anxiously.

"Ride carefully, watch out for cars, and don't forget to call Gamma. She called this morning, but I didn't want to wake you," she said quickly and backed away. "Remember, be good to those who are alive, because what good is it when they are dead?"

"I know, I know," I muttered, hearing that phrase from her for the hundredth time. "Bye, Mom." I smiled and pedaled my way to work on the red bike I had received last Christmas. Although I enjoyed riding, I was hoping to get a used car, or perhaps a new car, for my birthday. I didn't think I had ever pedaled so quickly in my life because I could feel my heart pounding in and out of my chest. I watched out for cars, just as I had promised. When I came to the first red light, I got off my bike and pushed the "walk" button. Impatiently, I pushed the button several more times, hoping that it would make the light change faster. I didn't know how these things worked, but I thought maybe it would sense my urgency.

Walking to school was much easier since it was a shorter distance, but it was just an excuse so that I wouldn't have to ride my bike to school. I just couldn't do it. Riding my bike to and from work was one concession I had to make to my mom. She'd rather have me ride the bike instead of walking home in the dark, since she usually worked the night shift. I knew it would put her mind at ease, so I didn't put up a fight. Patty lived nearby and we had planned to ride home together.

As I approached the building, a sense of excitement ran through me. On several occasions, I had visited Patty at her workplace, but it was always for a short time. Now that it was also my place of employment, I found a different kind of interest in the store. Patty saw me through the tall glass window and pointed her finger, directing me to park my bike next to hers. Her bike was black with yellow fluorescent lights in front and back. You could see that thing shine a mile away, but then again that was the whole purpose. It had an on-and-off button that controlled the brightness. I locked my bike next to hers, called

Gamma and exchanged a few words, texted Mom quickly to let her know I had gotten to work safely, and ran in.

"Sorry I'm late," I said still breathing heavily.

"You're here." She smiled. "No worries. Mrs. Lee had to leave, so I'm training you." She spoke while walking toward me to give me a big hug.

"Thank God. I didn't want to be late on my first day." I was relieved that I had just made it in time as I hugged her back.

"Now, let me show you around," she said enthusiastically.

As she spoke, I tuned out and observed the high ceiling and the huge size of the store. I guess I hadn't realized how big it was before. With this newfound interest, I observed where everything was: the bathroom, dressing rooms, storage room, light and music on-and-off switch, and the cash register, before Patty even pointed them out to me. Not only was it bright from all the lights, there was also a sense of comfort…maybe it was because Patty was around. Regardless, I was thrilled to be working and spending time with my best friend at the same time. Patty was right, what more could I ask for?

As Patty continued to talk, I noticed a few customers rummaging through the clothing racks. I also noticed a teenager in front of a mirror holding one of our shirts in front of her. As we passed her, Patty made a comment.

"That shirt would look really cute on you. Would you like to try it on? I'll take you to the dressing room, so you can see for yourself. My name is Patty, what's your name?"

"Clara," she said with spunk, obviously happy to have someone at her beck and call.

I followed them to the dressing room.

"Watch this," Patty whispered. When Clara came out with her new shirt on, Patty practically dropped her jaw with exaggeration, "Oh my gosh! You look sooo cute!"

"Yeah, I like it," Clara smiled, as she admired herself in the mirror.

"Like it?" Patty's tone begged Clara to say more.

"Okay, I love it...and...I'll take it," Clara said, wanting to please Patty.

"Great, let's take a look at some jeans to go with it. And we're having a sale on some jewelry as well."

Clara followed her like a lost puppy, and soon we were at the cash register. She bought two pairs of jeans, because she was undecided, three shirts, and a long chained silver necklace. Patty was such the saleslady. I helped her stuff the items into the Fashion Wear bag, a cheap gray plastic bag with the FW logo on it.

Patty looked into Clara's eyes with a big smile and said, "Thank you, Clara. Come again soon, and I'll help you with anything you need."

Clara looked so pleased and by now probably worshipped Patty for her expertise in fashion.

"Thank you, Patty, for everything. And don't worry, I'll come again soon. You were so helpful and very attentive."

Clara was gleaming with happiness and held the bag close to her, as if she had diamonds in it. After Clara walked out, Patty turned to me proudly and said, "And that's how you do it!"

"You were fabulous!" I said excitedly, thinking I had a lot of learning to do.

She giggled. "Thank you. With practice you'll be as good as me...well, almost," she teased.

"Maybe better," I teased back.

She gave a fake frown, and nudged my shoulder playfully and said, "It's always busy like this on Saturdays, but it makes the time go faster. Having fun?"

As I nudged her back, I replied, "I was so excited to actually have a job, and I didn't know what to expect, but it's so cool working with you. And you, my friend, are an awesome saleslady. Thank you for getting me this job." I smiled.

"Thank you, my friend, for telling me that I'm awesome. But you got the job yourself." She smiled back and bowed gracefully and walked away to attend to another customer.

"Regardless, thank you," I said, but I didn't even know if she heard me.

Throughout the day, I watched Patty work her magic. The day went by in a flash. I couldn't believe it when the clock said it was almost nine o'clock.

Patty's cell phone rang, and she answered. "Hi, Mom. You're what? How? I'm almost done. But, I…now? Okay, bye." She ran toward me looking very upset and confused. "My mom locked herself out, and she left the stove on. I've gotta go, but I'm suppose to lock up, or maybe you can, or…I don't know. I've gotta go. What should I do?"

"Calm down, Patty." I placed both of my hands on her shoulders. I caught on to what she was trying to tell me. "Don't worry. Show me how to lock up and go. I'll be fine. I just have to be here fifteen minutes and then lock up. No biggy. Just don't tell my mom I was here by myself, okay?"

She nodded quickly. "Okay. I'll make this fast. It's really easy. Nothing to it," she said, rushing. She opened the cash register and took out a key. "Use this spare key for tonight. Don't forget to bring it back with you tomorrow." Then she pulled me toward the entrance door. "Push this red button to activate the alarm, walk out, and lock the door."

"That's it?" I asked.

"That's it," she repeated. "Thanks, I owe you big time. Just text or call me if you need any help, and text me when you get home, or I'll worry, Okay?" She sounded frazzled as she looked at me for approval.

"Don't worry. Just go," I said. "What could happen in fifteen minutes?"

"I'm so sorry. Your first day at work and I have to leave you. Gosh, what was my mom thinking! Ahhh! I'm so mad at her right now."

"Don't worry about it. Don't be mad at her. She didn't do it on purpose. I'm a big girl," I said, smiling. "Now, go!" I said sternly. I practically shoved her out the door. Patty gave me a tight squeeze and left. Off she went pedaling as fast as she could. For her sake, I hoped she didn't hit all the red lights.

Fifteen minutes usually passes with a snap of a finger, so I waited for customers to enter while I paced through the rack of clothes, looking for something that might catch my eye. At least the music was keeping me company, but not a single customer walked through the door. Fourteen minutes. Thirteen minutes. I decided not to look at the clock every minute, but the longer I stayed here alone, the more anxious I started to feel.

Suddenly, I heard a loud BAM! It sounded like one of the dressing room doors had closed itself.

Stay calm. It's nothing. It's just the wind, I told myself.

I couldn't recall a customer being in one of the dressing rooms, so I guessed the door must have closed from the breeze that was coming from the air vent. Feeling more frightened than before, I quickly glanced at the clock. I decided to close five minutes early since nobody would notice, and that was when the music stopped.

I froze. My heart skipped a beat. It was like I was in a scary movie. I ran to switch the music button back on, then remembered that the control panel was located inside the dressing area. I stopped when I got near the door. I didn't want to go in there, but I had to prove to myself that it was a coincidence, and that the music was probably on a timer set to turn off at a given time.

As I slowly walked in, I looked around the five dressing rooms and saw that all the doors were closed. I was able to spot the switch quickly, as I remembered Patty pointing to the wall right next to the first dressing room. Just as I reached for the switch, the lights went off; it was pitch-black.

What was going on? This couldn't be happening. Maybe Patty forgot to tell me that the lights went off automatically. There had to be a reasonable explanation for this. Although I could see some dim lights from the parking lot glimmering through the windows, it was still dark, and I could barely make anything out. Then I heard a soft eerie voice call my name. "Claudia…"

I didn't answer. I thought I was losing my mind. Then I heard my name being called again in the same creepy voice. "Claudia…"

Hearing my name for the second time was a sure sign that I was not delusional. Immediately I panicked. I knew for a fact that there was no one here except me. I calmed down and decided to answer, thinking that maybe Patty was playing a joke on me. "He…ellooo. Anyone there?" I asked quietly.

"Claudia, commme."

"Who are you? How do you know my name?" I demanded. "Patty, is that you? You can stop now! I'm on to you! It's not funny anymore! You're scaring me!" I was envisioning Patty turning on the lights, laughing, and telling me it was her way of initiating a new employee. Please let it be her, I prayed.

"Follow the light," the voice continued, ignoring my request.

When it spoke again, I knew with certainty that it wasn't Patty's voice. The voice was very enticing and for some unknown reason, I wanted to go to it, even though I was scared for my life. Suddenly I was in a hypnotic state; I had no control of where I was going, though I could see and hear everything around me.

"Claudia, Claudia…come to me."

I was walking toward the light, which was glowing around a door. As I placed my hand on the doorknob, the bright light began to fade. I didn't want to move, but my body and mind were not in sync. I could see my hand twisting the doorknob, even though I was screaming inside telling myself not to open it. I could no longer resist, and I succumbed to the calling that would lead me into the darkness.

As I obediently walked into the room, the door behind me slammed shut. The loud bang jolted me out of the trance, leaving me to wonder why I was there. Immediately I turned to open the door, but it wouldn't budge. Twisting, pulling, and turning the knob every way possible was useless. With my back against the door, I searched the pockets of my jeans, only to realize I had left my cell phone next to the register. What could happen in fifteen minutes? I remembered telling Patty. I should've kept my mouth shut.

Feeling hopeless, I suddenly noticed something glowing down low, just adjacent to the door. It was something other than the moonlight beaming through the small window. Something was plugged into the wall, and the tip of it was bright so that you could spot it easily. As I reached to examine it with my hand, I was relieved to find that it was an emergency flashlight. I had never been so happy to see one. I grabbed it and looked around to see where I stood. Several tables were lined in the middle of this huge room with stacked clothes: jeans, T-shirts, dresses, and much more. I would have never guessed the storage room would be this big.

As I walked closer to the tables, I thought I saw someone or something. A rush of fear swept over me, and every nerve in my body awakened.

"Who are you? What do you want?" I said out loud, holding the flashlight closer and tighter to my chest as I trembled with fright. But there was no response.

I couldn't tell what it was at first, until it whooshed past me, almost knocking me over. My heart started thumping faster. A black cloud of fog was what I thought I saw. My eyes were glued to it as it swooped up to the high ceiling and then disappeared. Was it a ghost? I couldn't believe what I had just seen, but there was something definitely there, something menacing. As it materialized again and whooshed past me, I used the flashlight to hit it, hoping to knock it out or hurt it. But the flashlight went right through it. At that moment, the courage to fight back vanished.

Suddenly the room became extremely cold. It was so cold that I could see the mist flow out of my mouth as my breath became heavy with fear. Shivering, I hugged myself as I tried to find something, anything, to keep me warm. Then I thought of running to the window to scream as loudly as I possibly could in hopes that someone would hear me.

As I turned to run, the clothes on the table came flying toward me. I screamed out loud in panic. Using both arms to cover my face, I tried to reach for the door again. Even though I knew I wouldn't be able to open it, it was the only way out. I was confused, and I didn't know which way to go.

Suddenly the black cloud came at me even faster and harder. I kept backing away, shielding myself with my arm as I tried to escape, but it was relentless. It knocked the wind out of me, and I was gasping for air. Then it stopped. Feeling breathless and disoriented, I rubbed my sore arm and looked around.

Realizing I was now at the opposite end of the room from the door, I backed away slowly, taking one baby step at a time, afraid that it may sense my movement again. When I thought I had backed far enough away, I dashed for the door. That was when I felt something cold at my feet. It was already freezing in the room, but this coldness was directed solely at my feet, and the pain stung right through to my bones. I tried to run again, but it was no use. It felt like my feet were cemented to the ground. When I looked down, a long black fog that looked like a slithering headless anaconda started circling me.

The fog took the form of a snake, the thing I feared most. The one thing that would make my skin crawl inside and out was now taunting me, like I was about to be its next meal. The farther it moved upwards, the farther the coldness and the pain spread. As I stood there like a statue, a single nerve jolted through my body like lightning from my head to my toes. I tried to control my panic as my whole body trembled from the cold and fright. Trying to fight back, I looked around to see if there was anything I could use to defend myself against this attack, anything but this useless flashlight and my sore arm, but there was nothing.

The black smoke finally showed its face, but only for a split second before disappearing. Just a glance at the monstrous black face and demonic yellow eyes was enough to paralyze me. The fog seemed to be getting pleasure out of making my blood race with fear, teasing and taunting, shifting back and forth from a fog-like form to a snake. When it became the snake, it took a solid form with its red tongue slithering in and out, looking for the perfect place on my body to strike.

It began to squeeze tighter again, and I could no longer feel my legs. Blood rushed to my head, and I was certain death would be next. I wanted to grab the head of the snake, but I couldn't. The thought of touching it made me cringe, and I knew my hands would simply go right through it just as the flashlight had. Besides, I was a mere human next to this creature of immense power. There was no way I would win.

Let this be a dream, I prayed. Things like this didn't happen in real life. I needed to find a way to wake up. Wake up! Wake up! Help! Somebody help me! I screamed inside.

"No one can help you," it hissed wickedly.

I was so astonished to hear it speak that I was speechless. Then it hit me; hearing the snake fog or whatever it was speak to me was a sure sign that I was dreaming. Any minute now, I would wake up from this nightmare.

"I've finally found you," it spoke again.

I didn't wake up, and all I wanted to do was scream at the top of my lungs, but I couldn't. All I could do was scream inside my head. "I'm dreaming. I'm dreaming. Go away! Please, go away!" I finally managed to say in a hoarse whisper.

"Hisss. This isn't a dream, Claudia. I've been looking for you."

How did it know my name? What was it saying? It didn't make any sense.

"I'm going to enjoy you, slowly. I could end this in one strike to your heart, but I was ordered to bring you in alive. So, I am going to savor your moments of suffering. Each strike will deliver just enough poison to make you feel pain so intense, you will be begging me for death; but don't worry, I won't kill you. I just want to have a little fun before I bring you in. Let's play!"

Who would order her to bring me in? It didn't matter. I would rather die than be in the hands of who knows what. This was it. This was how I was going to leave this Earth. I was looking death right in the eye, and there was no one here to help me. I could imagine Patty finding me, and the guilt that would consume her for leaving me here alone. And my poor mom and Gamma, I was all they had. I would be another tragic death my mom would have to bear that would break her heart. As I closed my eyes to let fate take over, the creature positioned itself and was ready to strike.

"Please forgive me for all the wrong I have done," I prayed, hoping that the life I lived and the person I was would be enough to take my soul to a peaceful place, a Heavenly place.

"Hisss. How sweet, almost sad. God can't help you now." It was mocking me.

I opened my eyes again, hoping that the snake would be gone and this was just a nightmare, but it was still there. Without warning, it lunged toward me. I expected to feel pain beyond what I have ever felt or could ever imagine, but—nothing. Suddenly, the snake loosened its hold on my body, and then let go entirely. As I looked around me, I could not believe the sight that I witnessed.

Michael was wrestling with the fog, now in a beast form that looked like a hideous monster. I couldn't believe he was here. He wasn't just a dream; or was I dreaming now? My mind was frazzled. At one point, I had been so sure that he wouldn't lift a finger to help me, but I was so wrong. He was just as much in danger as I was, and he was here to save me. Every ounce of hope for survival that I had lost was regained.

Somehow the beast wrapped itself around Michael's waist. I could see Michael struggle to take control. I wanted to help, but I was unable to move or speak.

"Michael!" the beast said in surprise. "I thought you were dead."

Michael ignored her and started asking questions. "Why are you here? What do you want?" Michael demanded as he positioned his hands around the neck of the beast.

"I want her!"

"She is not an alkin! Get that through your head! Can't you tell the difference?"

Michael was angry, but he, too, was able to talk with the beast. I knew then that this was not my imagination. He spoke almost with familiarity. This beast was someone he knew, someone he was clearly trying to convince about my existence.

"Who are you working for? Who gave you the order?" Michael demanded.

"Hissss. You think I would tell you? Tell me, Michael. How did you get down here? How did you get through my barrier? I blocked anyone from passing through."

"You think I would tell you? You think you're the only one with that kind of power? I have my ways."

"Hisss. You used to tell me everything." Its voice was flirty.

"That was a mistake!"

"Hisss! Hisss!" It was livid. "Then you deserve to die!"

"Remember, Julia, I'm stronger than you! You can't win! Don't do this! I'll let you go!"

Julia? This beast had a name. This was more than an acquaintance. How did Michael know it? What did he mean by making a mistake? As Michael finished exchanging words with Julia, he grabbed the tail and managed to set himself free. The fog grew bigger, a huge shapeless blob, and swirled around like a tunnel as it slid underneath Michael. It pushed him up and slammed him against the wall. I gasped in horror as if I had been struck too. He got up as fast as he could, but he wasn't fast enough as the fog grabbed his leg and tossed him up to the ceiling. Michael fell flat on the ground, lying still. Imagining the worst and clearly not thinking about the fog, I ran toward where he lay.

The fog instantly sensed my movement, took the form of a snake, and lunged toward me like a bullet. Michael shot up and grabbed the beast just in the nick of time. He flung the beast away, but in that instant, it flew toward me and struck near my heart.

Even Michael's reflexes weren't fast enough. I lost my balance and fell hard onto the floor, crying out in agony.

Michael and I made eye contact, and I could see terror in his eyes. I tried to get back up, but I started to feel dizzy, and the room began to spin. My body began to thrash as unbelievable pain jolted me over and over again. I wasn't sure what I was seeing or hearing because by that time, everything was out of focus, causing me to collapse. The last thing I saw was a blurry vision of what appeared to be a sword between Michael and the beast, and I thought I heard loud screeching sounds that faded out.

"Michael," I cried inside, unable to speak. I prayed it was the beast's cry that I heard as darkness surrounded me. I felt like I was floating, as light as a feather. Death must have come; now the peace I had prayed for, that I hoped I had earned, would be my reward.

Chapter 7

As I slowly came out of the darkness, I couldn't open my eyes. Hearing jumbled whispers was a sure sign that there were people around me. But then again, was I even sure they were human? Panic struck me, and I desperately wanted to know where I was.

All my efforts to open my eyes did not work, so I decided to lay still and listen. I lay motionless, afraid to make any movement to show that I had awakened. Fearing that I may be paralyzed, I wiggled my fingers and toes slightly underneath the blanket just to make sure. As a sense of relief came over me, I began to wonder if I could even protect myself. So I listened intently, trying to figure out who was in this room and what they were saying.

Even with the bits of conversation I could hear, I couldn't distinguish their voices because they were whispering the entire time. For some unknown reason, these obscure conversations triggered my memories of why I was here. Thinking about what had happened, my guard was up again, and I didn't know for sure if I was completely out of danger.

"Is she all right?" I heard her ask loudly and clearly.

Instantly my spirits lifted and I relaxed, knowing with all of my being that I was safe. I was no longer in Hell's fury. I knew that voice. It was Vivian, and I knew I must be back in Halo City. She was standing at close range…I felt like I could reach out and touch her, but I dared not. I was afraid of how she may react to my display of human affection toward her. Excitedly, I attempted to open my eyes.

When my eyes opened, my vision was still blurry. I saw several figures standing next to where I lay. Slowly I began to focus, and I could finally see Vivian, Margaret, and Agnes. They were smiling at me. I smiled back and quickly looked for Michael. Although I was happy to see them, I needed to see him. Where was he? Had something happened to him? I became concerned and scared.

As I stirred to get up and look for him, I was quickly halted by the grasps of the three angels that were standing in front of the bed. I felt a tremendous sharp pain near my heart, unlike anything I'd ever felt before. I remembered at that moment that I had been attacked and bitten by Julia. Hazy memories of the black fog, the snake, and Michael flashed in and out, but were blurry. Panic struck me as I thought about Michael. My heart was pounding rapidly. I needed to see him, needed to know if he was alive.

"Be careful. You shouldn't move. You need time to heal," Agnes said as she placed her hands gently on my shoulders and lay me back down.

I didn't care what kind of pain I was in. I needed answers. "Is Michael all right?" I asked eagerly, hoping desperately to get the only answer I wanted to hear.

"Yes," Margaret said.

I let out a heavy sigh of relief. Now I knew for sure that it was the beast who had been wounded or killed, and not Michael.

"How do you feel?" Vivian asked as she placed her hand on my forehead. "Good, no fever."

"Except for the pain, I think I feel fine," I said, staring at her facial features, thinking how pretty she was. Her long brown silky hair dangled from side to side as she fussed over me.

"We got all the poison out, so you should be feeling better soon. Thank goodness Michael brought you back in time. We were all worried you wouldn't make it," Margaret said.

"Thank you." It was all I could say, feeling embarrassed that I'd caused so much trouble.

"Michael will be relieved to see you have awakened. He carries tremendous guilt for what happened to you. He is ashamed that he was unable to protect you better," Agnes said.

"But he saved my life," I spoke quickly.

"I think you should speak to Michael and tell him yourself. Your forgiveness will free him from guilt. I'll go get him," Margaret said.

They all left and I was alone, waiting for what seemed like an eternity for Michael to come. I felt my heart quicken, sending excitement and apprehension throughout my body. I looked around at my surroundings. Whose bed was I lying on, and whose room was I in? The furnishings were simple, but nice. My thoughts were interrupted by the sound of footsteps. My heart raced again with anticipation.

"Hi," said a small, sweet voice. A beautiful young girl peered through a sheer curtain that hung where the door would have been. It was Alexa Rose. She was dressed in a cute little white dress accented with a pink bow on the front.

"Hello, come in," I said with a smile.

"Are you hurt?" she sounded concerned.

"I don't remember quite all that happened, but I'm sure I'll be fine."

With some hesitation, she asked, "Are you an angel or a human?"

"Would that make a difference?" I responded. I wasn't sure what I wanted her answer to be.

"I don't know. I've never touched a human before or even been around any…and…and if you are a human, it's too dangerous for you to be here. You should go home to your mommy."

"Why?" I asked, trying to hold back a laugh. I was extremely amused by her adorableness and her concern.

"Humans can't come here. This place is for alkins only. It is the law."

"Don't worry. I'll be on my way soon. Are you the only child here?"

"No," she said, gently swaying back and forth. "I have many friends."

"How many friends?"

"Lots and lots of them. We go to school together. We learn how to be good angels, and we learn about all the rules we need to follow," she said, giving me a huge grin.

Her smile faded and she stopped talking, her face uncertain as she turned her head toward the sheer curtain and said, "Michael is coming."

With a snicker, Michael bent down to her level and said, "Hello, princess. I see that you've met our friend."

His appearance was a total surprise; I hadn't heard any footsteps. Had it not been for Alexa Rose's warning, I wouldn't have known he was nearby. I became breathless when his eyes flickered up and held mine for a second, and my spirits were lifted to know that he called me a friend.

She looked back at him with those puppy like eyes. "I like her. I know she can't stay here, but…but could she stay anyway?" Alexa Rose begged.

Michael looked at me and quickly turned to Alexa Rose. Very compassionately he said, "I'm afraid not. Humans just cannot be allowed to stay here. You remember the rules you learned at school, don't you?"

"Yeah, but how do you know if she is not an angel? Humans never come to visit, so she must be an angel," she challenged.

"That is true, but sometimes things just happen, and we can't always explain it."

"Okay, Michael," she said, sounding convinced.

Michael gave her a hug and stood tall. "Alexa Rose, I need to speak to Claudia alone. I will see you after school. I want you to find Davin for me, okay?"

She nodded, gave me a quick glance, and ran out the door. Then we were alone. There was an uncomfortable silence. As I struggled to find the right words, my whole body tensed, and I wondered if he would be nice, or if he would be back to his old cold self again.

"Hello," he said with a smile, still standing at a distance.

I was glad he broke the silence first. The smile confirmed what I wanted to know, and I immediately relaxed. "Hi," I smiled back, wondering if I looked presentable.

He brushed his hair back. He seemed to do that when he was nervous or uncomfortable. "I'm glad to see you awake. I didn't know how long it would take you to heal or let alone wake up."

"I actually feel fine. I mean, it's my first time being bitten by a humongous snake or whatever that fog-like thing was…something that doesn't exist in my everyday life, but other than that, I think I'm fine," I said, trying to sound humorous.

It worked. He chuckled softly. It was nice to see him lighten up a bit.

"Yeah, not normal for you humans, but I'm glad to hear that you're feeling better," he responded as he approached where I lay. "I know I told you not to come here, but I brought you here because the only person who could save you from my mistake was Agnes. She has the power to heal…sometimes…unsuccessfully. I was afraid that I didn't get you to her in time." He no longer looked me in the eyes; he looked down as if he was ashamed. "You may feel some pain from time to time, but the pain will go away soon, I promise. Some guardian angel I am." He paused, glancing sideways, and let out a soft sigh. "I failed you, and I would understand if you couldn't forgive me."

I couldn't believe what he was saying. I could see the guilt through his body language. He clenched his jaw, and his hands became agitated. There was anguish in his eyes. I wanted to touch his cheek, to erase the pain he was concealing.

"I'm sorry you feel that way." As I spoke, his eyes immediately found mine with a look of surprise. "You saved my life, and there is nothing to forgive. You did everything you could. So what if I got hurt? I'm still alive, aren't I?" I rethought my last sentence, realizing I didn't know the answer. Remembering the brief conversation with Alexa Rose, she had asked me if I were a human or an angel. Could it be possible that I was dead and they didn't have the heart to tell me? Was I, now, an angel too?

"I'm still alive, aren't I?" I questioned with an unsettling look.

He approached me, closing the gap between us as he leaned forward, and looked straight into my eyes and answered. "Yes. You are still alive." Amused by my question, he laughed and lifted his right hand, raising it toward my cheek. I could feel my blood fuse with excitement and desire. How badly I wanted him to touch me just once, if that was all it would ever be. Please don't stop, I thought to myself.

As he realized what he was doing, he immediately dropped his hand and backed away in surprise. A feeling of disappointment raced through me. I wanted to feel his touch, his warmth. I closed my eyes, knowing this fantasy I was having needed to stop. I simply breathed him in, enjoying every sense of his presence. I suddenly remembered that I hadn't called my mom and Patty, as I promised I would, when I got home. How would I ever explain?

As I started to say that I needed to call my mom and Patty, and that I needed to go home, he spoke simultaneously, "You need to go home."

"You took the words right out of my mouth," I said.

We both smiled, and he shyly turned away. I was seeing a whole new side of him. His sweetness made him that much more attractive, and his smile melted my heart. I thought at any given moment I would lose control—that is, until I tried to get up. Without realizing the depth of my pain, I turned to get up. I felt a blazing pain that ran through my body. It felt worse than the first time I had tried to get up. It was like being stabbed in my chest while my whole body burned. When he realized I was in pain, Michael immediately swept me off my feet and cradled me in his arms.

"Breathe…deep breaths…relax," he whispered into my ear. I weakened at the sound of his voice, and my body went limp. After the pain subsided, I turned to look at him to let him know I was feeling better, and our eyes locked. Everything went silent. In that moment, nothing else mattered. I felt like I was floating, as if we were dancing across the sky. It seemed never-ending as he stared into my eyes.

"Let's go," Davin interrupted, waving his hand while Alexa Rose stood right behind him. We quickly turned away, hoping not to get caught. With me still in his arms, we left the room. Phillip, Agnes, Margaret, Vivian, and Caleb walked in and smiled at me.

"I would like to take her back home, if it would be all right with Claudia?" Michael asked Phillip as he lowered me down gently.

Phillip was just about to say something when he was interrupted by Alexa Rose.

"Nooo!" Alexa Rose shouted. Everyone turned to look at her.

"I'll be right back," Michael said calmly.

"But, it's too dangerous." There was fear in her voice.

Michael picked her up and hugged her warmly. "You worry too much for a child. I'll be right back." He reassured her.

"Promise?" she asked as she placed her head on his shoulder.

"Promise," he repeated after her and gently placed her down. "I always keep my word."

Phillip turned to look at Michael, "Don't stay too long. Caleb, Vivian, and Davin have my permission to go down and help you if you need any assistance."

"Did I hear you correctly? Did you say my name?" Davin asked Phillip, unsure of what he heard.

"Yes, Michael may need your assistance, and if he does, Paul will take over as gatekeeper."

Then Phillip looked at me, "I'm sorry you had to experience such an ordeal. We hadn't expected that you would get noticed that soon. Michael and I already spoke about what happened, but do you remember anything the beast said to you?"

My memory was hazy, but I was a little surprised at the few details I could remember. "I don't recall much, but I do have some recollection of it saying something like it had been looking for me," I responded.

Phillip, Margaret, and Agnes looked perplexed by my words. They didn't say anything, no words of guidance or comfort, as if they were confused themselves.

Unexpectedly, Phillip placed his hand on my shoulder and kindly said, "Don't worry. We'll figure this all out."

Phillips words confirmed what I was thinking. We'll figure this all out meant they didn't know the reason why I was in danger. My gut feeling told me that this wasn't over, and I was still in the path of danger. Or perhaps I was overreacting.

"They need to get going," Davin interrupted.

"Very well, be safe." Those were the last words I heard from Phillip as Michael and I were transported back to Fashion Wear.

Chapter 8

"We're here," he whispered.

His muscular arms wrapped me tightly and I felt safe tucked in his embrace. I had expected he would release me when we got here, but he didn't. With my eyes still closed, all I could do was enjoy the moment. I could feel his firm chest rise and fall as his breathing synchronized with mine. The beating of our hearts was all I felt as neither of us moved. I couldn't look up; an overwhelming shyness struck me.

"You're safe," he finally whispered, breaking the silence. "You can open your eyes."

After I nodded, he let go. Michael and I stood outside Fashion Wear. It was the strangest feeling to be in one place one minute and somewhere else the next. All was peaceful in contrast to what had happened inside the store. The bright, almost full moon lit up the empty parking lot, overpowering the streetlamps. It was dark and I had lost all sense of time. "What time is it?" I asked in panic.

"It's 9:30," he said.

"How could that be? I was gone for a long time. What day is it?" I asked frantically.

"Don't worry, Claudia. In previous times, you entered Crossroads by yourself through your dreams. This time I took you. When an alkin or an angel brings you to our world, you return at the same time you entered."

Although I knew he wouldn't lie to me, I stood there in disbelief. "Oh…wow…okay. I need to lock up."

"Already done while you were resting. And don't worry about the storage room. Caleb put it back to normal, as if nothing ever happened."

"Oh, thank you," I said, impressed and dumbfounded, and perplexed by the idea that the storage room was back to normal. "I almost forgot. I need to call my mom and Patty."

"Yes, of course but," he was hesitant. "Vivian texted your mom and Patty for you. I hope you don't mind," he said as he handed me my cell phone.

"Thank you. I should thank Vivian," I said. Then I thought, How did Vivian know to text my mom and Patty? Then I remembered telling Michael earlier. I looked at my text messages and read out loud, "It's my mom. She texted, glad you got home safe. Patty texted, thanks for locking up, and I owe you one." I relaxed knowing they were not worried about me. If they knew what I had been through, would they believe me? I couldn't even comprehend it myself, let alone believe what was in front of my very own eyes. I looked up at him, waiting to see what he would say or do next.

He smiled. "I should get you home," he said, starting to unchain the lock on my bike.

I couldn't recall if I had told him the combination to my lock; regardless, I was more occupied by feelings of embarrassment knowing that he knew I rode a bike to and from work. It seemed childish, and I didn't want him to perceive me as one.

"How did you know the combination to my lock?" I asked, my eyes widened in surprise.

"I just know, and no, I'm not a mind reader. Why did you pick ten, two, and six?"

"It's my birth date, October 26," I mumbled, embarrassed to confess that I used such an obvious number.

"That's next Saturday," he said with enthusiasm.

"Yeah, but I really don't want to turn eighteen."

"Why not?"

"I think of it as more responsibilities, and plus I want to be a teenager as long as I can. You can't get this youthful feeling back later on...I mean...that's what I think." I quickly diverted the attention back to him. "Since you know my birth date, how about yours?" I asked.

He paused, appearing uncomfortable with my question. "I don't know," he said finally.

I should have stopped asking further questions, but I wanted to know more. "You don't know, or you don't want to tell me?" I asked carefully.

"No, I don't know. Birthdays are not of importance to us. We don't celebrate birthdays," he said, and looked away.

"Then you don't know how old you are?" I asked, not fully convinced he was telling me the truth.

"No," he said.

My heart sank, hearing that he didn't know his age or his birth date. Not that it mattered, but I was just glad he didn't look much older than me.

"I know one thing for sure; the alkins' ages vary, up to the late twenties."

"You are all so young," I said, thinking that was a dumb thing to say.

He gave me a look that said he wanted more explanation.

I had to think fast since I didn't know what I was talking about. "I meant...well...I thought the angels might look ancient or something."

He laughed. "You have a funny imagination, but you have to remember that we are not angels. We are alkins. There is a huge difference.

"I'll keep that in mind," I said, thinking I should just keep my mouth shut for a bit.

He began to chuckle, and I found myself staring at him. I studied his features and wondered to myself how it could be possible that someone of such perfection was in my presence. "Let's get going," I said, breaking my gaze.

We started heading the opposite way. Having been so caught up in my observations of Michael, it appeared I had lost my sense of direction. "Where are you going?" I asked, looking confused.

"I thought we'd take a shortcut." He tilted his head back toward a different direction.

"I never knew there was a shortcut," I said, taking several steps closer to him.

"That's because you probably never looked for one, and it is right through that park." He pointed this time toward a dark path.

I'd seen it before, but I never knew it was a shortcut. It was frightening, nowhere I would go alone, but I had my guardian angel to protect me, so I had nothing to fear. Unexpectedly, he linked my left arm through his right arm and pulled my bike along by gripping at the handlebar. I tensed up a bit and my hands felt tingly when I realized I was touching his bare skin. We headed toward the park, and I was amazed to find that it wasn't as dark as it seemed. Instead, it was magnificent. The reflection of the moonlight bounced on the lake.

"Look!" he said, pointing toward the lake. "Do you see the two swans gliding toward each other?"

I squinted to see where he pointed, but I couldn't see what he was seeing. "Where?" I asked. "I don't see them."

He pulled the kick stand down from the bike, moved closely behind me, and bent down to my level. I could feel his breath against the side of my face. Chills ran down my back, making me breathless. As his right hand intertwined with mine, he slowly guided my hand, then my index finger, to the location of the swans. "Right...there. Can you see them now?" he asked, turning his head slightly to face me.

Overwhelmed by his closeness and still breathless, I turned to speak to him. Our lips almost brushed together. I looked up, and our eyes locked for just a second before he dropped my hand and turned away. I could tell from his body language that he felt uncomfortable. Feeling embarrassed by what could have happened; I turned to look at the swans. They met beak to beak, creating a heart shape in the space between them.

"Look, Michael, that's so romantic. I've never seen such a sight," I said excitedly, hoping to make him feel comfortable again.

"Yes," he agreed, as his eyes gazed into mine so intently that it made me speechless. It was moments like these when I couldn't believe he was real, standing right in front of me.

"Even animals are allowed to feel love and give love," he said sadly.

In that moment, I felt his pain, but what did he mean by his words? I wanted to reach out to him, to comfort him, but could I? Although I knew that he couldn't show human emotions toward me, instinctively I showed mine. Unsure of what his reaction would be, I reached out and placed my hand on his shoulder. Slowly our eyes connected and there was no need for words. In an effort to lighten the mood, I did what I did best and started asking a bunch of questions. We continued to move forward, but this time we didn't link arms. Instead, I walked beside him as he continued to pull the bike along.

"The snake or the fog thingy, or whatever it was, spoke to me, didn't it?"

"Yes. She had the ability to turn into whatever you fear the most."

"Well, she was right on target," I said, still confused about what had happened to me. "I thought I was delusional." Then I suddenly remembered she had a name. "Why did you call her Julia?"

"You remember her name?" He sounded surprised. He paused and looked like he was searching for words. "Julia was a friend, a long time ago. She was one of the alkin officers. She turned her back on us and became a fallen."

"Oh," I said in surprise. "What did she mean by blocking your passage?"

"She had the power to confuse the location of where someone is. I couldn't find you. Luckily, Vivian is a locator, and she has the power to pinpoint the exact location. It took her a while, but she finally managed to bypass Julia's block."

"Wow," I said. "I'm grateful that you made it in time. I thought I was…dead," I said, trying to choose my words carefully so I wouldn't make him feel guilty.

"Claudia, you don't need to worry about her anymore," he said tenderly. "Her life was taken by me."

"How did you kill her? I mean, I tried to hurt her with my flashlight, but it went right through."

"When she struck or defended herself, she needed to take on a solid form. That was when she was most vulnerable. I had to wait for that precise moment to quickly drive the sword into her heart."

I vaguely remembered the sound of her cry, a painful screeching noise that I heard before I fainted. I felt so bad, but I was glad that he made sure she would never hurt me again. I didn't know what to say to console him or if he even cared that he had lost someone who was once an old friend.

Suddenly, my mind focused on what Margaret had said about Isaiah's descendants. She said we didn't need to worry about the one because it was slim chance to none that the one existed, since they were sure they had taken all the forbidden children. Although I was not even in a position to question her, I couldn't help myself as the thought of "what if" crossed my mind.

"Hypothetically, what will happen if the fallen find Isaiah's descendant?"

"The fallen cannot kill the one. The one must give one's soul freely. When the soul is released by the hands of fallen, this will allow the gates of the Halo City to be opened. There will be war, and humanity will be in danger."

"Ohhh," I said quietly. "How will you know that the one is Isaiah's descendant?"

"It is said that the one would possess a special birthmark. However, any descendant of Royal Council members would possess this special birthmark. Only the Royal Council, Margaret, Agnes, and Phillip know what it is."

"Why only them?"

"It is to protect the one. If an alkin decides to become a fallen, this information would fall into the wrong hands. Knowing what the birthmark is for sure would trigger the fallen to search every single human being on earth. Imagine what that would be like. Remember, they need the one in order to enter the Crossroads to Halo City."

"I see your point," I said, feeling goose bumps. "Why can't the angels come down here and find the one, if the one does exist?"

"Angels are not allowed to intervene with lives on Earth anymore; however, the Earth angels that already exist in your world can, but they are limited. Their primary roles are to help humans, guide them, and protect them. We're not allowed to be down here. It is one of the Ten Divine Commandments. The angels lost that privilege when they —" he was hesitant to say the last couple of words—"created us." His tone was soft, almost shameful. "Anyway, Margaret said they were sure they had taken all of them, so we need not worry."

Satisfied with his answer, I asked another question that needed further explanation. "Why was Halo City created?" I wanted to hear his side of the story.

He took a deep breath. "We didn't want to leave your world, nor did we want to exist in what you call Heaven. They didn't know what to do with us, so we made an agreement with the Royal Council. We would be allowed to stay at the Crossroads in Halo City. Phillip, Margaret, and Agnes were assigned to guide us and mentor us to be more like angels rather than humans."

"Do you age in your world?"

"Alkins remain the age we were when we entered Halo City, but the Twelve can be whatever age they want to be."

"What you are telling me is that you'll be young forever, and forever you will stay at Halo City?" I asked, amazed that such a thing could be true.

"Forever young," he said. "Some may think it is a curse, and some may think it is a blessing."

"Which do you think?"

"I thought it was a curse at first, but now I don't know anymore. It doesn't matter anyway. It's not like I can do anything about it," he said.

"How did you get to Halo City? Did they come down to Earth and just do their magic thing, and you're gone? Or, did they kidnap you? There are so many of you. How?" Trying to be sensitive and choose the right words, I stumbled on my questions.

"When the Royal Council knew of our existence and realized there were so many of us, they thought about cleansing the Earth and starting over again. Since flooding was used once, they contemplated earthquake or fire."

"Apocalypse," I whispered and gasped at the thought of what could have been.

"Yes," he nodded. "The end of the world."

"But why? Why couldn't we exist together? Isn't the Earth big enough?" I asked.

"It isn't about space. The alkins would overpower humans. Eventually humanity would be lost."

I soaked in his words, speechless, but Michael continued. "The Royal Council couldn't come to terms with what they thought was in the best interest for all, so they sent the Twelve Angels to search for us. They appeared in our dreams and took us. They stopped searching when they thought they had taken all of the forbidden children."

"Does the Royal Council know you are down here with me?" I asked.

"Phillip has contacts with the Royal Council. I don't know what he tells them, so I don't know if they know I'm down here or not. I don't ask too many questions because I don't particularly care for them. Don't get me wrong. I respect them, but it doesn't mean I have to agree with everything they did."

"You don't like them?" I asked.

"They took our memories of our life on Earth and made sure that we would not be able to stay in your world for a long duration of time."

My eyes widened in shock. "What do you mean? You don't remember your life on Earth?

"No," he said softly. "But ever since I entered your world, I've had a couple of glimpses of what I believe to be flashbacks of my time on Earth. They don't make any sense. It's a lot like déjà vu. It doesn't matter. It was many lifetimes ago. I think it's just that I want to remember, but I can't."

I didn't know what to say. What words could I say to make it better? There were no words that seemed to fit a situation like this. I felt so bad for him. I couldn't imagine not being able to remember my family and friends.

He continued talking. "If I stay here too long, and I don't know what too long is…hours…days…surely not months…I will die. I will be banished from Halo City." He was hesitant to say the last sentence.

I guess I wouldn't be too fond of them if they had erased my memory either. That would also explain why Alexa Rose was upset when Michael had to come to our world. She obviously knew that he couldn't stay down here that long and was worried for his safety. "Is Alexa Rose your sister?"

"We are all brothers and sisters in Halo City. We have no recollection of having any siblings on Earth."

"Sorry, I forgot," I said, thinking I should choose my words better. "I was just wondering because she seems very protective of you, and if I didn't know any better, I would think that she was your sister. She seems attached to you." I knew the reason why. How could anyone resist him?

"Yes, I'm afraid she is. I don't mind it at all. During the time of war, the fallen captured many alkins, including children. I rescued her from them so I take responsibility for taking care of her—not that anyone else wouldn't—but yes, she is attached to me."

"Since you can't stay long in my world, is that why I can't stay in your world?"

"Yes. Crossroads is like a second Heaven, or a place between Heaven and Earth. When humans are in a state of coma, or have near death experiences, their souls may wander, and sometimes they drift there, but they never cross over to Halo City."

"Unlike me," I murmured.

"Yes, unlike you. And because you are the first, we are taking precautions; that's why we make you leave as quickly as possible, for your sake."

As I realized we were halfway home, I became anxious, wondering how long he would stay with me, so I changed the subject. "Will I see you again?"

"As your guardian angel, I can come to you if you are in danger. I don't want to scare you, but you need to know the truth. They are after you for some reason, and we suspect the only reason is that you had contact with us. They can sense you easily now since you've been touched by an angel, thanks to Davin."

I turned slightly to smell myself. I wondered how I smelled to him. He chuckled loudly as he noticed what I was doing. "No, not like smelling you," he said laughing. "Let me try to explain. Humans have five senses, some maybe six. Angels have a lot more, and some more than others. Just like humans, we were not created to have the same talents."

"Wow," I said, as I recalled the miracles I had witnessed. Julia putting me under her spell, turning herself from a fog-like creature into a snake, Michael knowing the combination to my lock, Caleb putting the storage room back the way it was, and their overall speed and strength. I was sure I had only seen a glimpse of what they were capable of doing.

Then "touched by an angel" came to mind. When Davin held me at the Crossroads to make me feel better, he whispered in my ear that he would be in a whole lot of trouble for what he was doing. And I remembered that there was a light glowing, surrounding us, which instantly calmed my nerves. Now I knew what Michael meant by being touched by an angel.

I had already asked him so many questions and began to wonder if he was getting tired of answering them. He didn't give me any hint that he wanted me to stop, so I continued. "Can I ask you another question?" I asked politely.

"Sure. Ask away. I've got all night, I think." His brow was angled, his eyes uncertain, not really knowing how long he could safely stay on Earth.

"I was wondering if the fallen has a leader or someone they report to."

He held a steady gaze into my eyes and whispered, "The devil."

In sheer panic, my heart started racing, and I couldn't keep up. Either Michael realized how fast my heart was beating, or fear was clearly written all over my face. He placed one hand on my cheek and gave me a serious look. "I'm so sorry. I was just joking," he said seriously, trying to hold back a grin.

Initially, I was in shock that he could joke around like this; then I couldn't believe he was touching my face so tenderly the way he did. Afterward, I gave him a hard stare.

"Sorry," he said again, smiling innocently.

At times like this, it was easy to forget that he was not human. Regardless, I couldn't resist his smile. I let out a nervous laugh because anyone would be better than the devil. He put his hand down, and we started walking again.

"His name is Aden," Michael said gravely.

"Aden," I repeated. It wasn't the name itself that frightened me; just knowing that someone that evil had a name gave me the creeps.

"Have you ever seen him before?"

"Yes. He was one of the Twelve Angels. Aden was reassigned to Halo City just like Phillip, Margaret, and Agnes. But he rebelled. He believed we should be allowed to live freely among humans. So he started a war with the other angels. Because of this, his soul was stripped by the Royal Council. He may as well be the devil himself. But this happened ages ago. You don't need to worry about him. When angels lose their souls, their powers weaken."

As he said his last words, we approached the front of my house. I couldn't believe we were there already, and I had no recollection of how we had gotten there.

"Here we are," he said and set my bike adjacent to the door. Then he reached for the doorknob.

My eyes followed his hand and I wondered how he was going to open the front door. He turned the knob and pushed it open. I knew my mom would never leave the door unlocked, and he didn't use a key. I continued to stare at the door, wondering how it was possible, and looked up at him when he spoke.

"How are you feeling? I know it is too much to take."

"No." I nodded, looking down. I didn't want him to perceive me as a helpless human, but the truth was that it was a lot for me to take in. Even in my wildest dreams, I couldn't have imagined that I had a real guardian angel who was keeping me safe from the fallen. It was a nightmare.

"Then why are you shaking?" he asked, concerned.

"It's a bit chilly," I replied, not realizing I was shivering. It was partly from the cold and partly from my body reacting to how I was really feeling—terrified.

"I'm so sorry," he said, while holding me tightly with both arms. Then he rubbed my back and my arms. I couldn't believe I was in his arms again. I didn't know if he was going to leave me, so I had to think fast. The only reason he would stay is if I were afraid.

I looked up at him helplessly and said, "Yes, I'm afraid." Feeling ashamed for premeditating, I glued my eyes to the floor. I wasn't totally lying because I should be deathly afraid, although his presence gave me peace and comfort.

"Let's go inside and get you out of the cold. I'll wait until your mother comes home. Would that help?"

I nodded happily, suppressing a big grin as we walked in. It was a bit uncomfortable leading him toward my bedroom, but at the same time, I was feeling electrified. It didn't take me long to get ready for bed, and he was staring out the window the whole time. He didn't utter a word, and I didn't ask him a single question. His back was still toward me as I got into bed. I wondered what he was thinking about.

"Penny for your thoughts," I said cheerfully, trying to get his attention.

He turned to face me, still deep in thought. "I don't need any of your pennies, but you would go broke."

"That many?" I asked. I was hoping he would open up and tell me what he was thinking about, but he just stood there staring at me. Feeling uncomfortable, I asked, "Can I ask you a question?"

"No more questions. Lie down and go to sleep," he ordered.

He didn't sound friendly, and I was beginning to think that he didn't want to be here. I didn't move; I sat on my bed and glanced at him. He just stood by the window, with arms crossed, and stared back at me. He appeared to be looking straight through me, perhaps, searching for words.

He sighed heavily and finally said, "Life is so unfair, even for us. Sometimes the unfairness hits hard, like a ton of bricks. Sometimes, I wish I could be human and experience life again. I feel like we are being punished for who we are."

I felt horrible. His words struck right through my heart. He took a deep breath again and gave me a look as if he was about to confess. "All of this, it's my fault," he said, then looked away.

I was confused. What could this beautiful angel possibly have done to look so distraught that he felt like he had to confess to a human?

He continued. "I, alone, have put you in danger. If I had the will to just let you be, then you would not be in this position."

I gave him a puzzled look.

"You don't remember all the times you visited the Crossroads before, do you?

"No," I said, shaking my head. I felt confused and frustrated as I tried to remember how many times I dreamt about being there.

"Let me explain. You were just a child when I first saw you at the Crossroads. You only stayed there for a very short time, and you would disappear without warning. Periodically, you would reappear. And no matter how many times you visited, you always looked lost and confused. As I watched you grow up, I wanted to reach out to you, but I couldn't. I didn't tell anyone about you. I watched you from the other side, protecting you so you wouldn't be found. Somehow you entered the realms of our world while following Margaret.

"The first time you tried to enter by yourself, I should have let you be, and you would have just disappeared, but I let you in. It was me. I was being selfish. You made me feel things I didn't know I could feel. I didn't want you to leave, and when I knew you were about to give up, I stopped you from leaving. Now these evil beings won't leave you alone." He turned his back to me again.

I didn't know what to say. I couldn't believe what I was hearing. Although I had feelings for him, I was overcome by the thought that he could have those same feelings for me. He was an alkin. We would be impossible, but something inside me didn't care. Even if it meant that we could only be together for a short time, it was better than never being with him.

He continued. "Phillip asked me to be your guardian angel to look after you, not to complicate things. He trusted me to not let my human emotions get in the way. I told him I wasn't ready, but I don't blame him. He didn't know that I had seen you before. He didn't know that I had feelings…I mean…these human emotions are too powerful, and I don't know if I can control myself," he said, looking down ashamedly. "The Royal Council took away my memories of life on Earth. They should have erased my emotions as well. Then I would just feel nothing. Training to be more like an angel than a human is nearly impossible when you already have these feelings. How do they expect us to…? These temptations…we're half human."

I knew what he meant because I felt them too. In the midst of knowing that he actually cared about me more than a guardian angel should, I lost all sense of reasoning and blurted, "I'm glad you stopped me, and I don't care about the fallen!"

His response was not what I had expected. "You don't know what you are talking about. You almost got killed."

I was overwhelmed by all this. My head was spinning out of control. Feeling frustrated and struggling for the right words, I started to cry. As he saw the first drop of tears, he dashed toward me, wiped the tears off my face, and struggled to find a way to comfort me.

"I'm sorry. I'm so sorry," he said over and over again.

It should have made me stop, and I should have tried harder to control myself, but I couldn't, nor did I try. I cried even harder; I cried for his pain, I cried for my pain, I cried for the frustration and the unfairness of life. All of these thoughts circulated through my head. Suddenly I was lifted from my bed. He held me tenderly while my head lay contentedly on his shoulder. My sobbing softened as I tried to control the lingering, small gasps of air when I realized I was in his arms.

As he held me tighter, we stood there, our bodies melting perfectly into one. I could see a low beam of light projecting around us. It felt so warm and pleasant. I felt a sense of belonging I had never felt before. I had known him for such a short time, yet I felt like I had known him all my life. Both of us held on, not wanting to let go. Now we were cheek to cheek, my face rubbing against his affectionately, as one teardrop found its way to the ground.

The relentless thumping of my heart made me breathless. Butterflies in my stomach were fluttering a hundred times faster. I was panting with thirst — thirst for his love, and thirst for his kiss. As his lips started to inch toward mine, a sensational feeling shot through my veins from head to toe; I wanted so much to kiss him.

I couldn't believe what was about to happen. We both knew it was wrong, yet it was undeniably what we wanted. I could feel his breath on my lips. I could almost taste his sweetness. Then he stopped. He leaned his forehead onto mine and let out a frustrated heavy sigh.

"Thou shall not touch," he muttered. "I'm sorry. I don't know what's gotten into me. Please forgive me. It won't happen again." He was serious and sorrowful.

Realizing what could have just happened; he sat at the head of the bed and lay me down next to him, both of us silent and still catching our breaths. Forgive him? There was nothing to forgive. I wanted him just as much, if not more. The tone of his voice made my heart ache, and I realized I needed to be cautious of my own actions and lead him not into temptation. But I didn't know if that was possible. Every time I was around him, I was overflowing with happiness, and it was hard to control my desire for him.

He started caressing my hair gently, producing a different kind of pleasure. I wanted to hold on to him as long as I could, so I turned to my side and hugged his leg. Being able to physically hold him made this all so real. But it tortured me that I would only see him when danger arose. Gradually, my heart found its rhythm again, and at the same time, I was falling asleep. I didn't have the stamina to fight sleep even though I knew he would disappear into the clouds. Drained from all that I had endured that day, I eventually succumbed to sleep.

Chapter 9

I stared straight up at my ceiling, reliving the moment when we almost kissed. It had been exactly a week since I last saw Michael, but I could still feel the heat rush through my body and feel the excitement of what could have been every time I had these thoughts. He was my guardian angel. That was why he stopped. What was I thinking? Angels and humans did not have relationships. That was how this craziness all started in the first place. But I couldn't keep myself from thinking what it would be like to kiss him.

Then suddenly, Michael's words haunted me. Even animals are allowed to receive and give love. I tried to hide you and protect you from being found when you would mysteriously appear at Crossroads. Why was it that I couldn't remember how many times I had dreamt about being at the Crossroads, other than the recent visits? Still, with all that I had endured, it was hard to conceive that what appeared to be a dream was, in fact, real. What was real to me was the emptiness I felt after he had gone.

Why did Michael have to go back? As my guardian angel, why wasn't he allowed to stay with me at all times? Wasn't it reasonable, or was I being selfish? I stopped thinking when there was a soft knock at my bedroom door.

"Claudia, are you awake?"

I cleared my throat. "Come in, Mom," I said cheerfully and sat up.

The door opened. "Happy birthday, honey!" she said excitedly and planted a kiss on my cheek. "I didn't know if you were awake or asleep." She sat on the bed.

It hit me when I heard my mother's voice. It was my birthday. What should be one of the happiest moments of my life, turning eighteen, was not all that exciting. It was the last thing on my mind.

"Do you have any plans?"

"I do have to go to work today, and I promised Gamma that I would stop by her house afterward. That's okay, right?"

"Sure it is. She'll be so happy to see you."

"I see her every Sunday, but she called me to make sure I would visit her on my birthday. I'm planning on having dinner with you as always. Were you thinking I had forgotten to include you?" I asked, smiling.

"Well, I thought perhaps you wanted to spend the evening with your friends."

"No, Mom, it didn't cross my mind. That's our time together. After all, you did give birth to me. You deserve some credit," I said, teasing and leaning toward her. "Anyways, my friends and I are going out this Friday. I was gonna tell you about it. I mean, I was going to ask you if I could go out with them."

"Of course," she said.

She looked so happy. I was glad that I didn't make any plans. "Yes, I did raise you, no biggy," she laughed. "Where would you like to go?"

Just as I was about to answer her question, my cell phone buzzed three times, letting me know that I had three text messages. She nodded her head, giving me permission to check. "It's from Patty, Kristina, and Maggie wishing me happy birthday." I quickly texted them back and then faced Mom, feeling guilty for not giving her my full attention since we hardly got to spend time together.

Refocusing and thinking about her question, I asked, "How about the same restaurant we always go to on my birthday?" I really didn't feel like celebrating, but given the fact that she had made special arrangements at work just so she could take me out, I couldn't refuse.

"Are you sure?" she asked.

I nodded.

"Okay then, how about six?

"Sounds great."

"Maybe you can convince Gamma to go out to dinner with us. She already turned me down," she said as she placed a box in my hand.

"What's this?" I asked, blinking in surprise.

"Something that I've been saving up for, something you deserve. And it's about time you get rid of your bike." She winked.

I was completely stunned. Getting rid of my bike meant only one thing. Was it what I was thinking? Could it really be a car? I continued to stare at the box.

"Aren't you going to open it?" she asked excitedly.

I held the box with both hands. The beautiful design of the wrapping paper made it difficult for me to undo it. It was designed with my favorite flower—stargazer lily. I slowly untied the pink ribbon and carefully peeled off the layers of tape one by one. I paused for a few seconds, then opened the box. My eyes glued themselves to the object, and I was in shock, wondering if what I was seeing was real.

"I...I...don't know what to say," I said, feeling overwhelmed with excitement. I couldn't believe I was holding a set of car keys.

"Is this real, Mom?" I couldn't believe I said that. What a stupid question!

"Of course it is, silly! Do you think I would give you a set of plastic keys as your birthday present?"

I laughed. "No…no…of course you wouldn't, but I can't believe it's real. Oh my gosh! Oh my gosh! You bought me a car!" I shouted with excitement. "Thank you! Thank you!" I squeezed my mom so tightly she could hardly breathe.

"Let's go take a look," she said as she stood up from my bed.

"You mean, it's in the driveway?" I was beyond excited.

"Come on! What are you waiting for?"

I was in my PJs, but I didn't care. We both ran out as she pulled my hand, leading me out the front door faster than I could keep up. There it was…a shiny black Honda Accord EX. I must have given her a look that questioned if we were able to afford it, because she answered before I could even ask. "Don't worry. I got a good deal and sorry…it's not brand-new," she said apologetically.

I circled the car. I couldn't believe this thing in front of me was mine. I didn't care that it wasn't brand-new. I never even imagined I would even get a car. I didn't know what to say.

"Mom, don't be sorry. This car is perfect." I unlocked the door and got in. Looking around and touching everything made it so real. When I got out, I started rambling with excitement. "Mom, I don't know what to say. This is so cool. I…I…I'll pay for gas. I have a job. Patty, Kristina, and Maggie are going to totally flip. I can't believe it. I…"

She interrupted my chatter and hugged me. "Just say thank you, honey. That's all. You've been so responsible, and I'm so proud of you. You deserve it." I calmed down and tenderly hugged her back. "I have to go to work now, so I'll see you at six." She kissed me on my cheek and left.

I couldn't wait to go to work to show Patty my new car. I slowly got ready for work since I had plenty of time, repeatedly looking out the front window, awestruck by my car. I couldn't believe I had my very own wheels.

As I walked from my bathroom to the front window, I noticed a box on my desk. It was a plain beige box with a purple ribbon tied into a bow. I wondered who had placed it there. I had already gotten a gift from my mom. Then Michael crossed my mind. He knew my birth date, but he couldn't have, or could he? Then I thought how silly I was being. Why would he even bother to give me a gift? He was my guardian angel, not my boyfriend.

I held the box in my hands and took a deep breath. I slowly untied the bow while anxiety crept through me. Inside the box was the most beautiful necklace I had ever seen. A silver chain was looped through beaded crystals in the shape of a butterfly. I picked up a note that read:

Dearest Claudia,

To the world you are one person, but to me, you are my world. This crystal will warn you if any fallen are nearby. I will be there to protect you.

In my heart, in my soul – M

I couldn't believe it. Did I read this right? I read it again. I was his world. I kept saying it over and over again. I was floating in air. At least I knew that he was thinking of me. Carefully I held the necklace to my chest and took a deep breath. His words were so beautiful; it swept me off my feet. There was a strangeness about receiving such a beautiful gift from an angel. How would I explain this to those close to me? Keeping any guy in my life a secret would be virtually impossible. Yet one like Michael, who nobody was to know about, left me with uncertainty about how to handle the situation. Nonetheless, I happily accepted his gift.

Hearing rumbling sounds from my stomach reminded me I hadn't eaten breakfast. I went into the kitchen and got myself a bowl of cereal. Eating while admiring the necklace, I was unaware how much time had passed. I quickly got ready, jumped into my new car, started the engine, and just sat there, wondering if I could actually drive it. I had driven my mom's car with her, but this was different.

Realizing that the necklace was still in my hand, I placed it around my neck. I lowered the front shade and opened the mirror. Tiny little facets of light glistened inside the car. It reminded me of Halo City.

I raised the shade and mentally prepared myself so I wouldn't be late for work. I can drive this car, I thought to myself. There is nothing to it. As I talked my way through my apprehension, I set the shift to D and slowly stepped on the gas pedal. This was definitely faster than the bike, and I loved every moment.

What would have taken me thirty minutes on my bike only took me five in my car. I should have factored the time difference, but I'd rather be early than late. Patiently I sat in the car waiting for Patty. Feeling the extra weight on my neck, I looked into the mirror again. Just then I was startled by loud knocks on the window. Patty was jumping up and down with excitement. I almost knocked her over as I got out to join her.

"Happy birthday! You got a car! This is so cool! I can't believe it! Now you can pick me up! We can go anywhere!" she said as she hugged me.

She kept rambling about what we would do as we headed inside. As I walked behind her, a familiar scent sweetly danced around me. In front of the cash register was a vase filled with stargazer lilies and various colors of beautiful butterflies mixed in. The only people who knew that these were my favorite were my mom and Gamma. Patty was busy taking care of a customer, so I walked straight to the vase. I was curious who they were for. It was presumptuous to think that it was for me and not for Patty, but it was my birthday after all. There was a note,

Dearest Claudia,
Happy Birthday!
In my heart, in my soul – M
"In my heart, in my soul?!?! Who's M???"

My heart skipped a beat, startled by Patty's voice. She was reading over my shoulder. I hadn't noticed her behind me. My instinct was to hide the letter, but it was too late. She immediately crossed her arms, tapping her foot on the floor, while grinning from ear to ear.

"I…I…he—" She didn't even give me a chance to finish.

"I can't believe my best friend didn't tell me she has a boyfriend." She sounded disappointed.

"Boyfriend? No. Not at all. It's not like that. I…" I didn't know what to say. "I just met him."

"Okay, then at least tell me his name?"

I knew she wouldn't budge until I told her. "M stands for Michael," I said, giving her a look asking if she was satisfied.

"Nice name," she said, nodding and smiling. She didn't stop there. "Where does he go to school? Where did you meet him? How old is he?" She asked me a ton of questions.

How could I ever explain to her that I was in love with my guardian angel? She would think that I was crazy and needed some psychiatric help. "Do you believe in angels?" I asked, out of the blue, hoping her answer would guide me to what and how much I should disclose of my secrets. However, these were not my secrets to tell, so I decided not to say anything.

"I guess. I mean they did exist a long time ago. Why are you changing the subject?"

"No, I'm not changing the subject. I…um…" Should I tell her? I wanted to badly, but I knew that it would mean that I might be putting her life in danger, and I couldn't do that to her. I had to protect her, even if it meant keeping the truth from her.

"Why do you ask, Claudia?" Patty looked confused.

"I…well…nothing." I was searching for the right words.

Suddenly, her eyes narrowed on my neckline. "Who gave you that beautiful necklace?"

"What?" I was caught off guard. I had forgotten about it. I couldn't think fast enough, so I ended up telling her the truth. "Michael gave it to me," I said quickly as if it was no big deal. I felt guilty that I couldn't tell her the whole truth, but it was a small step towards the day I hoped to tell her everything.

"A guy doesn't give a girl a necklace like that one unless you mean something to him," she said with a smile. "Do you know in some cultures, a butterfly is a symbol for a young man in love?"

"Really?" I said in surprise, trying not to appear excited at the thought that Michael could be in love with me. Knowing Patty, she was trying to read my face. I had to give her my ultimate serious look.

"Nope," I said, plain and simple, while straightening out the shirts hanging on the racks, hoping she wouldn't notice my flushed face.

"Other cultures believe that the butterfly represents the soul. Maybe he's telling you that his soul belongs to you, huh?" she asked playfully, obviously teasing me. "How romantic," she said and let out a heavy sigh. Her elbow was lightly pressed on the rack, and she looked straight up to the ceiling, as if her dream man had appeared right in front of her eyes.

I looked at her and let out a small giggle. "In my culture, a butterfly represents a gift to say happy birthday, and that's it," I said and turned on my heel to move on to the next rack of clothes.

Patty shadowed right behind me. "So, do I get to meet him or what?"

"Meet whom?" I replied, pretending not to understand.

"I can't believe you! I get it. You're embarrassed of me!"

"No, it's not like that. You're my best friend. Stop being so ridiculous!"

"What's wrong? You know you can tell me anything, don't you?" Patty said tenderly.

"Yes, it's just that he is really nice, and I don't think this relationship will go far," I said, telling her the truth.

"Sorry, I didn't mean to upset you, especially on your birthday. I'm sure you'll tell me more when you are ready," she said, looking preoccupied. She walked toward the cash register and reached down.

I was relieved that she dropped the subject. What could I say to make her understand? I didn't even understand it myself. How could I explain our relationship—one that was forbidden? As I was pondering these thoughts, Patty stood up and surprised me with a wrapped box that had "Happy Birthday" all over it.

"Thanks, Patty!" I said while giving her a tight squeeze.

"Oh, it's nothing. I saw you admiring it, and I wanted to get it for you."

"Thank you so much. You are always so thoughtful." I hugged her again. I couldn't remember what I was previously marveling at; regardless, whatever it was, I was thankful.

"A friend hears unspoken words," she said and smiled back. "Open it and try it on before it gets busy again."

"What? What if Mrs. Lee walks in?"

"Don't worry, she won't be in. It's Saturday."

"Oh yeah, I forgot. You told me she never comes in on Saturdays," I said and started to open the box with anticipation. My eyes brightened as I pulled out a black chiffon dress with gold trimmings and a sash that tied at the back to accentuate the waist. "Patty!" I called her name with excitement. "Thank you so much!" I hugged her again. "I absolutely love it! Now I have something to wear to Ryan's birthday party."

"Ryan? Your ex-boyfriend?" She sounded disgusted and surprised.

"Yes," I said slowly, knowing she would disapprove. "It's at the Grand View Hotel, so I need something nice to wear."

"The show-off who likes to fan his money around? The one who thinks he is above everyone else?"

"Yes. No. I mean, he wasn't that bad," I said in his defense. "Anyway, I broke it off, remember. We're still friends. And plus, he invited practically the whole senior class."

"Yeah, the whole senior girl class," she said sarcastically. Then her eyes got bigger as she said excitedly, "Did you say the Grand View Hotel? The...Grand View Hotel?"

"Uh huh," I said slowly.

"Too bad I don't go to your school. Maybe I'll crash the party." She arched a brow. "See, show-off," she muttered.

I shot her a "give him a break" look.

"Okay , he went out with you. He must have half a heart."

I shot her the look again.

"Okay, he had a heart for six months and then lost it," she said giggling.

I shook my head laughing softly, grabbed the dress, and headed toward the dressing room. My heart pounded rapidly and I stopped abruptly, recalling that dreadful night. I took a deep breath and walked in. As I undressed in the dressing room, I could see what was left of the wound that had healed almost completely. The bite mark left four tiny scars; evidence of Julia's existence. I placed my hand over them as flashbacks of that terrifying night came to mind. I snapped back to reality when I heard Patty's voice.

"I'm waiting!" Patty yelled.

"Hold your horses. I'm coming out!" I yelled back.

"You don't have to yell, I'm right here."

"Sorry," I said, smiling as I stepped out of the dressing room. Turning side to side, I looked in the mirror and back to Patty to see if she approved. Patty looked proud of herself. "Thanks, Patty. I don't know what to say."

"You're welcome." She smiled. "I love it on you! This dress was meant for you. Watch out, senior class, here comes Claudia," she teased.

I blushed, but it wasn't the senior class that I wanted to see me all dressed up. Would I ever have the opportunity to show Michael? "Are you telling me the truth, or are you selling?" I winked.

"Look at yourself in the mirror, and there is your answer."

"Thank you for my beautiful gift," I said and gave her a long hug again.

"I'm glad you like it. Someone's gotta dress you pretty. Now get back to work."

"Yes, boss," I said sharply, and then we both laughed.

Patty attended to a customer who had just walked in, and I quickly changed back into my jeans and T-shirt. Since it was a typical busy Saturday, time flew. I was scheduled to work only a half day, since Patty knew that it was my birthday when she set the schedule. I was happy to get off work early, since I was eager to visit Gamma.

Chapter 10

Gamma lived in a two-bedroom house, a couple of blocks from where I lived. I could have parked my car at home and walked to her house, but I wanted to show her my new car. Anxious to see her, I quickly ran toward the front door and banged on it, as if I was going to break it down.

"I'm coming," she exclaimed in her loud voice, which wasn't very loud.

When she opened the door, I flung my arms around her tiny body and kissed her on her cheeks several times. It always amazed me how beautiful her short curly white hair looked on her. Most elderly people have gray hair, but her hair was a pure shade of white. And it was all natural, not dyed; that was the beauty of it.

"I missed you! It's been too long," I said even though I saw her practically every Sunday.

"Come in. Come in."

My eyes automatically went to her hands that were holding a wooden red rosary. I felt a little uncomfortable interrupting her, assuming she was praying. It amazed me how her house always looked so tidy, not a picture frame out of place.

"I see you got a new car, but then again, I knew before you," she teased.

"You knew I was getting a car?" I asked excitedly. "Mom told you."

Of course she would share that kind of information with her since they spoke practically on a daily basis. She led me to the window. We could clearly see my parked car.

"It's beautiful," she said, and I noticed the wrinkles on her forehead.

She looked tired and older today. She sat in her rocking chair and took a deep breath.

"Tired, Gamma?" I asked while I helped her place the blanket on her lap.

"I'm just old, honey. You know, I'm eighty-eight years old."

"You don't look that old," I stated.

She smiled, and her eyes fixated outside the window toward my car. "You know, when I was your age, I had a car too. It was the most exciting feeling. That was a very long time ago. Now, I'd rather not drive. Tell me, what are your plans?"

"I'm meeting Mom for dinner, but you probably already know."

She smiled. As I continued to speak, I sat facing her to give her my full attention, and that was when I saw her eyeing my necklace.

"Beautiful," she commented while placing it gently on the palm of her hand. I froze. I had forgotten to hide it underneath my shirt. I didn't want to make it obvious that I was trying to keep it a secret, so I relaxed after my initial shock.

"This gift was not from your mother. Who could have given such a beautiful gift to you? Perhaps a gentleman?"

I didn't say a word. I didn't know what to say.

"Love is everything when you find it. It can take you places and make you feel like you've never felt before. It makes you strong, and at the same time, it can make you feel vulnerable because you give all of yourself completely. Humans are unique because we can feel it and give it. Am I boring you with love talk?" Her eyes widened questioningly.

"No, Gamma, not at all." I knew what she meant because I felt it. I wanted to tell her the truth, but what would she think? When words fail me, my emotions take over. I didn't know what possessed me; I lunged into her lap and started sobbing. I couldn't stop. I was overwhelmed with all that I had endured lately, and I just broke down. I thought about my friend Claudia, angels, alkins, fallen, and Michael. Everything happened so fast.

"What's wrong, honey?" she asked, worriedly. "Did I say something to offend you?"

Gamma was always there for me when I needed a bandage on my cut. She was always there for me when I needed a good cry, and she knew how to comfort me and make me feel safe. This was the first time I couldn't open up to her, and I felt crushed. I felt like I was doing something behind her back, but this was one secret I couldn't tell her, no matter how guilty I felt. I couldn't answer her. I just continued to sob.

"Are these tears of pain, sadness, or happiness? I can't help you if you don't tell me," she asked tenderly.

They were tears of all the above. I finally managed to stop and wiped my tears. I wanted to ask her questions, but I didn't know where to start. I thought of many different ways to approach it, but I had to start with the first question that came to mind.

"Do you believe in angels?" I asked, hesitantly.

She looked stunned, and answered with a troubled look on her face. "Yes."

"Why? How do you believe in something you cannot see?"

She was searching for words. She closed her eyes tightly, then reopened them. I don't know what I had expected her to say, but I was disappointed. I thought, being as religious as she was, she would have some answers.

"Well, I…that's a good question. I just do, honey. Why do you ask this question? Did something happen?"

I didn't answer her, instead I immediately asked another. "Do you believe in God?"

"Yes," she said, as I had expected.

"I don't know what I believe," I said, worried about what she would think of me. "I don't understand why He would allow bad things to happen to good people and why He would allow good people to suffer." I was thinking about Claudia and her tragic death.

"Well, it is difficult to believe in someone you can't see. I don't know why some people just believe and some people question His existence, but you wouldn't be human if you didn't question it. It doesn't make you a bad person. Humans are special beings because we have the freedom to make good or bad choices. Bad and good things happen to all people. If things happen beyond our control, then it was just meant to be. Everything in this universe is about balance. If there is good, there must be bad. If there is happiness, there must be sadness. But one thing is for sure, there is always a light at the end. You just have to be patient and believe. Humans are all different, and life experiences mold us to become who we are. I cannot tell you to believe or not to believe. You, and only you, will find the truth. It might be tomorrow, or in a year. Who knows? It is something you will find in your own time."

"Do you think less of me?" I asked, not able to look her in the eyes.

"Of course not, Claudia," she said, lifting my chin. "You have much to experience, and I will never judge you."

She had never judged me. I had been perfect to her in every way since the day I was born. In her eyes, I was special, and I could do no wrong. She was my comfort zone, and that was one of the many reasons why I loved being with her. Listening to her words of wisdom, I placed my arms around her small belly and lay my head on her lap again. As I let Gamma's words sink in, I felt like a little girl longing to feel safe and accepted.

We continued to enjoy each other's company, with me chatting about school and work, when we were interrupted by Gamma's phone. I immediately thought of Mom. I hadn't realized that I had been there for two hours, and I was late for dinner.

"I'll tell her to meet you there," she said quietly. "No, no, no…you girls catch up. I'm sure. Talk to you later," she said and hung up the phone.

I stood up, not wanting to leave. Gamma walked me to the door.

"Why won't you come out to dinner with us?" I asked.

"I want you to have your time with your mom. I'll only get in the way."

"Gamma, that's not true," I said, thinking she was always considerate of other people's feelings. She wanted Mom and me to have our quality time together, since I didn't get to see her that often. And I knew that once she made up her mind, she stuck to it. I knew there was no way I could convince her to come out with us, so I didn't bother to pursue it.

Gamma opened the door. "Have a wonderful dinner with your mom. Oh! I almost forgot," she said as she placed an item around my wrist. "I had this made especially for you. It was blessed by Father Roy. May you find comfort and peace in whatever lies ahead."

It was a bracelet made with brown-colored stones. In the center was a cross that blended with the bracelet so it was hardly noticeable. There was a symbolic meaning behind her gift, and it was a fashionable way for a teenager to hold a rosary.

"This one is for you to wear, and this one is for your car."

They looked exactly alike. "Oh Gamma, they're beautiful. I will wear it all the time, and I will put this one in my car." I placed my gifts over my heart to show her how much I appreciated her thoughtfulness. "I love you," I said, as I kissed both of her cheeks and hugged her before I headed out to my car.

"Happy birthday!" she said excitedly. "And drive carefully! Don't stay out too late! And call me later!"

I turned to wave good-bye, blew a kiss, and drove away to meet Mom for dinner.

🦋

"Mom!" I waved to her where she was seated at a booth waiting for me. "I'm sorry. I lost track of time."

She got out of her seat to hug me. "It's all right, honey. It's been a while since you got to spend some quality one-on-one time with Gamma. How is she?"

"She's fine, but she looks so frail," I said worriedly.

"That's what happens when you get old. Don't worry. I'll go check on her later. She is strong, and you know how stubborn she is. I guess you couldn't convince her to come out with us."

"Nope."

"What would you like to eat?" she asked, changing the subject.

"The usual, the house special hamburger, please," I replied. "I'm so hungry, I could eat a horse."

"That hungry, huh?" She laughed softly. "Anything else?" she asked lovingly.

"How about some curly fries?"

"Anything for the birthday girl."

The waiter came by our table. I didn't look up at him until I heard his voice. He was tall with a cute, friendly face.

"Hello. I'm Austin. I'll be your waiter tonight. Care to order your drinks first while you decide on what you would like for dinner?"

"Sure," Mom and I answered back simultaneously.

"I'll have the peach iced tea," I said, looking straight at him.

"Good choice," he said quickly and smiled. "And how about you, ma'am?" he asked Mom politely.

"That sounds refreshing. I'll have the same, but could you take our orders too?"

"Sure, what would you like?"

"The house special burger for my daughter, with curly fries, and I'll have your cob salad with chicken."

"Thank you. I'll be back with your drinks first."

As he walked away, Mom giggled like a teenager gloating over a cute guy. "I saw the way he was looking at you, honey."

"Mom!" I hissed quietly, leaning against the table with a shy smile on my face. Although I was flattered, I felt uncomfortable talking to her about guys.

"Whaaaat?" she asked. "Can't a mom say something when a good-looking guy seems interested in her beautiful daughter?"

"No, especially not on her birthday," I whispered.

"All right," she surrendered and changed the subject, becoming serious.

She leaned toward me as if she was going to tell me a secret. "How are you, honey? I mean, you look so tired these days. Is everything all right?" She placed her right hand over my left hand that was resting on the table.

I wasn't all right. I was hiding a secret, a kind of secret I couldn't even share with my mom. "I'm fine, Mom," I answered, unable to look her in the eyes.

"Honey, you can tell me anything. You know that, don't you? We didn't get to talk much after Claudia's death. How are you dealing with it?"

"Of course I'm sad, and I miss her, but it's a bit easier to let her go since our friendship had drifted apart. I know she will always be a part of me, but I'm dealing with it, so don't worry," I reassured her, forcing a smile on my face. "Don't worry too much, it's not good for your skin," I teased, trying to lighten the mood. "But seriously, I'm fine. Better than I thought I would be." And that was the truth. When Claudia had given me the last hug in my dream, I was able to let her go in peace.

Mom squeezed my hand before letting go. "Okay, take it easy. I don't like seeing you like this."

Did I look that bad? I didn't even notice.

Austin came to our table with our food, smiling. "Let me know what else I can help you with."

"Ketchup and Tabasco, please?" I asked.

"Anything for you. I'll be right back." His tone was flirtatious. I shyly looked down as he left.

"I told you he's interested," Mom teased.

"Mom," I said, feeling my face get warm.

"He has a nice, toned body too," she added.

Before I could say anything, Austin returned. "Here you go." He placed the ketchup and Tabasco bottles gently on the table. "Anything else I can do for you?"

"No, thank you," I responded. I noticed his smile as he walked away.

Mom and I had such a wonderful time eating and bonding that we promised to do it more often. As I lay in bed that night, I stared out the window, recapping what a peaceful night I'd had. I was wishing it hadn't ended so quickly. Then thoughts of Michael burned through my mind, as they always did when he was away. I rubbed the crystal necklace he gave me as if I was rubbing a magic lamp, wishing for him to appear. He was my first thought as I woke in the morning and my last thought as I fell asleep at night.

Looking in the darkness, I could see a few glittering stars, and wondered if Michael was looking at them too. I couldn't help but be amazed every time I thought of him. Why me? What was so special about me that I was able to cross over from my dream to his world?

🦋

The next day, after church, Patty and I went to work. Sundays were usually slow, but it was fun for us because we got to catch up on our gossip and even try on a few new clothes.

"I have something else to give you," Patty said, gleaming.

"Another gift? But you already got me something," I said, thinking about the dress she got for me on my birthday.

Patty looked very nervous and started to play with her hair. That told me that she was up to something. "Okay, it's not new. In fact, I'm just letting you borrow it. I… well…I knew you wouldn't go, so I'm making you go 'cause you're my best friend…and…I really would like for you to be there."

"Where?" I was short with her, wondering what on earth she was talking about.

"Camping! I know you don't like camping, but —"

I didn't let her finish. "That's right." I agreed quickly, and pretended to be busy with the cash register.

"Come on, Claudia. It will be fun. It's only for two days. Please!" She begged with her hands clasped together.

"You know I don't like bugs, bears, and especially snakes!" I grumbled with a disgusted look, envisioning the night I got attacked by Julia, the demonic snake.

She gave me a pleading look. "You'll be sleeping with me, and I'll take care of you."

"Bathrooms?" I asked.

"For sure, toilets and hot showers. I promise." She gave me the sign of the cross.

"I'll think about it." I said, to get her off my back.

"Well, don't think too hard because…you see…I kind of…sort of told Mrs. Lee that we needed next weekend off."

"You did what?" I was furious. I hated it when she made decisions for me without consulting me.

"I'm sorry, but I really want you to go. I know you'll have a wonderful time, and plus, when will we get this opportunity again? I know your mom will be fine with it since we would be going with our church youth group."

"It's not my mom I'm worried about. You can't mention a word to Gamma."

"Don't worry; I know how protective she is of you. A bit too much, if you ask me."

"She's just old-fashioned. But seriously, I don't want her to know. She'll get really upset and I don't want to disappoint her."

"What are you going to tell Gamma? What excuse are you going to give her for not being at church on Sunday?" Patty asked, worried for me.

"I don't know. I guess I'll tell her that I'm sick or something, and Mom will have to cover for me. We just have to be careful and not mention the word 'camping' around her," I said, already feeling guilty for contemplating the lie I was going to tell Gamma.

"Don't worry. I'm not doing anything to ruin our chance of going camping together. You turned me down several times before. I know it's because Gamma thinks it's too dangerous, but it's not. I've been so many times, and I'm in one piece."

I frowned, wondering if this was a good idea. "All right then, I'll go since you took such great efforts to arrange all this," I said, debating whether I should be mad at her or thanking her.

"Open!" she said with a huge grin. She placed an oversized box in front of me.

I was hesitant to open it, but I did as told. It was a dark brown sleeping bag that looked very warm. I didn't bother to take it out, knowing I would have to fold it back into the box.

"Sorry it's not new, but you know how expensive these things are."

"Yes, I do. I have tons of these," I said sarcastically. "But don't worry, I promise to take good care of it, and I'll return it back in mint condition," I said, this time more obligingly.

"So, are you going to bring him?" she asked, as curiosity sparkled in her eyes.

"What?" She completely caught me off guard.

"Michael. Did you forget about him already?"

She had no idea how much he was embedded in my head. "No. He won't be going." My voice was low.

"Oh, that's too bad." She looked disappointed and strolled away.

Several customers walked in, and we went back to work. We were busy, which was odd for a Sunday, but I didn't mind because it distracted me from my thoughts of him.

Chapter 11

Mom was thrilled that I was going camping with Patty. We agreed not to mention the word "camping" to Gamma and that Mom would tell her that I was too sick to attend church. I felt bad about lying to her, but I knew she would be adamant that I shouldn't go. Patty was right. She was always overprotective; more than Mom ever was. Patty had asked me to go camping with her several times before and I might have gone, but Gamma insisted that it was not a good idea. I wasn't allowed to do anything that was considered dangerous in her eyes. Regardless, I obeyed because she was my godmother, and I didn't want to start a fight about something that I would eventually be able to choose for myself.

"Over here!" Patty waved her hand.

I tossed a small black duffel bag over my left shoulder, tucked Patty's sleeping bag under my other arm, and casually walked toward her. "Hello," I said and hugged everyone standing near Patty.

"Glad you could make it, Claudia," John said with a smile.

"If Patty snores too loudly, you can come to my tent." Chris was flirtatious.

"That's not funny." Patty frowned while looking irritated. "I don't snore!" She crossed her arms.

Something about snoring made females seem less attractive, and Patty was not going to allow that to cross anyone's mind about her. I spoke in Patty's defense. "You won't get a visit from me, Chris. Patty doesn't snore." Patty looked my way with a smile to say thanks.

"Let's go! Last one on the bus does the dishes the first night!" Andrew, our camp director, joked to get us on the bus.

"Come on, Claudia!" Patty linked my arm to hers, pulling me toward the bus. "I hate doing the dishes."

"I'm walking as fast as I can." I reshuffled the bag on my shoulder. "I have extra weight on me," I said, insinuating that it was her fault.

"Wimp," she teased and pulled me even faster.

"Don't forget to take the front seat," I reminded her while we placed our things inside the storage compartment of the bus. Patty knew I suffered from motion sickness, particularly in the back seat. Being car sick was not how I wanted to start this trip.

As I climbed the steps, excitement ran through me. I had never been on a tour bus like this before. Patty had told me that Andrew rented a Greyhound bus, but I wouldn't have imagined it to be this spacious or look so nice. It even had a bathroom in the back.

"Here," she said as she patted the first seat on the bus.

I plunked myself down next to her, taking the window seat.

After the last person got on, Andrew counted heads to make sure everyone was on board. "Twenty and I make twenty-one. Great! Let's get going." He motioned the bus driver to start moving. He sat at the only empty seat available, which was right across from Patty. I knew she was thrilled since he was her secret crush that only I knew about. It was her ultimate secret, something so sacred to her that I could dangle it over her head if I were that kind of friend. I could feel Patty stiffen uncomfortably.

I whispered in her ear. "He doesn't know, so lighten up, or he'll sense something is wrong."

She nodded and loosened up and even started a conversation with him. While everyone was having fun laughing and chatting, my thoughts were elsewhere. Feeling slightly carsick from the bumpy ride, I placed my head against the window. I didn't realize I was drifting off to sleep.

Darkness surrounded me. I didn't know where I was. Then out of nowhere, my friend Claudia Emerson appeared and started speaking to me. "Claudia, why don't you come home? I need you. Why did you leave me? Don't you care?" she asked.

I took a few steps toward her, even though the sight of her frightened me. She looked so pale and ghostlike.

"What are you talking about? I am where I belong. This is home," I replied.

"No, you're wrong. You belong in my world."

"I don't understand." I walked right up to her to calm her down, but she snatched both of my wrists with so much strength that I shrieked in pain.

"Stop! You're hurting me!" She didn't let go, and the pain was excruciating. I didn't care at this point whether I was using good manners to a dead person and I shouted, "You're dead! Go away!"

At that moment, Claudia's face transformed into an unrecognizable man's face. His face expressed intense anger, and if looks could kill, he would have done it. There was a deep, sharp tone to his voice; it sounded familiar, almost like Julia's, but huskier.

"We're coming! We're coming!" he said over and over. I knew I was dreaming, and I wanted out. I tried screaming, but I had no voice. Drifting in and out of a dreamlike state, I fought with every part of my body to get myself to wake up from this nightmare. He was fading away, but the image of his face was permanently etched in my head.

Someone was shaking me. "Claudia, Claudia, are you all right? Wake up!"

"Patty," I spoke softly as I awoke to a few of my friends sitting near me, looking concerned.

"We're almost there. You were dreaming. Wow! It must have been some wild dream. Everything okay?"

"Yeah, I'm fine…thanks," I said, feeling self-conscious. I wasn't fine; the nightmare made me nervous for the rest of the ride to the campsite. I kept replaying it in my head, trying to find the meaning behind the dream. Nothing made sense, and I couldn't shake the image of the man's face.

It took us two hours to get there, and it was all a blur to me. As I stepped off the bus, the whole uncomfortable idea of camping started fading away. We grabbed our gear and headed toward the campground.

The bathroom, with hot showers, was located on the campground just as Patty promised. There were picnic tables and tents that looked spacious enough for four campers. I was happy to see only a few trees and shrubs. I disliked shrubs because they provided a home for snakes and insects. The weather was just perfect, not too hot and not too cold.

"So what do you think?" Patty nudged my shoulder.

"Not bad. Not bad at all. In fact, I may like it here." I pointed to the tents that were scattered around the campfire. "Who put up the tents? Or are they up all the time?"

Patty chuckled lightly. "Mike, the other camp director and his friends left early this morning to get the tents ready for us. Believe me, it can take hours to put up the tents," she explained, leading the way to ours.

Patty unzipped the front of our khaki tent, and I followed her in. It was spacious, yet it felt cozy. Although I knew we were exposed to whatever was out there, like bears, snakes, and who knows what, being inside the tent somehow made me feel safe. As

Patty placed her bags down, so did I. Then I copied Patty as she unrolled her sleeping bag, seeing as I didn't know if there was a proper technique to unrolling one. After all, it was my very first time.

"Here." She grabbed something out of her bag and tossed it to me. "I brought this for you."

It was a flashlight. It fumbled in my hands and I nearly dropped it, not realizing how big it was. Useless thing, I thought, reminded of that dreadful night when one went right through the black fog. Then again, it did provide some light. Patty's flashlight was mega big.

"You can light the whole campground with this thing," I said as I turned it on and off.

"That's the point. It gets really dark here, but no one can miss you with my flashlight...not that you would get lost, but just in case you need to use the bathroom in the middle of the night or something."

"You know you're coming with me, even if I have to wake you up in the middle of the night, right?" I asked matter-of-factly.

"Of course. I promised I would take care of you. Now let me unpack some of this stuff." She reached into her bag again. "Here," she said again and tossed more items at me.

"Thanks," I said, picking them up. "Sunscreen...need that...bug spray? Yuck! But I guess I need that too."

"Oh, here, I almost forgot," she said and tossed me several packs of something.

This time I caught them. They were giant chewy Sweet Tarts. "Oh my gosh! You brought my favorite candy!" I squealed. Any feelings of irritation toward her for bringing me camping disappeared. She was always thoughtful, whether the thoughtfulness was to my liking or not.

"I had to make it up to you somehow," she said, smiling. "Let's go. We need to meet the others by the campfire."

We all gathered around the campfire while the blue group was getting dinner ready. Andrew gave us some rules to follow,

"Stay in the tents you were assigned. Don't wander by yourself, and especially don't go into that area." He pointed to the woods to the left that looked to be about a mile from here. "It says to keep out, so do as the sign says. Is that clear to everyone?"

We all agreed. "Yes!"

As I was thinking to myself that I would never go in there, Marie said it aloud. "I wouldn't go in there if someone paid me. It looks deadly."

Marie was like a perfect doll; perfect skin, perfect body, perfect clothes, and even her hair was perfectly silky and shiny. Others made fun of her behind her back, saying that she practically lived in the bathroom. What she lacked most was the confidence to be herself. She was very competitive and had to be the best at everything. Her need to have the last word irked all of us.

"I dare you to go in there tonight," John teased.

"No way!" Marie replied back. "It looks like something straight out of a scary movie. Why don't you?"

"I'll go if you pay me a million dollars," John suggested playfully.

"That's enough. I want you to stay out, and if I hear of or see anyone even going near that area, I'll send you home." Andrew looked as serious as he sounded.

As Andrew was speaking, we were distracted by the smell of spaghetti and food was the only thought at that point.

"Dinner is ready!" Chris shouted, wearing an apron and holding a spatula in one hand.

As we all sat around the picnic table eager to eat, Andrew prayed. "Thank you for allowing us to get here safely. Please help us do the right thing and help these teenagers control their hormones, and make them listen to their camp director so they won't get into trouble," he said with one eye open to see if we were looking at him. I loved that he put a twist of humor into his prayer.

"Amen," we all replied.

After dinner, the red group was assigned to wash the dishes. So Patty, John, Marie, and I went straight to the kitchen area. There wasn't much to wash since we used mostly paper plates and paper cups; only a few pots, pans, and utensils. Patty was busy flirting with Andrew, and John and Marie were in a heated conversation about who knew what as they helped "clean up".

It seemed my group was busy trying not to wash the dishes, so that left me to carry out the duty. I filled the sink with warm water and allowed the pots and pans to soak. After I wiped the working area around the sink, I dunked my hands with a sponge to scrub them. I was thinking idly about Claudia, and how it would have been nice to have gone camping with her, when I felt someone's arms around me. A pair of big strong hands was gently rubbing and cleaning in unison with my own, as if our hands were one.

I was flushed with embarrassment. Who would come behind me and invade my personal space like that? Wanting to see who was rubbing my hands that way, I looked up accusingly into his deep dark brown eyes. An unfamiliar face stared back at me. I jumped with fright, backing away with a sudden jerk, and accidently splashed water on him.

"Ahhh!" I screamed. "Oh my gosh! I'm so sorry!" It took me a second to realize that he was the waiter who had waited on my mom and me at my birthday dinner.

"Kinda late for a water fight, don't you think?" His lips curled into a smile. "Or is this how you greet your friends?"

"Hi...ummm...you shouldn't scare people like that." Surprised to see him, I almost choked on my words. "What are you doing here?" I demanded, as I grabbed a towel and handed it to him.

He took it and wiped his face and shirt. "Claudia, right?"

I was surprised that he knew my name. "Yes. And you are the waiter from...?" Still in shock from seeing him here, I lost my train of thought and forgot the name of the restaurant.

"Austin. My name is Austin. Anyway, didn't look like anyone was helping, so I decided to jump in. Unless you prefer to do it yourself?" He was right. Nobody in my group was helping, but I didn't like the way he was helping.

"No. I didn't mean...I'm just surprised to see you here. I didn't know you went to the same church," I said, trying to find the right words.

"I don't. Andrew is my good friend. He invited me, so I drove up here after work."

"Oh, I see." Learning that he was Andrew's friend, my heart returned to its steady beat.

"Well, it looks like you're done, so I'll help you dry the pots and pans."

"That's okay. I'm sure you're not here to dry the..." Before I could finish my sentence, he had already grabbed a towel.

In no time we were done, and everyone was curious to meet the new person at our campsite. I could hear the girls whispering and giggling about how cute he looked, and wondering how I knew him.

Marie walked right up to him and introduced herself. "Hello there, my name is Marie," she said, batting her eyelashes while extending her hand to greet Austin.

I couldn't believe she did that, but then again, it was Marie. I wanted to throw up. I thought he would flirt back, but instead he shook her hand politely and immediately turned my way, which made her furious. She walked away pretending not to care, but I knew deep inside it bruised her ego. Andrew walked toward us to greet his friend, with Patty following behind.

"Hey, glad you made it," Andrew said. They exchanged a quick manly hug. He noticed Austin's damp T-shirt. "I see you already got acquainted with Claudia, and had a little fun with the water," he said, insinuating that we were flirting. Patty's eyes immediately widened.

"No, no, no...," I whispered to Patty. I didn't want her thoughts to wander to something that didn't happen, but she kept smiling and wasn't listening to what I was trying to tell her.

Suddenly Andrew jumped on a wooden table to get all of our attention. "Everybody, this is Austin, my best friend! He will be joining us this weekend! Austin, this is everybody!"

Austin waved.

"Hey, Austin!" everyone shouted as they welcomed him.

"Dishes are done! Great job, red team! Let's meet at the campfire!" Andrew spoke, always short and to the point.

I hadn't realized how dark it was. The only places that gave light were the campfire and the kitchen area. A dark blanket covered the "unsafe" areas that at one point looked pleasant; the darkness was now uninviting. This eerie feeling was so strong that I didn't want to expose my back to the absolute darkness.

The crackling sound of the burning wood sent a warm feeling through my body. It was starting to feel chilly as the night crept in. Many had already changed into sweats or heavy jackets to accommodate the cold. We all huddled for warmth near the campfire. I huddled between Patty and John. Just as I decided to get my jacket from the tent, I felt someone behind me.

"Excuse me, may I squeeze in?" Austin asked John.

I could tell John didn't want to, but he moved over anyway. I looked over to see Austin smiling, but I just ignored him. Unexpectedly, Austin threw a light blanket over my shoulders. I didn't even know he was holding one.

"Thanks," I said, thinking that I barely knew him and feeling uneasy about him becoming so personal with me. However, I was cold and it was thoughtful of him. Patty looked at me with a huge grin on her face.

"You looked like you could use one," Austin commented.

"Thank you," I said warmly, giving him a quick smile, and turning my attention back to Andrew's scary story.

"Let's go get some hot cocoa. That should warm you up a bit more," Austin whispered.

"What?" I asked, surprised that he asked me.

"I could use some help in the kitchen," he said, with pleading eyes.

"Oh, sure," I said, not wanting to go with him, but thinking I should since he had helped me with the dishes.

"Where are you going?" Patty whispered.

"Hot cocoa," I whispered back.

She smiled and pointed to Andrew and herself. "Bring us some."

As we walked toward the kitchen, the cold air made me shiver. I gripped the blanket by my neck, wrapping it completely around me.

"That cold?" Austin asked when we reached the kitchen area.

"I'm fine," I said eyeing a couple of pots boiling on the electric stove.

He gestured to the stove. "I started boiling the water when you went toward the campfire. I hope you don't mind?"

"No, it's fine. I mean, thank you for thinking ahead."

"Hot cocoa will help," he said as he placed the cups on the trays. He scooped the cocoa powder into the cups, poured the hot water, and stirred them with a spoon.

"Is there anything I can help you with?" I asked, feeling awkward just standing there watching him do all the work.

I looked up for an answer. He turned to face me, but I quickly looked away when his eyes met mine. Before I could move, he placed his warm hands gently on my mine, still gripping on the blanket. For a minute, I thought he was making a move on me, but instead he let go of my hold on the blanket and placed my hands straight down. He fussed over the blanket and finally managed to tie a big knot by my neck area. The blanket still enclosed me, but left a slit in the front, which allowed my hands to be free.

"You can help by holding this," he said, handing me a cup of hot cocoa. "Now your hands are free, and you can drink."

"Thanks," I said softly, with a quick smile. "How about I help you hold the other tray?"

"No worries. I got it. Remember, I'm a waiter." Somehow he managed to hold two trays. I couldn't believe he was able to hold both of them; not a drop spilled from any of the cups. As I walked behind him, I took a sip and thought to myself, Ahhhh…it really does hit the spot. I couldn't help notice his muscular arms that held the trays tightly.

Austin passed out hot cocoa to those who wanted it. You could hear everyone savoring the taste and graciously taking warmth from it. Some were exchanging scary stories as well as funny ones. It was a joy just sitting around the campfire among my friends, and the best part was, no parents! I thought about how glad I was that I came to experience camping and why I had dreaded it so much before; it wasn't so bad after all, besides the fact that Gamma didn't want me to go.

Many of our friends had left for their tents, except for Andrew, Patty, Austin, and I. We were the last ones left. Andrew offered to walk Patty to her tent, and I stayed behind, so I wouldn't be a third wheel. I wanted to give Patty and Andrew some space. Feeling a bit nervous, I sat there wondering what I should do or say. I looked straight up to see the night sky filled with thousands of luminous stars. They were so mesmerizing that I couldn't peel my eyes from them. Thinking it was about time for me to head to my tent; I was just about to excuse myself when he spoke.

"Beautiful, isn't it?" He leaned closer and pointed up to the sky, invading my personal space again.

"It is," I agreed, looking up again and slowly widening the gap between us.

"Do you know that there is a myth about how the stars came to be?" he asked.

"Really? There is a myth about the stars?" I asked excitedly. Curiosity got the best of me, and I wanted to stay and listen.

"They say when humans go to heaven, their souls turn into stars. Each star's purpose is to guide other humans still on Earth.

It acts as a beacon that guides them to the right path so that he or she can become a star when they die."

"Wow! I've never heard of that." I was fascinated.

"Well, I don't know if that's true, but it sounds interesting."

"I guess I'll never look at the stars the same way again," I stated.

"Can you see Orion?" Austin asked.

It was hard to distinguish at first because of the many stars that sparkled clearly that night. They seemed to be closer and brighter in comparison to the way they looked at home. "Orion, the hunter. I think…it's those stars…connecting there." I pointed to several stars, not realizing I had leaned close enough to almost touch his lips. I jumped from what could have happened and slid further away from him. I saw a smile on his face from the corner of my eyes. That was pretty tricky, I thought. I'm gonna have to be careful with this guy.

"Pretty impressive. You know your stars," he praised.

"Orion is one of the most recognizable constellations besides the Big Dipper," I said proudly.

"Do you know the myth behind Orion?"

"You sure know a lot of myths."

"Yeah, I read a lot and hear about these things. I think it's interesting. There are different versions of Orion, but there is one particular version I like the best. Orion, the hunter, hunted various celestial animals, including Lepus, the rabbit, and Taurus, the bull. According to Greek mythology, Orion was in love with Merope, but Merope would have nothing to do with him. Orion's tragic life ended when he stepped on Scorpius, the scorpion. The gods felt sorry for him, so they put him and his dogs in the sky as constellations. They also put all of the animals he hunted up there near him. Scorpius, however, was placed in the opposite side of the sky so Orion would never be hurt by it again."

"Wow! That's a cool myth, but sort of tragic."

"I think he's one stupid hunter for stepping on the scorpion," he said.

"Well, maybe he stepped on it on purpose. Maybe he wanted to die because Merope didn't love him back the way he wanted her to."

"Perhaps, or he was just stupid for killing himself over a girl."

"But when you're that much in love, who knows? Like Romeo and Juliet."

"Yeah, I don't understand that one either," he said, shrugging his shoulders.

"Okay…" I smiled, amused by him.

"I don't know if you know, but when you smile, you shine like the stars. Your eyes twinkle especially when you talk so excitedly," he said, looking straight into my eyes.

Feeling more nervous than before, warmth quickly spread all over my face. I was too embarrassed to say anything, but I didn't want to be rude. Why was he saying this to me? He hardly knew me at all. "Thank you." I quickly turned away.

"Andrew speaks very highly of you. He says that he has never heard you gossip or speak badly about anyone."

"Really? Andrew said that?" I was surprised. Patty must have said something nice on my behalf. "Well, I was taught never to judge a person unless you've walked in their shoes."

"Good rule. I'm glad you won't judge me because I've done many bad things," he said, arching his eyebrows.

I was stunned by his words, which was clearly expressed through my facial expression. What bad things was I not to judge him about? Seeing the expression on my face, he immediately eased my mind.

"Relax, I'm joking." He nudged my shoulder. "I'll walk you to your tent."

"It's okay. I can walk there myself. Good night." I started walking away, but he caught up to me. I thought I should take this opportunity to ask him about Andrew's feelings toward Patty. I didn't know if he would share that kind of information with me, but thought I'd try. "So, is Andrew leading Patty on, or is he really interested in her?"

"I'll tell you this much, Andrew doesn't lead anyone on. He wouldn't let Patty follow him the way she does if he wasn't interested in her."

"I just wanted to make sure."

"I understand. You're just looking after your friend's interests," he said.

"Well, I'd better get some sleep since we're hiking tomorrow, and I've never hiked before. This trip is pretty much a first all the way around for me. It's also getting awfully cold." I used my free hands to hug the blanket even tighter around me. "Aren't you cold?" I asked.

"No. It doesn't bother me."

I couldn't understand. It was freezing to me, but he was only wearing a pair of jeans and a T-shirt. He stopped walking.

"Seriously, you've never hiked before?" he said, looking surprised.

"Surely I'm not the only person in the entire universe that's never been hiking," I defended myself.

"Either that, or you are very sheltered."

"Well…" I started to say and lost my words when I realized we were at my tent. "Here we are. Thank you for walking me," I said politely as I tried to untie the knot he made with the blanket.

"Anytime," he replied.

I turned around to give his blanket back, but he had already disappeared. I tried to look for him, but there was no sign of him, not even the sound of his footsteps. How odd, I thought. As soon as I got into my sleeping bag, Patty immediately rolled over next to me and shone her flashlight on me. "Wow, what are the odds of you liking the best friend of the guy I like."

"What! Whoaaa, Patty I never said I liked him."

"Well, you could have fooled me the way you were flirting with him and getting him all wet."

"What?! I was not flirting! Not at all. And getting wet was by accident. It was his fault for scaring me. You weren't even there. I was being nice." I emphasized the word "nice."

"Well, he was definitely into you," she smiled, grinning from ear to ear.

"Really?" I pretended to be surprised. "Well, I'm sorry to disappoint you and him, but I'm not remotely interested."

"Anyway, that's all right. I'm just so glad you came. Are you glad you came with me, Claudia?" She suddenly sounded concerned.

"Yes," I replied, not wanting to admit she was right. "It's better than I thought it would be."

"See!" she said loudly, sitting up with excitement. "I knew you would! And you didn't want to come. See what happens when you listen to me? You always end up enjoying the things I make you do!"

"Hey, quiet in that tent! We're trying to sleep!" someone yelled.

"Shhh," I said to Patty as we both laughed quietly.

After the laughter subsided, I realized I was extremely tired. Feeling a bit uneasy about sleeping outdoors, I wiggled myself closer to Patty. I needed to feel her presence close to me, and I thought that physically touching her sleeping bag was just what I needed to make myself feel secure. Still feeling uncomfortable, it dawned on me that I was actually sleeping on the ground. Even though Patty's sleeping bag was plush, soft, and warm, sleeping on the ground was not what I was used to. I was out of my own comfortable bed, and I needed to readjust myself to my new environment. Thank goodness it was just for one night.

"You okay?" Patty whispered, probably wondering what the heck I was doing tossing and turning so much. "You're not scared, are you?"

"I'm fine," I replied, not knowing exactly how I felt.

"Just go to sleep, and before you know it, it will be morning."

"Okay," I answered. "You know what?"

"What?" she asked, as if anticipating that I was going to tell her something important.

"I feel like a hot dog lying here all bundled up."

"What? You're hungry?"

"No, that's not what I meant. I'm the hot dog, and the sleeping bag is the bun."

Patty busted out laughing and then covered her mouth as soon as she realized how loud she was. "I know what's on your mind," she finally managed to say after she calmed down.

"What?" I whispered out loud. But I started laughing too, thinking how silly my words were.

"Okay, but I want to know who you are thinking of, Michael or Austin?"

"What! Gross, Patty. Just because your mind is there doesn't mean mine is."

"Oh yes it is, 'cause if it wasn't, you wouldn't know what I was talking about. And since you know what I'm talking about telling me that you are not talking about it, then you are thinking about it."

I was really confused and too tired to try to figure out what she just said. "Good night, Patty," I said, giggling and ignoring whatever we were talking about.

"Michael or Austin?"

"Good night, Patty." I ignored her as my eyes became heavy, and I couldn't fight to stay awake any longer. The last thing I remembered was Patty rambling on and on about hiking in a whisper as I dozed off to sleep.

Chapter 12

I was in a deep sleep, exhausted from the day's excitement, when I was suddenly awakened with a jolt. I didn't know if a couple of hours had passed or if it was the middle of the night. A strange noise disturbed my sleep. I realized it was the sound of Patty's snoring. After I turned her head slowly to the opposite direction, the snoring stopped, so I tried to go back to sleep. As I turned around, my back to Patty, I heard a faint voice.

"Claudia…come."

At first, I thought it was Patty. I turned to look at her, but she was snoring again. Not knowing if the voice was real or just my imagination, I hesitantly stepped out of the tent, holding Patty's mega flashlight. The flashlight was so bright that I felt like I was holding a spotlight. I could clearly see what was around me. Since I couldn't see anyone, I turned to go back inside, when the voice called me again. It became stronger and more intense, and I felt a force. I found myself being pulled toward the forbidden area.

I stepped into the forest, holding Patty's flashlight with a tight grip. I could see the intricate branches tangled in all directions and it took every ounce of my strength to push my way through. As I got in further, the branches slowly slithered away like snakes, welcoming me as if they knew that I was coming. It gave me chills. The trunks of the trees were so huge that it would take ten of me with my arms extended just to measure half of its width. The height of the trees was even more remarkable; they could have touched the stars.

Although the trees looked intimidating from the outside, I was mesmerized by their beauty. Moving deeper into the forest, these colossal trees became less apparent. The combination of the full moon and Patty's mega-light provided enough brightness so I could see where I was going. I didn't know where that was, only that I was being led to the one place Andrew said not to go.

Oddly, no movement was visible and no sound was audible from this peculiar forest. I wasn't sure if it was my imagination, but I had an eerie feeling that I was being watched from the darkened woods. I walked the twisted trails, and noticed that the path was leading to a cliff ahead. My body kept on walking, like a puppet being pulled by its strings. Without warning my crystal necklace began vibrating softly. I looked down; it had turned jet black. I heard his voice, the same voice I had heard on the bus in my dream.

"Claudia, come to me."

Where was this voice coming from? What did he want with me? I needed to hide. It suddenly hit me that I wasn't dreaming, and it might be one of the fallen. I was terrified, and adrenaline began fiercely running through my body. As I was trying to catch my breath, I could see the cold mist finding its way out from my mouth. I hadn't noticed how chilly it was. I didn't know if the shaking of my body was from the cold or the absolute fear of what was to come. Every time he called my name, my body involuntarily succumbed to his calling. I knew I had to fight with everything I had because with each passing second, I was getting closer to the edge of the cliff.

"Claudia, come home to me, and let your soul be free. Give me your soul."

I could see everything, but I felt like I was sleepwalking. Mesmerized by the sound of his voice, my eyes were finally fixed on him. He was floating out beyond the cliff. It was hard to distinguish the shape of his face or his body, but my body stiffened to see such a sight. It was like something you would see only in the movies. Who was he? Why was he trying to hurt me? I was only a few feet away from my demise, and no one would ever find me. I was screaming inside for help when I heard Michael's voice loud and clear.

"Stop, Claudia!" His voice pulled me out of the trance.

Knowing Michael was there, my heart found a steadier beat. The stranger froze, and his eyes gazed past me. He looked in disbelief at the sight of Michael, as if Michael was the last person on Earth he would have expected to encounter. "Michael, it's been a long time." He was pleasant, almost friendly.

"Sorry. I can't say the same," Michael said, moving steadily toward me.

"Did you stop by to help?" he asked sarcastically, still floating in midair over the cliff.

"Yes, as a matter of fact. I came to help you leave."

"Now, now, don't be rude, Michael."

"I'm going to give you a chance to leave, and make it quick," Michael said sternly.

Fear emanated from the stranger's eyes when he realized Michael was closer than before. He glided further back and cried out furiously, "Michael, it's too late!"

"Aden, you don't have to do this. What do you want from her?"

This man was Aden, the fallen's leader. Terror began running through my body, and the temporary calm brought on by

Michael's presence had now turned to absolute horror. It was Aden who was after me.

"Back off, Michael, if you know what's good for you! I'm not alone. You remember your friends, don't you?"

Curiously, I looked behind, but I couldn't see a thing. Were they hiding? Aden floated in an astute manner, looking proud, like he had won this fight.

Michael didn't flinch. He chuckled stoutly, "And that's supposed to scare me? They are not my friends anymore!"

"Is that why you killed Julia?" Aden asked.

Michael's eyes grew wide with the sudden revelation. "So you were the one! You sent Julia instead of coming yourself! I should have known. Your powers were weakened when you turned against your own kind, leaving others to do your dirty work, like a coward."

"Julia would have brought her to me. When she didn't come back, I thought she had betrayed me, but it was you. You, Michael, ruined my plans! I should have made sure you were dead. When you escaped, you were badly wounded. I was certain you wouldn't survive. I was mistaken in thinking the Royal Council would have finished the job."

"I asked for forgiveness. The Royal Council doesn't consider me as one of the fallen like you anymore."

"Fallen," Aden laughed, mocking Michael. "Is that the best you can do?"

"I have other names, but it would be inappropriate to say them in front of a lady, now wouldn't it?" He arched his eyebrows intensely.

"Silence! No more talking! Move out of my way! You're forgetting who you are talking to."

"I do remember, too well," Michael said with a smirk. "I remember how you trained me to fight. Do you remember telling me I was the best?"

Did I hear that right? Aden trained Michael? How? When? I was beyond confused. Surely Michael wouldn't associate with an evil being like him. As these thoughts ran through my mind, Michael took a stance as if he was ready to do battle. I could feel the tension in his muscles even from a distance.

"Stop. Don't come any closer!" Aden yelled, ignoring Michael's question.

"Are you afraid?" Michael said, taunting him. "You should be."

"You dare to threaten me. Very well then. So be it." Aden gave a wicked smile. "Kill him!" Aden shouted forcefully, screeching with anger that shot a pain through my ears.

Then countless fallen came flying toward Michael, and my prediction of him collapsing didn't happen. Out of nowhere appeared Davin, Vivian, and Caleb. I was overwhelmed to see them. Michael didn't have to fight alone. Their attack was such a surprise to the fallen that even Aden was taken aback.

Even though Phillip had already told me that I wouldn't be able to tell the difference between an alkin and a fallen, it was confirmed as I watched the battle. They looked just like the alkins. The fallen and alkins fought with swords. Watching, I noticed that Michael had one too, but where had it come from?

"No!" Michael shouted, suddenly standing directly in front of me. "You don't need her. She's just a human."

"Get them!" Aden shouted again.

The fallen and alkins were battling; all the while, Michael continued to stay by my side, protecting me. They fought so swiftly that even with my flashlight; it was hard to distinguish alkins from the fallen. I focused intently, trying to figure out who was who, but it was no use. They were too fast for human eyes. Then I pointed the flashlight, hoping to blind or distract them, but that also proved to be pointless. It was only useful for my vision.

With a blink of an eye they were here, there and everywhere. All I could hear was the clanging of swords colliding against each other. The swift, sharp noise of metal slicing against metal was painful to hear. As the screeching sounds continued, all I could see were sparks as the swords made contact. It looked as if we were in the middle of a lightning storm. Fearful of any alkin getting hurt, I covered my ears, hoping that it would end soon.

Suddenly, Aden raised his hand toward the stars, and the fallen stopped. The sounds of the swords crashing against each other came to a dead halt. Aden started circling around Michael and me. As he drew closer, I could see that he looked exactly as I remembered him from my dream. The wrinkles on his forehead defined his age, and although I conceived of him as being evil, it was his voice that scared me more than his appearance. Aden never lifted a finger to fight, but instead he relied on the fallen to carry out his battle strategies.

"Michael, come with me. I'll give you anything you want."

"There is nothing I want from you!"

"They've turned you against me. I should have killed you when I had the chance!" Aden was raging with anger.

"They didn't turn me against you. I did it of my own free will."

"Move out of my way!" Aden shouted.

"You'll have to go through me first!"

As Aden was circling around us, I could sense movement from the fallen, edging closer to Michael and me. The alkin must have sensed it too as they positioned themselves right behind us and immediately began to attack the fallen. Michael moved me to the left and then to the right, fighting while shielding me. Although the fallen were fewer in number than before, they were fighting in full force. In the midst of all the chaos, I lost my grip on the flashlight, and it tumbled off the cliff. Instinctively, I reached for it, and in a split second, I began to fall, along with Michael. Gravity was pulling me faster than my body could resist. I've always heard that at the moment of death, your life flashes before your eyes; all the moments that brought you to this point, big or small. All I could think of was death itself and the one person who had changed my life forever—Michael.

Chapter 13

Complete darkness engulfed me; I couldn't see a thing. I was afraid to move, especially since I didn't know where I was. But I felt an indescribably soft object encircling me, and it made me feel so warm. Whatever it was gave me such comfort, and I felt safe wrapped inside it, like a cocoon. So soft and featherlike, it felt like velvet or the stuffing of a goose-down blanket. As I realized I wasn't dreaming, I panicked and tried to wiggle my way out. It didn't work. Feeling claustrophobic, I lost my breath, which made me fight frantically with all my might, pushing and punching, then finally surrendering when I heard his voice.

"Claudia, you're safe. It's me, Michael." Michael peered in.

"Michael?" I was so relieved to hear his voice. Pulling the crystal toward Michael, I asked quickly, "What color is it?"

I could tell he was trying to hold back from laughing. "It's clear," he said.

I relaxed. Pulling the crystal into closer view, I squinted my eyes to confirm what Michael had said, but I couldn't see a thing.

Not that I didn't believe him; I was just amazed that he could see in the dark.

While holding the crystal in my hands, I remembered that I hadn't even thanked him for my gifts. "I should have thanked you sooner, but I want to thank you for my birthday gifts. It was a pleasant surprise, but you didn't have to," I said in the most sincere way. "I thought alkins didn't celebrate birthdays."

"We don't, but the Divine Commandments didn't say anything about celebrating a human's birthday." He winked.

"So, you kind of make up your own rules, huh?"

"I guess you can say that. By the sound of your voice, you sound fine, but how are you feeling?" Michael asked, changing the subject.

"I don't know. I guess it would depend…" I paused with a terrible thought. "Am I dead?"

"You think you're dead." He chuckled. "Why is that always your first thought?"

"Well, I guess because I'm always blacking out or waking up somewhere else. This isn't normal by human standards."

He laughed out loud.

"Hey! This isn't funny. And…and where am I? I want out!" I started pushing him away from me, but he was way too strong for me and he didn't even budge. I stopped when I realized how close his face was to mine. I became breathless as he continued to look at me with such tenderness. My mind wandered with impure thoughts and I had to force myself to snap out of it. With my head clear, I remembered what I wanted to say. "Please," I asked warmly.

He let out a heavy sigh.

"Something is wrong, isn't it?" I asked. "I'm dead. I'm really dead, and you don't have the guts to tell me," I said louder, angrily.

"No. Nothing is wrong," he said, and his eyes grew bigger. "You don't think I saved you?" he asked, looking hurt.

Immediately I relaxed. It was not my intention to offend him. I should be thankful. "I didn't mean it that way. I'm sorry," I said as I ran my fingers through his hair. I was shocked that I touched him that way; immediately I placed my hand down and refocused somewhere else.

"Claudia," he called gingerly.

I looked at him, marveling at how his voice saying my name sounded like a beautiful melody to my ears. He looked so serious that I refocused my attention. I had to prepare myself for whatever he was going to tell me. The delay must mean that something awful had happened.

"I'm going to open up, but you have to promise me that you won't freak out...Promise?"

What could possibly make me freak out? All sorts of nonsense started racing through my mind. Was I hurt? Or was Michael or the alkins injured? I imagined the worst, just like the pictures I saw in my history book with the wounded soldiers during the war.

"You promise, Claudia?" he asked sternly.

"Okay. I promise," I lied, not knowing exactly how I would react to something he told me not to freak out about.

As I prepared myself for whatever it was, something held us tighter and moved us upward. Slowly, I was released from his hold. I stood right in front of him with my mouth opened so wide that I could have swallowed the forest. He slowly moved his wings up and down. They were grand, bigger than Phillip's wings. Michael's were as white as the clouds. I couldn't believe how strong they were, to be able to hold me the way they did. His wings were magnificent, but how? "Alkins don't have wings," I whispered. I stared into his eyes to get an answer.

"This one does," he responded and turned away.

"They are..." I was lost for words as I continued to stare, enthralled by him.

He continued speaking, unwilling to make eye contact. "My father is or was one of the Twelve. That's all I know." His voice was low and indifferent.

Michael's father was one of the Twelve, and the Twelve have wings. Then Phillip's words flashed through me. Phillip, Margaret, and Agnes are part of the Twelve. Aden, who had become a fallen, was one of the Twelve. That left eight of the Twelve Angels still on Earth to carry out their duty. Who could his father be? And was his father still alive, or had he died? This happened before the Crossroads was created. It could be any one of them. Regardless, I could only imagine how difficult this must be for him. Although there were so many unanswered questions, now didn't seem like the right time to ask them.

I started walking in circles around him, engrossed by his wings. His shirt was torn on the back. From where the wings protruded out, there were long slits to form an upside-down V. He was beautiful, his wings were beautiful, and I was even more in awe of him. Perhaps my reaction embarrassed him, as he quickly closed them. It was amazing how they completely disappeared without a trace of their existence. Even his shirt showed no sign that it had been torn to allow such a phenomenon.

"May I please take a look again? For me, please?" I pleaded.

"You're not freaked out?" he asked, looking astonished.

"Should I be?" I asked, wondering why he felt embarrassed with his precious gift.

"I thought it may freak you out. Something not by human standards," he replied.

I leaned closer and place my hands on his shoulders. "I'm not freaked out. I think you are amazing just the way you are. I wouldn't want you to be any other way," I said tenderly, trying to sound convincing with my words and through my body expression.

His eyes were still steady on the ground. I needed to try harder to make him understand that there was nothing freakishly wrong with him, and that his wings were just as incredible as he was.

"Michael, please, open for me," I pleaded, with my hands still resting on his shoulders. Then I gave him the biggest smile, hoping he couldn't resist and would do as I asked.

He opened gracefully, slowly expanding, not to rush the excitement of what I wanted to see again. I placed both of my hands gently on this mysterious gift and stroked it like it was gold. I was amazed by the many delicate layers of feathers, soft as cashmere and smooth as silk, but equally taken aback by the power and strength they exuded. The same wondrous feeling had rushed through my senses when I was wrapped inside them after the fall, just before I had panicked. Had I known then that they were Michael's wings, I would have stayed there for eternity.

Slowly I turned my back toward him and tried to wrap myself inside his wings again. I wanted to be back in the arms of an angel, back to the feeling of peace that was so desired. As he fidgeted away from me, he mumbled, "This is too dangerous. I won't be able to control myself." His voice was worried and low.

I didn't heed his warning. As I pulled him closer, he ultimately gave in. He held me gently with both of his arms and wings this time. All I needed was his touch, for him to hold me that way; it made all the difference in the world. I was safe again. Without thought, I turned toward him. The look in his eyes was so tempting, telling me that he wanted me too. I knew it was impossible for him to want and need me the same way, but his eyes told me something else. The depth of my yearning and what I wanted to do at this very moment was undeniable.

I leaned toward him and tenderly placed a kiss on his supple lips to thank him. It was an innocent kiss. What was the harm in just one small kiss? I was extremely surprised that he didn't push me away. I was even more surprised at myself. I was never the type to make the first move.

"Thank you for saving me," I whispered, looking straight into his soulful eyes, as something came over me. Uncontrollable heat ran through my body. He was right. It was dangerous, but it was me who couldn't control myself. His eyes gave me permission to continue, so I gave him another kiss, but slower and longer this time. He kissed me back, but with much hesitation. His lips were warm and sweet like honeysuckle, just how I imagined they would be. The warmth spread all over my body like a blazing fire.

Still holding me, he pulled me away with a sudden jerk, his eyes piercing into mine with anger. His left hand was tightly wrung around my hair and the other gripping my shirt so I could feel the tightness from it. Panting, wanting more of him, I forgot how to breathe, and so did he. His eyes, still fierce with anger, gripped me even tighter as he slightly pushed and pulled me, fighting and uncertain of what he wanted to do. Feeling petrified, I had to prepare myself for the consequence of my actions, for I knew I had crossed the line.

I was waiting for him to release me and push me away. I also anticipated the lecture he would preach about how humans and angels couldn't have any physical contact. Remembering the last time, he suddenly stopped as we almost kissed. Then, he drew me even closer, and kissed me back hungrily. Passionate kisses that I never knew could be possible claimed both of us. My toes curled, feeling immense pleasure that tingled to the very depth of my being as my fingers tugged lightly on his muscular shoulders. Then his wings were totally wrapped around us. We were in the dark, just Michael and me inside the cocoon of his wings. I couldn't believe what was happening. It was our first real kiss. He pressed his whole body against mine and I could feel his heart racing just as fast as mine was. We both lost control, and every part of me shivered with intense pleasure I had never felt before.

"Hellooo," someone said, clearing his throat.

Michael immediately unfolded his wings and exposed us. We were both in shock to have been found. Nearly falling and out of breath, I was trying to gather myself together. What had I done? As I looked around, turning my head in every possible direction, I didn't see anyone.

"Hellooo," the voice said again. I recognized the voice. It was Davin.

Glancing past some of the trees, I saw some alkins, smiling and sitting on top of the branches.

"Caleb? Vivian? What are you doing here?" I asked, surprised to see them. They glided down toward where Michael and I stood. They both smiled at us, but Caleb raised an eye upward at Michael.

"Where's Davin?" I asked casually.

"Previously saving your butt, but I'm here," Davin said from a distance that seemed to come from a tree above. He swung around a branch and landed right next to me. He then placed his arms around my shoulder. "Miss me already?" he mumbled, with a cigarette at the tip of his lips.

I wasn't surprised by their actions only because I had seen what they were capable of doing. Their strength and speed were incredible. Davin was still holding his sword. It was the length of an arm, with golden designs and beautiful indescribable markings on the handle. When he realized my eyes were focused on it, he placed it behind his back and said a few words in Latin, and it magically disappeared. Fully amazed by his little trick, I became distracted by the smell of cigarette smoke. Without hesitation, I immediately pulled the half-smoked cigarette out of his mouth and stomped on it.

"You know how bad that is for you, and plus I can't stand the smell of it," I said with a disgusted look.

He frowned first, then looked shameful. "I know, but I think I wanted to be a human again and do things I had forgotten about. I don't know where this sudden urge came from. Maybe I smoked when I lived here once upon a time. It's strange, like déjà vu."

I didn't realize how much I missed his friendship and his sincerity. Davin having the urge to smoke might be the same connection to Michael's experiencing glimpses of his past here on Earth that didn't make sense to him. Perhaps the longer they stayed, the more they might remember here and there.

"I thought you all had left," Michael said. I could tell he was uncomfortable, clearly embarrassed at being caught.

"We decided to stay since it was our first time being here," Vivian said, smiling. Then she turned to me. "Do you remember what happened?" she asked tenderly.

I dug deeper into my memory, trying to remember what they wanted me to. "I remember some now. Fallen pushed us. I fell. I mean, we fell! Michael and I fell…but Michael didn't fall, did he? He has wings. He fell to catch me." Now it was all coming together. "Then, I think that's when I blacked out."

I looked at the cliff and got a glimpse of what could have been. I knew one thing for sure…I would have fallen to my end had Michael not intervened. Now I knew why this campsite was called "The Cliff." It became clear why they were here. I looked at all four of them, one at a time. They were here to save me from the fallen.

"Thank you," I said, feeling embarrassed. I didn't know why I felt that way. Perhaps it was the trouble I was causing.

Davin placed his arms around my shoulders again. He was friendly and charming as usual. "Nothing to it. It was kind of exciting." He was trying to make me feel better.

"What happened to the fallen after I fell?" I asked.

"After we got rid of all of them, Aden disappeared," Davin replied, seeming quite proud.

"Let's hope we did enough damage so that it won't happen again," Caleb said.

Hopefully, but in danger or not, I wouldn't mind coming down to Earth once in a while just to pretend we still exist here," Vivian said, looking straight ahead, deep in her thoughts.

Curiously, our eyes followed the direction of her gaze, and we were all captivated by the exquisiteness of what we were witnessing. A small ray of light was stretching and yawning, making its way through the coat of darkness, little by little, peeling layer by layer to reveal the beauty of nature and its creatures. Night and day had met, but never touched or overlapped as the morning sun conquered the night once again. Motionless, our view looked like a giant frameless oil painting. The hills were vast, yet they all looked miniature; I could almost reach out and touch them. The curves of the lake wrapped around like a snake, seeming endless and smaller as I looked farther out into the distance.

"Wow! This view is magnificent," I said softy. But it was nothing compared to what I witnessed with Michael.

"I'm loving my view too," he whispered into my ear, as his eyes never left my face.

I turned to stare into his eyes, and I could see how much he cared for me.

"Well, we better get going," Caleb broke the silence.

Davin spoke with sadness, "The longer I stay here, the harder it is to go back. I just need one more puff." He looked at me to see how I would react. I gave him a disapproving look.

"Well, it doesn't hurt to ask. Come on, Claudia, I'm half dead anyways."

I didn't realize until he said those words that he was right. They were half humans and half angels. What did that mean? I felt for them. I could only imagine what they were feeling and wanted to reach out and comfort them—but how?

Caleb got up from the rock he was sitting on. "Well, I'm glad we're all safe, but he'll be back. We're going to have to discuss this with Phillip."

Michael didn't say anything. He didn't even look at him.

"Michael, Caleb is right. We're here to help, but the next time Aden comes back, he'll be back with more fallen. We're going to need more help. We're talking about Aden!" Davin said.

"No! Not yet! I need more time to figure this out!"

"How long? And what is it that you need to figure out?" Caleb fired back. "You're not thinking straight! Your human emotions are slowly taking you over! You need to follow the Divine Commandments!"

Michael didn't like his response. I could feel the tension, and everyone was silent. He found his calm voice again, "Please, just do as I ask. Phillip doesn't need to know about this, and I won't ask any of you to come with me next time." He looked at Caleb and then at everyone else.

"Michael, I didn't mean it that way," Caleb said. "I'm just worried for your safety, and Aden…"

He never got to finish his words. Michael looked at him coldly as soon as he heard Aden's name. "Don't worry. He has no effect on me. I'm not going down that route again." Michael reassured him.

I wanted to hear more. I was curious to know how Michael and Aden were connected.

"Like I said, we better get going," Davin interrupted.

Vivian spoke next, "I agree. We don't even know how long we could survive here, so let's get going."

They all stood up and got ready to be transported, their faces expressing mixed emotions.

Vivian waved, "See you later, Claudia. Hopefully under better circumstances next time."

Davin looked at Michael. "Coming?"

"You all go first. I need more time."

"Michael," Caleb said. "Don't forget, thou shall not…"

Michael put his hand out to stop Caleb from finishing. "Whether I do or not is none of your concern," he said calmly.

"You want to be kicked out of Halo City because of her?" Caleb raised his voice; his eyes flickered at me for a second, before refocusing on Michael. "You need to release yourself from her."

"It's too late. Don't worry about it. They won't know unless you tell, now will they?" Michael said calmly.

There was dead silence. Caleb didn't say a word, but he was right. Michael wasn't supposed to kiss me the way he did. I'd caused him to stray. What was I thinking? But I couldn't control myself, nor did I want to.

Davin spoke with a concerned voice. "Don't worry, we won't tell Phillip about any of this, but Alexa Rose will be waiting for you. She worries for your safety."

"I know. Tell her I'll be there soon."

They all stood close to Davin. I never had the chance to witness his magic until now. With his eyes closed, he mumbled a few words in Latin, turned to me with a wink and said, "See you when I see you." Before I could say a word, puff! They were gone, leaving a trail of rainbow rays that lingered for a split second before disappearing at the speed of light towards the direction they were headed.

I stood there feeling dumbfounded, looking into the empty space where they had stood. They had vanished right before my eyes. A part of me felt empty. I hadn't realized I had grown attached to them, even though I had only seen them a couple of times. It was quiet and still for a few seconds, until Michael broke the silence. "Hello."

I looked at him. "Hello there." I knew the inevitable would happen, and I had to prepare myself for the emptiness I would feel when he left me again.

He cupped both of his hands around my face. "I'm sorry. Are you all right?"

"When you leave, I won't be." I didn't want to make him feel guilty, but I wanted to tell him the truth.

"I'm sorry for all this. Sorry for doing things that make it harder for both of us."

"It's not your fault," I said.

"If it would be easier for you, I could talk to Phillip and appoint you another guardian angel."

"No," I pleaded. I couldn't bear the thought of never seeing him again. Then I crossed my arms, looking quite upset. "You expect me to go on living as if I've never met you?" I spoke angrily.

"Well, perhaps time will set you free. It looks like I have done too much damage already for you and me."

"You could forget about me that easily?" I was hurt by his words.

"Of course not, but my pain doesn't matter. Yours does. I don't want to see you waste your life wanting something that cannot be."

"There must be a way, Michael."

"Impossible. You are a human, and you belong here. I am an alkin, forced to live elsewhere."

I could feel his pain and I didn't want him to think that this was his fault. "I'll be fine. I'm not as fragile as I look, and I promise I'll be fine when you leave, so don't send anyone else, please!" I demanded.

He gave me a huge smile. "Then let us not waste a minute. What would you like to do?" he asked.

"I think I should go back and explain my absence first," I said as I realized I had left my cell phone inside the tent.

"Don't worry, already taken care of."

"How and when?"

"Before you awakened."

"What did you tell them?"

"I spoke with Andrew. I basically told him that I was in charge of the campgrounds, you had a slight accident, and you were to stay with me for medical observation.

"And he believed you?" I asked, surprised. "He didn't ask any questions?"

"They actually had no choice. I used my angel power on them. They were instructed not to come and not to ask any questions. Something like "Just do as I say.""

"How do you do that?" I asked, astonished by his power.

"The best way to explain it is that it's like being in a trance-like state, the way Aden lured you to this place. We are not allowed to use this power unless it is absolutely necessary, and I thought it was."

"Wow," I said softly. Then I realized that I didn't have to go hiking and felt delighted. Without a word, he grabbed my hand and led the way.

"Where are we going?" I asked.

"Hiking. That was on your agenda today, but we are going on a different trail."

"What?" I couldn't believe what he had just said. I gave him a big frown. "I hate hiking."

"How do you know? Have you been hiking before?

"No."

"You'll love the places I'm going to take you," he said, grinning.

He knew I didn't like hiking, but he was taking me anyway. As I slapped his arm lightly to let him know I wasn't happy, he immediately fell to the ground. Surprised by his action, I reached for him. "Michael!" I shouted.

Then next thing I knew, I was lying wrapped inside his wings as he floated slightly above me. We had locked eyes, and everything else ceased to exist. All my senses had shut down, and I couldn't control the emotion that had taken me over. I was utterly and completely head over heels in love with him. He was right. It would cause me too much pain if I could never see him again. The damage was already done.

"Hey, you tricked me," I said, smiling, not minding at all what he had just done.

"There, much better. You shouldn't frown, even when you are upset, because you never know who is falling in love with your smile. And you…have a beautiful smile. It's brighter and warmer than the sun. It lights up the sky. And your smile warms me up in many different ways," he said, lifting his brows wickedly. "Let me show you one way," he said, and lightly caressed his lips to mine.

That sent shivers up my spine, and I melted deep into the Earth. He can show me more, I thought. Next thing I knew, I was standing upright still dazed by his tender kiss. It was one simple kiss, but that was all it took to make me feel as light as a feather.

He started walking without me. "Don't worry; like I said before, you will love the places I'm going to take you! Trust me!" he shouted with excitement from afar.

I ran to catch up to him. "Great!" I mumbled, not feeling pleased at all, but at the same time, it didn't matter what we did, as long as we were together.

Chapter 14

Walking along the edge of the cliff turned my stomach inside out. Why is it that some of us are afraid of heights and others not? I couldn't recall any terrible incident; I only knew I was one of many who was terrified of heights. Every nerve in my body was telling me to back away to a place more in my comfort zone, but I had to do this for Michael. He wanted to take me somewhere that was special to him. Aside from my fear, I couldn't wait to get there. I kept telling myself not to look down, so I tried to think of other things. The best distraction was the view.

"Hurry up, slowpoke," he said jokingly, walking right behind me.

"Hey…just because you're not afraid of heights. I could just pee in my pants right now."

"What are you afraid of? Falling? You know I'll catch you if you fall."

"Don't tempt me. I might purposely fall just so I don't have to endure this," I replied, feeling slightly queasy.

"Hold my hand, I'll help you up."

"No, thanks, I can do this," I replied with a little attitude, wondering if I would regret the response I had given just to sound tougher. "Are we almost there yet?" I asked, feeling hopeful and out of breath.

He laughed hard. "Almost; that's like the tenth time you asked me."

"Maybe it's because you keep saying…almost."

He laughed again, "I promise this time, we're almost there."

"Okay, we better be, or else you'll be in big trouble."

"Oh really? What will you do?"

"I'll…I'll…" Then I realized that I didn't know much about him; his likes or dislikes. "Well, it's a surprise," I said, like it was something big.

"I don't know if I like surprises. Make sure it's a good one."

The view was magnificent, but the heat was starting to make its way up. Sweat was already dampening my skin. Michael must have noticed because he gently wiped several drops that were trickling down my forehead. I brushed my bangs back with my hands to allow the heat to escape. How was it possible that he didn't even break a sweat? I knew the answer, but I couldn't stop marveling at his capabilities.

We walked while holding hands and enjoying each other's company. Then, it suddenly dawned on me that I wasn't wearing any makeup and that I was wearing the sweats I had worn to sleep. I quickly sniffed my sweatshirt to make sure I didn't smell bad.

He gave a crooked smile as he eyed my actions. "Don't worry. You smell nice, even when you are sweating."

I blushed from embarrassment. He noticed everything, even when I tried to go unnoticed.

Timidly I asked, "Can I ask you a question?"

"Of course. What's on your mind?" he asked, giving me his full attention.

I wasn't sure if this was the right time or place to ask personal questions; maybe it was because I was afraid of what his answer could be.

Hesitantly I asked, "How did you know Aden?"

He looked straight ahead. I thought he was trying to find a way to avoid my question.

"To make a long story short, Aden strongly believed that we should live freely among humans. Shortly after we were taken to the Crossroads, Aden convinced many alkins, including me, to follow him. This is what I meant when I said he brainwashed us. I thought the world of him. He was like a father to me."

He paused, looking heartbroken. I wanted to reach out and console him. I didn't want to see him like this.

He continued, "I didn't like the things Aden did. He killed alkins who wouldn't follow him, and many of them were my friends. I tried to stop him when I realized what we were doing was wrong. There are two separate worlds for two kinds, angels and humans. Alkins weren't supposed to be born. We were created in sin."

I placed my hand on his arm and said compassionately, "No, Michael. You were created by love. How could you say that?"

"I shouldn't exist. We're nothing. I'm not a human, and I am definitely not an angel."

"You were created by two people who loved each other."

He interrupted. "Or maybe lust or temptation."

"Regardless of the reason, it's not your fault. You didn't create yourself. And it's not like the Earth angels or any of the Twelve Angels who were on Earth were emotionally detached. They were able to feel as humans, correct?"

"I suppose," he said nonchalantly.

"Then in order to understand us, they needed to feel what we feel–anger, hatred, lust, greed, sadness, and even love. And it's not like they had an emotional button they could just turn on or off."

"You need not make excuses for them." His voice was low.

"I'm trying to understand them, and so should you. You need to forgive them so you can be at peace with all of this."

"I did many bad things for Aden." His eyes were filled with anger and regret. "I don't know if I'll ever find peace in what I did for him," he said sorrowfully.

"But you are not that same person." I cringed for saying the wrong word. "I mean, alkin. So what happened after that?"

"It becomes hazy after that. Aden knew I was turning against him, and I was attacked by numerous fallen. I know for sure that Aden pierced me with his sword, and I was badly wounded, but then I woke up in Halo City. I don't know how."

"So Phillip, Margaret, and Agnes took you in?"

"Yes. They gave me a second chance, and I'm very grateful."

"They saved you because you are worth saving. They saw good in you as I do," I said, gazing deeply into his eyes, trying to read his thoughts. Pain and anger were in his eyes. Could he ever forgive them? Could he ever forgive himself? "What happened to Aden?" I asked, changing the subject.

"Aden was banned from the Crossroads, and his soul was stripped."

"What does it mean to have your soul stripped?"

"Having a soul grants you permission to have life after death. If you have no soul, you simply vanish. Some believe soulless beings are banished to a lifetime of punishment. Humans call this place "hell." When an angel's soul is taken, their powers are weakened. That is why Aden needs the fallen to do his dirty work."

"Do you have your — ?"

He didn't let me finish. He knew what I was going to ask him. "Yes," he said looking down, but his tone revealed he didn't think he deserved to have one.

I tried to make him feel better. "See, those evil beings don't have souls. You're not like them."

He gave a half smile and said, "I see your point."

I didn't believe him; his eyes said otherwise. I could imagine his guilt for killing who knows how many alkins. I could also imagine the pain of trusting someone like Aden, only to discover that he was brainwashing you to do his dirty work.

"So Aden can't just appear at the Crossroads like I did," I confirmed.

"No, but now he is out for revenge and it doesn't matter who gets in his way."

"Is that why you have that glowing ring around Halo City?"

"Yes. That glowing ring around Halo City is what keeps soulless beings out. You're very observant."

"It's not like it's not obvious or anything. It just sticks out like a sore thumb. How can anyone miss it? It glows brighter than the sun."

Michael laughed. "Yes, it is, but it's not as bright as your smile."

I smiled, flattered by his words, and looked away shyly.

"What pleases your eyes?" he asked.

"You," I said without hesitation.

He smiled. "Besides me, what pleases your eyes?"

My hands immediately touched the crystal necklace he gave me. "Butterflies," I said quickly. I didn't know why he was asking me that question.

"Butterflies it is, then."

I gave him a look that questioned his reply, but he didn't answer, so I didn't pursue it. As we continued to walk, I guessed it was probably almost noon. That would explain the rumbling sound coming from my stomach. Suddenly he covered my eyes with his hands. "We're almost there, and I want to surprise you, so don't peek."

I nodded as he slowly guided me, directing me with his hands. Although I totally trusted him, something about walking blindly made me hesitant.

"Where are you taking me?" I asked curiously.

"Shhh…," he whispered in my ear. "We're almost there."

"Why are you whispering?" I asked, whispering back.

"We don't want to disturb them."

My mind ran rampant trying to figure out what he wanted to show me.

"Close your eyes, and keep them closed," he demanded as he scooped me off my feet.

I guess I should be used to having him carry me that way, but it amazed me how effortlessly he did it. I wasn't sure, and my mind could have deceived me, but I felt like I was floating. My sense of smell was out of control. A rich, pleasant scent was filling the air around me. "Open your eyes, Claudia."

It took me a few seconds to readjust my sight, but it was worth the journey to be here. I was surrounded by a variety of flowers. The beauty of their colors and the variations were indescribable. I was amazed by the splendor. I stared at Michael smiling, and I was speechless.

"How?"

"Shhh…"

Now I knew why he was whispering and hushing me. Gradually he walked away from me, tiptoeing. He started to brush the tops of the flowers with his hands, and hundreds and thousands of butterflies fluttered off the ground right in front of my eyes.

"Wow!" My whole body exploded with joy and excitement to see this magnificent sight. Overwhelmed by their presence, my stomach fluttered right along with them.

Butterflies of every color, looking as if they were painted with patches of bold bright reds, oranges, blues, purples, and yellows, all intertwined, overlapping each other. As I continued to follow their path, I squinted at the brilliant sun in the cloudless sky. It blinded me for a split second, and then I saw that the butterflies were returning, circling around Michael and me—all of them dancing in the sky. Each knew its location and position with such precision, never colliding while reaching higher and higher to form a tunnel.

Countless butterflies, circling around us, gave me chills as I could feel the air gently flowing from their wings. It was incredible to experience such beauty of color and grace so close within reach. Gently Michael embraced me from behind and extended our arms, which allowed them to brush against our skin. I giggled as the soft wings tickled us through and through. Shortly after, they disappeared, moving upward until I could no longer see them. I turned to face him and looked at him inquisitively.

He immediately responded as if he could hear my thoughts, "No, they do not belong in your world."

I didn't ask any more questions about them because I knew it was his way of showing me how much he cared. It was a gift, and I wasn't about to spoil it. He grabbed my hand and led the way again. "Let's go. You must be starving."

"Not really," I lied.

How could I think of food when I was at a place full of magnificence? Even though I had lied to Michael and to myself about not being hungry, loud rumbling sounds gave away the fact that I was starving. He frowned and glared at me for not telling the truth.

"Okay…I'm starving," I said while rubbing my stomach as it continued to rumble. We couldn't help but laugh. As we continued to walk, I had a thought. "So if I told you that frogs pleased my eyes, I would have had countless frogs in front of me?"

He chuckled, "You don't look like the type of girl who would actually like frogs."

"Well, only if one could turn into a prince," I said with a smirk.

"Too bad, princess, because the only frog you'll ever see is this one," he said, planting a kiss on my forehead.

He led me toward some trees, and I was happy that I didn't have to step on the flowers. Instead, there was a path, one so small that you couldn't see it from a distance. He led me under a tree and it was impossible not to appreciate its beauty. The grandness of the tree and its leaves provided us shade from the sweltering sun. I was startled by the unusual size of the leaves. They were quite large, like nothing I had ever seen before. Michael was watching me, seemingly amused by my delighted reaction. He pointed to the ground. "Let's eat."

In front of me was a blue blanket with a brown wicker picnic basket on it.

"How? When?" I asked.

"I knew you would be hungry, so I asked Davin to whip up something to eat. Are you okay with this?" he asked.

"Okay with this? This is perfect," I said, tugging at him to sit next to me.

The picnic blanket was so soft, and the aroma bursting around me made me spin out of control with hunger. I didn't want to be rude, so I waited patiently for him to move first. I watched him take a few items from the basket, placing the containers in front of me.

Wanting to help, I carefully opened the lids so I wouldn't look clumsy. Inside the containers were various dishes: fried rice, Kung Pao chicken, and vegetables.

"I can't believe he cooked all this, but where?" I asked curiously. I made a mental note to myself that I should thank him the next time I saw him.

Michael looked amused, trying to hold back his laughter. I began to wonder what was so funny.

"It's called Chinese takeout," he finally said, smiling.

I sat frozen, feeling like a huge dork. I had to redeem myself, but I didn't know what to say. After I cleared my throat, I said, "Good choice." Then it dawned on me that I didn't know if he actually ate. "Are you going to eat with me?" I asked indirectly, hoping he would understand what I was trying to ask him.

"I'm not hungry," he said, taking a fork and a napkin out of the basket, placing it next to my plate.

His answer did not satisfy my curiosity. While I glanced at my plate, I was dying to ask him the question. I wasn't sure if he would feel comfortable answering, but curiosity overwhelmed me; I had to know. I asked hesitantly, "Can you eat?"

He gave a big grin. "Took you long enough to ask me."

"I…what? I…" I fumbled my words from his unexpected comment. He knew what I was trying to ask him, but he was playing games with me. He didn't let me finish.

"Yes, if I wish. But I wouldn't starve to death like you if I didn't." He winked. "One of the perks of being who I am."

I grabbed the fork as gracefully as I could, and positioned myself to eat like a lady. I didn't want to embarrass myself again. He lay on his back, arms behind his neck and legs crossed. He looked relaxed as he watched me eat.

"This is sooo good," I said, speaking nervously. He focused his eyes on me more intently, readjusting to his side, lying there comfortably.

Suddenly, he got up and wiped a bit of sauce from the corner of my mouth with a napkin. How sweet, I thought, relishing this kind of attention. After I ate the last delicious bite, he tapped the blanket next to him, motioning me to lie down. As we lay, he opened a container that was next to him. Inside were the biggest strawberries I had ever seen. My eyes opened with delight, like a child who was given a huge lollipop.

"Strawberries are my favorite fruit," I said excitedly.

"I know," he replied. He immediately placed one in my mouth. Every bit was amazing, and every bite was sweet as any other.

After he watched me eat a few, I seductively brushed a strawberry against his lips. He moved slightly forward, ready to take a bite, when I pulled it back playfully. His eyes widened in surprise, and then he gave a loving smile. I teased him once more, but this time he was too fast for me. "Delicious," he said and ate the whole strawberry.

"You can eat after all," I said, giving him a sly smile.

"Poor Adam. Now I know why he couldn't resist taking a bite of the forbidden apple from Eve. Women are dangerous," he said and gave me a playful look. Without warning, he flipped me over onto my back. His hands pinned me down as he straddled lightly on my hips.

"Hey, no fair." I tried to wiggle myself out of his hold, but it was no use.

"You're hot," he said, out of the blue.

I blushed at first, but then understood that he meant the literal meaning of hot. He noticed my flushed face and the dampness on my body. I didn't care about the heat since I was too absorbed in being with him.

"I'm fine." I lied again. "It's probably the sweats I'm wearing."

"You can take it off. I promise not to look," he said, teasing me as he released me.

"What?" I said.

"Well, either way, I can see right through your clothes if I wanted to," he smiled and turned.

"What? Seriously?" Quickly I placed both of my arms in front of my chest and grabbed the blue blanket to cover even more. "You're like Superman or something?"

"Superman? Who is Superman?"

"Never mind. He's not real," I said, feeling irritated that he didn't tell me earlier.

He looked confused. "I guess I didn't tell you. Don't worry. That would be an invasion of privacy, and I wouldn't do that to anyone. I can control my vision." He blushed.

"That's some power," I said, wondering what else he was capable of doing.

"Sometimes I can't."

"What?"

"Just kidding. Don't worry."

"Can you see through walls?" I asked, fascinated.

"Yes, but let's not talk about it. I know a perfect place to cool off. Here." He reached for me, wanting me to get up, but I continued to hold onto the blue blanket. I didn't budge.

He reached for me again. "Trust me," he said with a serious tone.

When I extended my hand, he grabbed it and pulled me up. Unexpectedly, he ripped the bottom half of my sweat pants with his hand. I was surprised how perfectly he cut them. He did it so fast that I didn't have time to react. Then he took off his T-shirt. It was the first time I saw his perfectly ripped muscular chest. His tight, cut, defined six-pack abs, flawless in form, and chiseled biceps, were unforgettable. The sight of him shirtless made my temperature rise. I had to fan myself with my hands, pretending it was the heat, and not him.

I felt extremely embarrassed and looked away. It was hard not to stare. He looked so sexy. It took some self-control not to throw myself at him.

My eyes glued to the ground and I said, "Just because you can see mine doesn't mean I want to see yours."

He chuckled. "Here, put this on." He grinned as he handed me his T-shirt. "I'll turn my back. I promise not to look."

"Oh, thanks," I said, wanting to kick myself for saying something stupid.

When his back was to me, I asked half jokingly, "You don't have eyes behind your head, do you?" I knew that question was ridiculous, but I asked anyway. After all, I didn't know what else he could do.

He laughed again, turning his head slightly and asked, "Do you wish I did?"

Shocked by his response, I fumbled my words. "I…umm…no…of course not," I said as I quickly put on his T-shirt. It was more like a dress on me, but wearing something that belonged to him made me feel that much closer to him. "You can turn now," I said.

"A bit big, but it will do. Kind of sexy, if you ask me," he said with a wink.

His comment was so unexpected that I flushed. He started gathering all his belongings from the blanket and placed them neatly near the tree. Then everything disappeared. Stunned, I looked at him with my eyes bulging out and my mouth dropped to the floor. I had just witnessed something else he could do.

He winked and shrugged his shoulders. He looked so cute with his innocent smile that I couldn't help but stare at him.

"I want to take you to another place. Let's go, it's not that far," he said excitedly as he broke the stare. "I'll race you."

"Race me? That's not fair." He had already started running before I had the chance to tell him I preferred walking. "You're too fast," I said, running after him.

He ran in circles around me like a bullet train; he was so fast that it caused a cool breeze to toss my hair from side to side. It helped me cool off a bit. How I wished I could run with him. He was my Superman, whether he understood what that meant or not.

"Show off," I said out loud, laughing.

Gradually he slowed his pace, and we were walking together. It didn't matter where we went or what we did because I was with him. Every step, every touch, every minute was a gift, and I was thankful.

Chapter 15

"We're almost there," Michael said, smiling.

"I didn't ask you if we were almost there," I replied, knowing he was teasing me.

"I know, but I wanted to beat you to it."

"Fine, you got me. I was just about to ask," I said playfully.

He had offered many times to carry me, but I didn't want to look helpless. I never wanted to be a "damsel in distress" kind of girl. But I was so glad to hear that we were close; I didn't think I could take another step. A sudden burst of energy hit me as the sound of a waterfall came closer and closer. I could almost feel its cool mist.

He's taking me to a waterfall, I thought to myself. When we reached our destination, he held my hand as we climbed some oversized rocks. Right in front of me was a single waterfall. It was not as big as I had imagined from the sound, but regardless, it was refreshing and spectacular. The roar of the water falling made me feel vulnerable to the power of its strength. As the water crashed to the bottom, the mighty waves lessened and trickled peacefully. There were many trees, rocks, and bushes that surrounded the waterfall; it would have been difficult to find this place, even for an experienced hiker.

"Sit here!" Michael waved at me.

He sat at a distance from where I was standing, dangling his feet into the water. As he kicked higher, I could see his jeans were rolled up neatly. I was so preoccupied with admiring my surroundings that I hadn't noticed he left my side. Michael splashed some water with his feet; it looked just like the crystal-clear turquoise water you see in vacation magazines. The heat and the atmosphere brought on such temptation; I wanted to jump in, even though I was not a good swimmer. Wanting to feel the water, I kicked off my shoes and headed toward him. I didn't realize how hot the path was. I looked like I was doing the chicken dance, jumping up and down as the heat shot through my bare feet. He laughed so hard watching me that it nearly threw him off balance.

"You think that's funny?" I said, giggling. I plunked myself down at a distance and started kicking and splashing water at him.

"Okay, okay, you win!" he said, sounding defeated.

We sat there enjoying the peace, when curiosity kicked in, and I began to ask him more questions. I remembered Michael telling me that he had no memories of his life on Earth, but he also told me that he had glimpses of flashbacks that made no sense. I wanted to ask him again, just in case there was something he could remember, but didn't want to share with me before. So I thought to rephrase my question.

"Do you remember your parents?" I asked, then instantly regretted asking that question for fear that I may be touching on a sore topic. He may even wonder if I had memory loss too.

He didn't look at me, nor did he act surprised by the question. He paused for a few seconds. "No, I don't at all," he said blankly, staring out into the distance.

"Does that bother you? I mean, that you don't remember much of your past?"

"It did, but I've learned to live with it and try to hold onto the memories that I have now. I'm making new memories with you." He looked at me and gave me a warm smile. "Every memory and every day that you live should be cherished. It is a gift. We all take it for granted, until it's too late. We don't appreciate what we have and always want what others have. The grass is not always greener on the other side."

"Do you know if your friends remember anything from their past?"

"Not at all."

"Not even a little glimpse?"

The look in his eyes told me he was thinking about something.

"Perhaps, I'm assuming, but maybe they do. Davin had the urge to smoke. It must have come from somewhere. This is our first time being down here since we were taken; I guess time will tell if it will bring back our memories, but I doubt that it will. I don't question the Royal Council. They know what they are doing. But who knows?"

I felt horrible. No memories of their parents, friends, or life on Earth. This wasn't fair, but then I remembered Michael saying that life isn't fair. You take it for what it is, and you make the best of it.

"If life is a gift for humans, what is it for alkins?" I asked.

He turned to me quickly and looked deeply into my eyes. As he gently caressed my hair, I closed my eyes to control my heart from racing, but it didn't work. So I opened them slowly, only to see Michael's eyes locked on mine.

"I don't know about the others, but I found mine. You are my gift. I never dreamt that I would feel this way. You make me feel human again. You make me smile. You make me laugh. I've broken some Divine Commandments, but I don't care because it doesn't feel wrong to me. How could something that feels so right be so wrong? I will treasure every second we have together, even if it's for a short period of time. These happy memories you are giving me are worth it all. I promise to protect you and even lose my soul if I have to. I will not lose you to Aden or anyone else. If that happens, I will have lost myself."

I was completely speechless. All I could do was throw myself at him. He immediately responded, and we were locked in the sweetest embrace. Neither one of us moved as we sat there, listening to the sounds of the waterfall.

Slowly, I could feel him leaning in closer, his face pressing against my hair. "I love the way you smell," he murmured as he dug his head deeper. I felt his sweet breath on my ear as his lips lightly caressed it. Then his lips moved up to my eyes. "I love the way you look at me. I love the way your eyes flirt with mine." Slowly, his lips moved down to my lips. "I love the way your lips feel against mine. You are all that I need. And it's extremely difficult to control myself around you. This feeling is too powerful. I'm under your spell," he whispered. "Tell me...to stop."

Feeling breathless from his words, I whispered, "I...I...can't." I lost all my sense of reason as he continued to press his face against mine. He wasn't fighting it, like he did the last time, and I wasn't about to stop him. I managed to mumble a few incoherent words. "If you can't...I..."

Before I could finish my sentence, his lips had already conquered mine. Gently, softly, they moved in unison. He pressed deeper, and our tongues moved in ways I never knew possible. I didn't realize we were standing until his wings enclosed us in complete darkness. I felt weak as his hands moved inside my shirt. Quivering from his touch, every part of me awakened. He glided his hand down my spine, to the small of my back and then stopped from going down any further. Tingling sensations ran through me wildly, and I was enraptured by his touch; I wanted even more of him. I couldn't get enough.

My hands tenderly ran up the smooth, strong chest that I'd wanted to touch for so long, down to his muscular arms, and then met at the fingertips, where they intertwined perfectly. "Don't stop," I whispered as I guided his hand down a little lower. Our bodies were pressed intensely, and the only thing between us was my bra and my sweat shorts. I had no recollection of how my shirt was taken off. He pulled my right leg up to his hip and wrapped it around him. Slowly he lowered me and gave me tender kisses down my neck. Arching my back, moaning with intense pleasure, I forgot everything outside our cocoon. Nobody was around to stop us. How far would we go?

"Hello there, you two lovebirds! What are you doing in there?" The voice came from the direction of the waterfall.

Startled by Davin's voice, our breaths still heavy, we stopped and calmly fixed ourselves to look presentable. Michael was in control this time and opened his wings slowly, so I wouldn't lose my balance. "Impeccable timing as usual," Michael muttered under his breath.

Flushed with embarrassment for getting caught doing something he wasn't supposed to be doing, he said loudly with slight irritation in his voice, "Hello there yourself, peeping Tom. How long were you there eavesdropping?"

Davin leaped from the top of the waterfall and landed right between us. "Don't worry, not long, just long enough to be disgusted. Actually, it was more like rated G since I couldn't see what was happening inside. I'm sure you were discussing something important and not doing things I would do with a beautiful woman." Davin arched his brows and faced me. "Sorry, just having fun with Michael. I missed him too much."

"I didn't miss you," Michael said jokingly to Davin.

"Yeah, I wouldn't miss me either," Davin said, chuckling.

Davin was about to reach for Michael and give him a hug when he stepped back, looked at my T-shirt, and looked at Michael. "Whoaaa! Claudia stole your shirt?"

I looked at what I was wearing and immediately blushed. I had forgotten I was wearing Michael's T-shirt.

"You talk too much," Michael said and pushed Davin playfully.

Then he was no longer shirtless. I blinked my eyes in surprise to witness a magical moment.

Davin pushed back. "Ready to leave? You've been here for quite some time. They were worried about you. I told everyone you were fine, but Alexa Rose begged me to come and get you."

"There is one more thing I'd like to do with Claudia," he said. He grabbed my tennis shoes, helping me slip them on.

I was extremely touched by his sweetness. Even though he told me that he cared for me, it was his actions that spoke louder than his words. It was the simple, caring things he did that made me crazy for him.

"We'll be right back," Michael said to Davin.

Before I even had a chance to ask him where we were going, his wings fanned open in a flash. Michael lifted me off the ground, and I started screaming at the top of my lungs. It was like riding a roller coaster, only faster.

"Hold on tight! You know I wouldn't let you go!" he said as we continued to fly straight up to the sky. "Open your eyes, Claudia…fly with me," he said.

I didn't realize my eyes were closed and immediately opened them. That's when I began loving every moment of this rush. What an amazing feeling it was to fly. I completely let myself go. I was one with him and one with the wind. We looked like two birds gliding across the sky. It was almost the same sense of freedom I felt when I first drove my car, but this was a million times better.

Words could not describe how I was feeling and what I was seeing. To see the splendor of nature from the sky was unbelievable. I completely forgot about everything, and a tranquil feeling rushed through me. Michael's grin continued to hold the whole time as he never left my eyesight. I didn't know how long we were flying, but knowing we had to come down saddened me deeply.

"Thank you," I whispered. It was all I could say. There were no words to express how grateful I felt. He had already given me so much. I would never forget today.

As we spiraled down slowly, I could see the tired look in his eyes, and his body showed some fatigue. Although he tried to conceal that he was getting weaker, I couldn't bear to see him that way. I knew he had to go back quickly, and I was afraid for his life. Without warning, he collapsed to his knees.

"Michael!" I yelled as I fell to my knees next to him.

"I'm alright," he lied, trying to hide the worried look in his eyes.

"Davin!" I called, afraid that he had already left.

"Right here," he said. With a blink of an eye, he appeared next to me. "We should leave now, Michael," Davin spoke, looking very concerned. "I'll take her back to the campsite. It's getting late. She should have been back by now."

I could tell Michael was not happy, but I knew he completely trusted Davin.

"I'm sorry, Claudia, I always have to leave you," he said, struggling to stand up.

Davin tried to help, but Michael just pushed him away. Michael somehow managed to get up, but he moved in a pained way. When he finally stood up, he fixated on me with such intensity. "I've changed my mind. I'm going with you. I can manage," he said, sounding strong again.

"I don't think it's a good idea, Michael. Let me take you first, and then I'll be back," Davin replied.

"Don't worry. I'm not that weak. I can manage to go on my own. If you take me first, Claudia will be left alone. And that's all it will take for them to get her. I know my body. I'll be fine," Michael said.

"We'll do it your way, but we need to hurry," Davin replied.

Michael and Davin grabbed me, and we glided across the field. They brought me back to the same place I had entered. The soaring trees looked a lot friendlier than when they were seen at night. When we neared the campsite, all that was on my mind was Michael's safety.

"Your campsite is in between those trees," Davin said, pointing toward two trees that were in front of us. "We'll wait until we know you are safe."

"I don't want to leave you," Michael said, still holding me.

"Don't worry, Michael. You need to go. I'll be fine." I tried to sound strong.

"I'll be back as soon as I can," Michael said. "I'll think of something to say to Phillip. Nothing can keep me away from you."

"I'll be waiting as long as it takes. But…make it quick."

I turned to Davin. "Thank you for being my friend, and thank you for understanding. I know we are asking a great deal of you to keep our secret, but—"

He interrupted, "It's too late for me to intervene. He's already lost to you. He's already feeling human emotions that we have tried so hard to suppress all these years. I don't blame him. I think I would too. How could you not? I know Michael far better than anyone else. As you already know, he doesn't follow the Divine Commandments. He makes up his own, which can get him into trouble if he's not careful, but who am I to judge? I think in some ways we all make up our own rules. As long as you are both aware of the consequences, then so be it.

"Regardless, human emotions or not, he is your guardian angel. He is the most qualified one. His powers are stronger than any alkin I know. Sometimes I envy him. I wish I knew what it is like to fall in love. Don't worry, I don't blame you. It's not like you both planned this. This kind of love is something you cannot control. I understand that. It makes you a better human, or alkin. That's what I see from Michael, and that is my opinion. I've never seen him happier and full of life. Evidently, love knows no boundaries. Anyway, no puff this time," he laughed. "See, your friendship makes me care about my health even though I'm already dead."

I didn't know what to say. I quickly gave Davin a peck on the cheek, "Thank you."

He was in slight shock. Immediately he placed his hand on the cheek I kissed and smiled.

As I turned to face Michael, Davin spoke again. "I almost forgot. Here's your flashlight. Can't get any brighter than this one."

He wasn't holding it before; it was as if it magically appeared in his hands. It seemed they could make things appear and disappear, like Michael with the picnic basket, their swords, and now with this flashlight. "Thank you!" I said excitedly and grabbed it out of his hands and hugged it. "I thought I lost it. I was sure it fell over the cliff."

"It did, but Michael retrieved it, thinking it was important to you. He just asked me to hold on to it. Michael was right. It is important to you," Davin replied, giving me a funny look.

Then I thought how ridiculous I must look hugging this thing. "It belongs to my friend, and I would like to take it back to her."

"Now I understand. Well, we better get going. See you when I see you," Davin said.

I turned to Michael and placed my head on his chest. His hands ran through my hair and back to my face, as if trying to memorize every detail.

"See you soon. I promise," he said. He pointed to the crystal. "I am with you."

"I know," I said, looking straight into Michael's eyes. "I love you," I said, shocked at myself for saying it. The words flowed out of my mouth so effortlessly. I immediately looked down after I said it, fearful of how he would respond.

He lifted my chin, and our eyes met again. His face lit with a broad grin as he said, "I love you more."

Feeling relief that I hadn't made a big fool of myself, I returned a heartfelt smile.

"You're doing it again," he said.

"Doing what?" I asked, wondering if I had done something wrong.

"Melting my heart with your smile," he said.

"Okay, enough with the mushy stuff. Time to go, Michael. Now I'm getting really disgusted," Davin said, laughing.

I looked at both of them, blew them a kiss, and said, "Go, I'll be fine."

"He loves me more" were the words I held on to, but he didn't know it was me who loved him more. I took a deep breath and walked toward the campsite.

Chapter 16

I reached the campsite filled with anxiety. I needed an explanation. What was I going to tell Andrew, who had told us explicitly to stay away? Oh no, how would I tell Patty? From a distance, I could see Patty running toward me. Her smile was a good sign and I was able to slowly release a bit of my anxiety.

"Are you okay?" she said, squeezing me tightly. "We were so worried about you. Did you fall hard? You must have, for the ranger to keep you that long."

As usual, Patty had too many questions, so I simply nodded. "I'm fine. I don't remember much," I lied. I was hoping that would be the end of it, but I knew she wouldn't let me off that easily.

"Now that you're fine, what the heck were you thinking?" Her voice was steady. "Who goes there in the middle of the night?" She pointed toward the off-limits area. "Are you crazy? What possessed you to go there all by yourself? And to top it off, you got hurt. Do you know how worried I was when I couldn't find you in the middle of the night? I thought you were kidnapped or…and…I just had these images of something horrible," her voice trembled, holding back her tears. "For goodness sake, I'm the one who made you go camping!"

Filled with guilt, I felt sick to my stomach that I had put her through all of this. The whole time she was giving me the third degree all I wanted to do was to tell her the truth, but I couldn't. There was nothing that I could say now to make her feel better, so I just grabbed her and held her tightly. "I'm so sorry," I said. "I'm so sorry, Patty. I don't know what came over me. I promise never to scare you like that again."

She let out a heavy sigh. "Okay, don't scare me like that again, ever. You nearly gave me a heart attack," she said as she let go and looked at me. My heart sank to the ground, seeing her eyes slightly teary. "I'm never bringing you camping again," she said, nudging me on the arm.

Although she seemed to feel better, I continued to feel horrible, and I had to find a way to make it up to her. One thing about Patty, she doesn't hold a grudge.

"So, you were with that ranger, Michael, all this time?"

"You…you met the ranger?" I said in shock, and I felt my face flush with guilt. I knew Michael had spoken to Andrew, but I couldn't recall Michael mentioning anything about meeting Patty.

"Sort of. He spoke to Andrew, and Andrew filled me in."

"Oh," I said.

"So, were you with the ranger the whole time?"

"Yeah. He wanted me to rest," I said with a straight face. I knew Patty could see right through me if I was not careful with my facial expression and my choice of words. Patty knew I wasn't a good liar, and I thought she was going to get mad at me for not telling her the truth, but she didn't suspect anything. Either that, or she decided to let it go.

"I would rest all day if he looked after me," she said. "He is one hot ranger." She looked at me from head to toe. "He gave you his shirt too? And what happened to your sweat pants? Looks like he cleaned you up pretty well." She moved her brows up and down, insinuating there was more to my disappearance from the camp.

I blushed and lost my words. "I...umm...he had to cut it, and...I tore my sweatshirt from the fall." That was the lamest excuse, but that was all I could come up with.

"Uh huh..." Patty smiled.

I hated lying to her, but what choice did I have? Patty started to say something else when Andrew interrupted. "How are you feeling?"

"I'm good as new," I said cheerfully.

"Just stick to the perimeters, please," Andrew said blankly and walked away.

I looked at Patty. "Is he mad at me?"

"What do you think? He was worried because you sort of went in there when you weren't supposed to," Patty said, pointing to the forest, trying not to sound accusatory. "Don't worry. He's fine. I told him not to be mad at you, and that I would handle it since I brought you here."

"Oh," I said, feeling guilty for not sticking to the rules. I was just glad Andrew didn't give me the heat like Patty did.

As Patty and I walked toward our tent, she finally noticed the flashlight I was holding. "So, you made use of the flashlight," Patty said suddenly.

"Oh, this thing. It's pretty useful. Very bright."

Patty just smiled. "I'll wait for you outside."

As I changed into my jeans and T-shirt, I quickly reached for my cell phone, wondering if I had any missed calls. Several missed calls from Mom. Then I looked at my text. It was from Kristina. Don't forget to RSVP to Ryan's B-day. Missing U at the movies. Hope U R having fun camping!

I texted back. Amazing! We sud go. Say Hi to Maggie for me.

Just as I stepped out, Patty approached me with her cell phone.

"Please don't tell me you called my mom!" I whispered.

"No, I didn't," she replied with a stone-cold look on her face.

I was glad she didn't, but wondered why she had that expression on her face. "What is it?" I asked immediately.

"Talk to your mom." She handed me the phone and left quickly.

I cleared my throat and tried to sound cheerful, "Hi, Mom! How are you?"

"Hi, honey. Are you okay?"

Immediately I was furious with Patty. How could she just lie to my face? "Yes, I'm fine. It's nothing. Who called you?"

"Andrew called me."

As soon as I heard his name, I felt bad for thinking Patty was lying. I was glad that I was thinking it and didn't say it out loud. I should have figured that Andrew would have called since he was our camp leader. She immediately changed the subject, which I thought was strange. I thought she would beg me to come home; instead her voice sounded different. "Mom, what is it? What's wrong?" I asked as I walked further away from my tent to get more privacy.

"I tried calling you many times."

"I'm so sorry. I forgot to take my cell phone with me," I said.

"Honey, I don't want you to worry. Everything is fine. It's just that she is in the hospital, and I—"

I didn't let her finish. I immediately knew. "How is Gamma? And just tell me the truth." I sounded firm.

"She had a stroke, a massive stroke in her brain. She is in a coma. I don't think she'll make it."

As she spoke, streams of tears fell down my cheeks, much like the waterfall I had seen earlier. Guilt pounded through me, knowing that Gamma would have been against me going camping and that Mom and I had told her that I was sick. I lied to her so I could go. Had I stayed, I would have been with her the whole time. She needed me, and I wasn't there for her. Could I ever forgive myself for this?

"Honey? Claudia? Are you there?"

"Yes." It was all I could say without sounding like I was crying.

"I know you'll be home soon, and I'm sure Gamma is waiting for you to say good-bye. I know this is hard, honey. She had a wonderful life. We all have to be happy for her. She'll be in a much better place. I'll see you when you come home…okay?"

"See you at home," I said, my voice trembling.

As soon as I hung up, Patty ran toward me and held me tight. "I'm sooo sorry!" she whispered.

I knew I didn't have to say a word. Everyone already knew. I was too busy elsewhere. I felt guilty for not being there for her, and I would feel worse if I didn't get to her on time. I realized at that moment that everybody was already packed to leave. They were just waiting for my return.

Patty had already packed my bags for me while I was on the phone with Mom. What would I do without her? What would I do without Gamma? With Gamma on my mind, I immediately sat at the same seat on the bus. I knew it would happen someday, but not now and not like this, when I was not with her. It felt like a dream. Was Gamma really in a coma? I closed my eyes and tried to come to terms with reality. Just then, I heard a voice. It was Austin.

"Claudia, Andrew said it was fine for me to take you home since I can get you there faster in my car."

The idea of riding with Austin didn't appeal to me, but it would be faster than the bus. I looked at Patty questioningly. She nodded and motioned for me to go. "I'll call you later," she said. Then she grabbed my wrist when I was halfway out of my seat. "Don't worry about your bag. It will slow you down. I'll drop it off later."

"Okay, thanks," I said, as I headed out of the bus.

"Drive carefully, Austin. Remember you are fully responsible for her," Andrew said.

"Yeah, yeah, yeah!" Austin replied back. "Talking like a true leader."

"Thanks, Andrew," I said. I was glad he was sensitive to the urgency of my situation, and then I felt terrible again for not following his rules. "I'm sorry about not—"

"Don't worry about it. I'm sure you had your reasons. Anyway, I hope you get to see her in time," Andrew said sincerely, placing his hand on my shoulder.

"I hope so too."

"Let's go, Claudia, before the bus gets there before you do," Austin said. He opened the car door like a gentleman, and I got into his black Infiniti Coupe. It was sleek, and the body of the car looked futuristic. Everybody was looking at me from the window of the bus, including Patty who was waving and smiling. We drove for a little while before Austin broke the silence.

"Sorry about Gamma," he said tenderly.

"Thanks," I said.

He continued. "I know what it feels like to lose someone."

"You do?" I asked curiously.

He stared straight into the window and sighed. "My dad passed away, many years ago."

"I'm sorry to hear that."

"That's okay. I've learned to deal with it. We all have to in order to move on with our lives. I'm sure my dad didn't want me moping around for him. He would want me to be happy and continue with my life while I hold on to his memories."

"You're right, but it must have been extremely difficult."

"You have to grieve. It's part of the healing process. I cried. I cursed. I was a bit rebellious at times, and I didn't make things easy for my mom until I realized that she was feeling the same as me. She had lost her husband. I was being too selfish thinking about what I had lost."

"So it's just you and your mom?"

"Yeah."

"Brother or sister?"

"Nope. Only child. Thank goodness I have good friends. Andrew was there for me. I'm lucky to have a friend like him."

I knew what he meant. Patty was the same way for me in many different ways. I only hoped that I was the same kind of friend for her as well. The motion from the car made me sleepy, especially since I had hardly slept at all the night before. As my thoughts turned to Gamma and Michael, I drifted off to sleep in the soft leather reclined seat, and the sounds from the cars on the highway faded.

Chapter 17

"Claudia! Claudia!" It was Gamma calling me, but I couldn't see her. Where was I? My vision cleared as I looked around, only to realize that I was at the same unpaved road. It suddenly came to me that I was at the Crossroads. Why were we here? Then I heard Gamma's voice again.

"Claudia! Claudia!"

"Where are you, Gamma?" I yelled.

I started walking around in circles, looking for her. I was about to give up when I saw her at a distance, inside the field.

"Gamma?" I shrieked in disbelief.

She walked toward me with a horrified look in her eyes. Her expression frightened me.

"Run, Claudia!" she yelled. "You don't belong here."

My mouth dropped in shock from what I had seen and heard. I didn't want to run. I wanted to hold her. She said it again, but this time with more urgency.

"Run, Claudia! They're coming for you."

I did as told. I didn't know why I was running or whom I was running away from, but my heart was pounding. All of a sudden, I couldn't breathe; I grabbed my throat, gasping for air.

"Wake up, Claudia." I recognized his voice. Austin was shaking me. "Are you all right? It must have been some dream."

I roused from sleep and realized we were still in his car. "Yeah…um…sorry…didn't mean to scare you like that," I replied as I sat up, feeling embarrassed. I quickly rubbed the back of my palm to my mouth to make sure that I wasn't drooling.

"It's okay. It looked like you couldn't breathe. I thought I was going to have to do CPR on you." He winked with a smile.

"Very funny," I said, fixing my hair.

"Well, here we are."

He had driven me to the hospital instead of my house. I couldn't remember what I had asked him to do, but I was glad we were at the hospital because this was where I wanted to be. "Thanks, Austin." I dashed out of the car, anxious to see Gamma. "I really appreciate it." I closed the car door behind me. I was just about to walk away when he rolled down the window.

"Glad to help. I would go in there with you —"

I interrupted because I didn't want him to feel like he had to act like a gentleman and walk me in. He had done enough. "No, don't worry. I should face this alone. I wouldn't want you to see me…" Searching for the right words and anxious to get going, I said quickly, "You know what I mean. See you later." I took a few steps, but he wasn't finished.

"Claudia, I'm not saying that she is going to die, but you have to prepare for the worst too."

I nodded, half listening. "You're right," I said quickly.

"You can call or text me anytime," he said.

"Thanks," I replied and walked away quickly. I didn't mean to be rude, but I was anxious to get to Gamma before it was too late.

I took a deep breath and headed toward the hospital entrance. I felt tiny approaching this huge building. I glanced at all the windows and wondered which room was Gamma's. In the middle of the hospital building was a big and bold sign that read General Hospital. A person would have to be blind to miss it. A security guard at the entrance stopped me and asked what the purpose of my visit was.

"I'm here for Gamma, I mean, Lucy Reed."

I was so used to calling her Gamma that I had almost forgotten her real name. I was also quite shaken up by the fact that I was actually here, which meant that it was real. As I was waiting for him, I squinted for fear that he would inform me that I was too late. Instead, he gave me a long plastic strip.

"Please place this on your wrist. Here, I can help you. Go straight through the door, hang a right, then a left. And a lady will be there to help you."

"Thank you," I said, feeling relieved.

He gave me some hope that I was not too late, but then I wondered if he even knew anything about the patients in intensive care. As I walked further in, I discovered I was alone. There weren't any other visitors. For a hospital this big, I would've expected to see many more; however, it was dark and I was sure visiting hours would be ending soon. Go straight through the door, hang a right, and then a left, I repeated his instructions over and over in my head so I wouldn't forget. Every which way I looked was a corridor leading to another hallway. It was like a maze in here. A lady was behind a counter, seemingly not very busy.

"Yes…?" Her voice lingered, as she looked up at me, appearing to be annoyed. "May I help you?" she asked in a rather snobbish manner.

How rude! I thought. No wonder people don't like going to the hospital. "I'm here to see Gamma, I mean, Lucy Reed."

"Who?" she asked again, looking irritated.

"Lucy Reed."

She quickly looked at her chart, flipping through a few pages. "Fifth floor, room 512," she said, pointing straight ahead.

"Thank you," I said, as I moved ahead anxiously.

The long hallway seemed endless as I stepped out of the elevator. Curiosity got the best of me as I quickly glanced at the occupied rooms. I couldn't help but feel depressed by the ambiance, although it was comforting to observe the families caring for their elders. My mom always reminded me to see Gamma as much as I could. Her words were strongly embedded in my head, "Be good to those who are alive, because what good is it when they are dead?" It made more sense to me now, knowing that it may be the last time I would see her. I wanted to be able to tell her and show her how much she meant to me.

The numbers read closer to 512; I was almost there. I could feel my heart racing. I concentrated on the room numbers, afraid that I would pass her room. As if my heart wasn't racing fast enough, it started beating even faster and louder, so that I was certain the nurses could hear my anxiety attack. Finally—room 512. Apprehensively, I walked in; it was a sight I hadn't prepared myself for. Gamma looked lifeless and motionless. She was hooked up to an IV, with an oxygen tube in her nose, and a tube running down her throat, forcing her mouth open.

"Oh, Gamma." My heart sunk to the floor. I thought I was going to lose control, but I forced myself to feel nothing. I was afraid to touch her or to hold her; she appeared so fragile. Gently I reached for her hands, but they were cold and unresponsive. Softly I cupped them with my two hands to give her some warmth. I took a deep breath, not wanting to have a breakdown. I completely blocked myself from reality and pretended she was asleep.

"Can you hear me?" I asked softly. "It's me, Claudia."

Startled by the twitches from her fingers, I immediately dropped her hands and stood up. Was that her way of communicating with me? I was hopeful that she would wake up, so I asked again. "Can you hear me, Gamma? Please wake up. I'm here. I know you've been waiting for me. Let's go home," I pleaded, touching her forehead, her cheeks, and finally, her hands.

Upsettingly, there was no response. I looked at her intensely, as to not forget her face. I realized the deeply rooted wrinkles in her forehead had eased. Was she in pain? Could she hear me? Many thoughts ran through my mind. Just then, a doctor entered, and I jumped with surprise to see someone come in. I was startled to see such a young doctor. Would he have the experience to help Gamma? He was attentive and tried to answer all my questions to put my mind at ease. He started off with words I could not understand, all that medical jargon, but immediately realized I wasn't comprehending.

He paused and spoke again. "Basically your grandmother had a massive stroke. She is unable to breathe alone, as you can see. She is hooked up to an oxygen tube. Given her age, surgery would only complicate the situation. Most likely, if she even wakes up from her coma, she will be severely impaired. To what extent cannot be determined. I am very sorry."

"I am sorry" meant that she didn't have a fighting chance of recovery, and hearing those words from her doctor made it that much more difficult to bear. "Thank you, doctor," was all I could say.

"Excuse me," he said. He shone a light in her eyes and nose, and shook her for response. I was upset by the sight of him shaking her like that. I wanted to yell at him to stop, but I knew he was doing his job. I couldn't bear to watch, so I turned around. Then he headed for the door.

"I'll be with other patients, but if you have any questions or concerns, just have any one of the nurses page me."

"Thank you," I said solemnly.

Focusing on Gamma, I started speaking to her again. "Please, wake up," I said, as if she could hear me. I had read an article about a patient being able to hear their loved ones while in a coma. Whether this was true or not, I had to try.

I sat there for who knows how long. Mom had texted me back to let me know she had been here earlier, but had to leave because of an emergency at work. They needed additional nurses, but she said she would meet me as soon as she could. It didn't bother me; in fact, I was happy to have this time alone with Gamma. I wasn't sure how long she had. I embraced her with my arms gently around her shoulders, trying not to disturb the tubes that were keeping her alive, and rested my head lightly on her chest. As I told her that I loved her, I didn't even fight the tears; instead, I welcomed them.

"Come on, fight!" I said out loud to her. "You still have much to live for. You can't leave me, especially now!" I wanted to tell her about Michael, and about speaking to the angels. I knew she would be fascinated by my stories. Suddenly, I felt movement and then a light grip on my shoulders; I looked up to see Gamma's eyes, opened wide and alert. The tube in her mouth was out. She must've pulled it out just before she grabbed me.

"Gamma!" I couldn't believe my eyes. I was ecstatic. Either the doctor had misdiagnosed her, or this was truly a miracle. "Do you know where you are?" I stared, waiting for her to respond.

Without warning, she pulled me closer. "Claudia, listen carefully. I've been waiting for you. I can't wait any longer. Please listen carefully as it may come as a shock. I've been protecting you."

Protecting me? Was she hallucinating? What was she talking about? I listened intently, trying to make sense of what she was saying.

She continued after a pause. "I knew your mother. I promised your mother…would look after you…keep you safe."

"My mother? Of course you know her," I said, reassuring her that she did, thinking she was out of her mind.

"What I'm about to say…difficult to believe…listen carefully. You need to know. The mother you live with, Ava Emerson…not your real mother. Adopted."

My eyes widened with shock at first. Then I thought something must have happened to the part of her brain that held her memory. I just sat there, listening to humor her, and didn't say a word.

"You were sent from the clouds, Ava would say. She named you Claudia."

"Yes, Gamma, I know the story. Mom told me she thought she couldn't have children and that I was a blessing from above," I said, caressing her hands, trying to play along with her made-up story that I was adopted.

She shook her head. "I'm not making this up. Your real mother, Sophia, was my dear friend. She had a short relationship with a man, but he was not an ordinary man. Your father was one of God's first angels. And because only God's first angels or their offspring have the soul of the Holy Spirit, I had to protect your soul."

"My father was one of God's first angels," I mumbled. I was trying to make sense of all this while I was in complete disbelief. I had to decide whether she was telling me the truth or losing her mind. But God's first angels and having a soul of the Holy Spirit was something she couldn't just conjure up in her mind. If she was telling me the truth, why hadn't she told me sooner? Not that this kind of news was easy to explain. I already had background knowledge of what the Holy Spirit's soul was, so I could understand the severity of what she was telling me.

Every fiber in my body was fighting back the shock, confusion, and anger brewing inside me; but Gamma was sick, so I had to watch my tone. "What do you mean by protecting my soul?" I asked calmly, although I was fuming. I was nearly having a heart attack. It was too much to bear.

She didn't answer my question. Instead she started talking again. "This may come as a surprise to you. I don't have time to explain. I'm an earth angel."

"Earth angel?" My eyes widened with disbelief. I remembered Phillip telling me about them, but it was unfathomable that Gamma was one.

Gamma continued, "You were in danger. I knew others would be looking for you," she said.

Aden popped into my mind. My mind was being pulled into all different directions, wanting to know more, not knowing what questions to ask. Gamma snapped me out of my thoughts when she continued to speak again.

"Sophia, your birth mother, told me that a fallen angel was after your soul. You were just a baby when your birth mother was murdered by him. I'm sorry that I couldn't save her. I promised her that I would watch over you and find a nice family for you so that you could have a normal life."

I placed my head down on the bed to soak all this in. Immediately Gamma placed her hand on my head. She was trying to comfort me, and for the first time, she couldn't. I needed to be strong and get more answers, so I refocused. I looked up. Gamma had her eyes closed.

"Gamma...Ava Emerson, my mom, does she know any of this?" It was strange to ask this question. I had known her all my life as my mom.

"No."

"So, she thinks I'm her biological daughter?"

"Yes."

"Is Ava Emerson human?"

"Yes."

"Sophia, my real mom, was she human?"

"Yes," Gamma said quickly, and gasped for air.

I was trying to find a way to help her through this, but all I could do was watch. She took a deep breath.

"Are you all right?" I asked compassionately.

She nodded.

"My father is one of God's first angels?" I asked nervously and swallowed hard.

"Yes."

I paused, looking at her with narrowed eyes, wondering if I had heard what she had just said. I had no words. She kept nodding her head, trying to reassure me that what she was saying was true. I looked away. I didn't want to believe her. I didn't want it to be true. How could this be?

She continued. "I know you've been to the Crossroads."

I blinked my eyes at her in alarm. "What?" I whispered. How did she know?

"When you were a child, you would dream about the Crossroads, and you would travel there through your dreams. Somehow, subconsciously, you knew such a place existed. But I stopped you. I pulled you back. The last time you went there was about a year ago. You stopped going there, so I didn't monitor you any longer, but I should have continued. You found your way there again, didn't you?"

"Yes," I nodded. At that moment, I remembered Michael telling me that I would disappear without a warning. It was Gamma who had pulled me away. "How did you know?"

"It is difficult to explain, but I knew when a fallen angel named Aden tracked me down. I thought you were safe. This is my fault. I could have prevented this if only I hadn't stopped monitoring you. My poor judgment has caused this."

"But why? Why did you pull me away? Why must I stay away from the Crossroads?" I asked.

"Going to the Crossroads is not the problem. Sometimes, human souls wander there when they have near death experiences. It's when you crossed over to Halo City; I was trying to protect you from crossing over, but I was too late," she answered.

"Why must I not cross over?"

"When you cross over to Halo City, your aura becomes different. And having the soul of the Holy Spirit complicates things. You hold the key to our survival."

I couldn't believe my ears. Then, I remembered Phillip telling me that the fallen may be after me because crossing over to Halo City will cause my aura to stand out. "No, no, no!" I shook my head vigorously. "It's not me. It can't be me. Why me? I'm not special. I have no powers."

"It's you," she said.

I didn't want it to be true. "Make it stop. I don't want this," I said, not realizing my grip had tightened on her blanket.

"You have your father's soul. You can't stop, or fight, destiny. Don't fight what you cannot control. Fight for what you can. It's too late. It has begun. The fallen are multiplying by the hands of one angel. He is creating his army now that he knows you exist. We have to stop them, or humanity will be lost forever."

"Soul of the Holy Spirit" now registered loud and clear. Feeling dizzy again from information overload, I felt the room closing in. Covering my face with the palms of my hands, I saw my whole life flash before me, realizing that my life was a lie.

Now I knew why Aden was after me. Inside me was the soul of the Holy Spirit. He needed my soul not only to open the gates to the Crossroads, but to regain his powers. There was nothing I could do about it. But there was one thing I could control; I had to give my soul to Aden willingly, and I was not about to give him that. He could hunt me down for the rest of my life. I would never give him my soul.

She turned away from me. "Claudia, my time has come," she said sorrowfully. "I must leave you now."

"No, Gamma, please! Don't leave me! I need you!" I begged, wrapping my arms around her, even though I knew it was useless.

"I'm too old. I can't help you anymore. I'm so sorry that I won't be able to protect you, but I asked someone to watch over you so I can leave you in peace." She spoke so softly, it was hard to hear her words. "You are a miracle. I'm so proud to have watched you grow into a fine young woman. You have a big responsibility ahead of you. You must have faith in yourself, faith in others who want to help you, and especially faith in the one you cannot see. Find my letter, and everything will be clear."

Before I had a chance to ask her who she had asked to watch over me and where I was to find her letter, her eyes widened and her face elongated with terror. "Run, Claudia! They're coming!"

"Who's coming?" I asked anxiously.

Beep! Beep! Beep! The heart monitor beeped out of control, alerting the nurses.

As the nurses rushed through the doors, I stepped out of the way. They were trying to revive her when I heard the heart monitor sound go flat. It was a while before one of the nurses turned to me.

"I'm so sorry. I'll give you some time alone."

I knew what "I'm sorry" meant. I just couldn't believe it. What made everything worse was that I had many questions, and Gamma was the only one who could answer them. As the nurses left, I reached for Gamma again. Knowing she would go to a peaceful place gave me a sense of peace.

"Good-bye, Gamma. I love you," I said quietly and kissed her on the cheek. As I gave her a last hug, I closed my eyes tightly to stop the tears from falling. Unbelievably, I had none to shed. I rested my head on her chest, but could hear no sound. All the monitors that kept her alive were turned off, and the room was still and quiet. I thought my ears were playing tricks on me when I suddenly heard Gamma's voice again. "Run, Claudia!"

Surprised to hear her voice, I looked at her, but she was lifeless. Was I hallucinating? Just like in my dream, she was telling me to run, but there was no sign of evidence she was alive. Unexpectedly, a low beam of light glowed from her body. My eyes widened both with astonishment and fear, and I backed away. Her spirit was being lifted right out of her body. Her radiating soul rose higher and higher. Her body was in perfect form, burning like a star. "Run, Claudia. Now! They are coming!" she said once more.

Frightened by Gamma's warning, I ran to the door. I looked to the left, then to the right, but I didn't see anyone, not even the nurse that was stationed at her desk. Then the lights in the hospital went off, and the only lights visible were the emergency lights, situated dimly on the floor. It was dark, but there was just enough glow for me to get around. Strong warning signals were shooting through my veins. The crystal on my neck vibrated and turned black. I knew what that meant — the fallen was near.

"Go right!" Gamma was directing me.

I didn't listen. Curiously, I looked left and what I saw paralyzed me with fear. It was Aden, with at least twenty others. They stood at a distance making it difficult to recognize their faces, but I knew who they were. I turned once more to face Gamma, and that's when her spirit vanished, her body remaining still. I was petrified by what had happened. Her spirit was gone, and I was left alone. There would be no more guiding words from her, and fear overtook me.

I turned right just as Gamma had instructed, and I ran for my life. Afterward, I didn't know which way to go. Gamma's only instruction was to turn right. Do I turn left or right again? Then I realized the sounds of their footsteps stopped. It was silent, and the only sound was the beating from my own heart. I could imagine them gliding after me. Periodically I turned my head, only to see them closing in on me. As I turned again, all of the fallen were gone except — for Aden.

Chapter 18

Frantically looking for a place to hide, I turned the corner and saw the elevator. I pushed the up button many times in panic. To my surprise, it opened immediately. There were twelve floors. Unsure of which floor to exit on, I pressed the twelvth floor. The twelvth floor was just as dark. Did I make the right choice? Should I have gotten off at another floor? It was too late.

Closing the gap between the wall and me, I ran faster down the hallway, looking for a place to hide. As I tried to enter a room, the door was locked. Then I tried another one, it was locked too. This floor seemed different; there were no patients on this floor. When I finally found a room that was unlocked, I realized I had entered a storage room. It was filled with various medications, shots, monitors, IVs, and things whose purpose was a mystery to me. Regardless, I thought I could use them if I needed to defend myself. At this point, I didn't care where I hid as long as they couldn't find me. I knelt down behind a storage container in an effort to be invisible. Where are you, Michael?

All was quiet and still. I was sitting here like a target duck. My heart could no longer take the anxiety attack I was having. I couldn't breathe. The room was spinning, and I couldn't focus. Then I heard footsteps, and I froze in absolute silence.

"I know you're in here, my little angel." His voice was strong and sharp.

He made me shiver with just the sound of his voice. Uncontrollably my body trembled from fear and my hands felt clammy. I contemplated my next move, knowing this was now a life-or-death moment. But I was unable to move. I didn't know what to do. I was scared out of my mind.

"Don't be scared. I sent my friends away so you and I could have some alone time together. We need to get better acquainted. This room isn't big enough for you to hide in forever." He laughed slyly.

A large dimmed emergency light hung overhead, and I could see his shadow cast on the walls around me, getting larger and closer by the second.

"Your friends have some surprise visitors. I'm afraid you are on your own. Well, not quite alone, you have me. So why don't you come out and end this cat-and-mouse game." He paused and waited for me to show myself. "I'm running out of patience. If you don't come out now, I'm going to have to hurt you, and that is not my intention." He was getting irritated, and his voice was getting louder. "Come out now, Claudia!"

He sounded so forceful that I wanted to dig myself further into the ground. Suddenly all the tables and containers were lifted, and I was exposed. Stunned by the power that I had witnessed, I curled myself into a ball. He stood, smiling through narrowed eyes, focusing solely on me. "There you are."

The items, still hovering, were tossed to one side of the room, leaving me wide open and vulnerable. I cringed and covered my ears to block out the noise.

"It doesn't have to be this way. I didn't want to scare you. Come to me," he said gently.

"Michael," I whispered. Not knowing what else to do, I stood slowly, sliding up against the wall to balance myself, as my legs were still shaking. Even though I knew he would win, I had to fight with everything I had.

"Come, Claudia."

My mind begged me not to move, but slowly my body, against my will, led the way as I struggled to resist every step. I was fighting inside my head, but he was too strong. I surrendered, unable to fight any longer. I was certain all hope was lost, and then he called my name.

"Stop, Claudia!"

Hearing Michael's voice triggered a sense of hope. I snapped out of the trance, but remained motionless. Aden's hold grew stronger and more intense. Unable to turn even my head, I fought against his power. It felt like I was dreaming with my eyes open. No matter what I did, I could not wake up.

"Michael!" Aden yelled, sounding appalled. Aden spread his brilliant alabaster wings, lifting him just above the ground. He was the worst form of evil; a dark, soulless creature, undeserving of such beauty.

In an instant, Aden released his hold on me. I swiftly ran toward Michael. In my peripheral vision, I noticed Davin, Vivian, and Caleb. Although terrified, I was overwhelmed with relief to see them all again.

"Too bad your puppets were cut from your strings. We enjoyed sending your friends back to hell," Davin said, as he crept closer to Aden.

Davin's remarks infuriated Aden, triggering a strange phenomenon. His hair and wings that were so beautifully pure in their color turned jet-black. I was astonished to witness such a quick transformation. How was such a thing possible? It was surreal. He began elevating himself higher off the ground. You could almost feel his temples pulsating as the blood rushed through his veins, full of hatred and rage. He looked like he was about to explode out of his body.

"You're outnumbered, Aden. Turn yourself in, or I will have no choice but to kill you. This is not my intention, but I will do what needs to be done," Michael attempted to reason with him.

"You're a fool to think this is over," Aden replied.

Sure enough, it was too good to be true thinking it was over. Numerous fallen appeared out of thin air, surrounding Aden. They, too, made their swords magically appear in their hands. Immediately, I knew something was different about them. One looked directly at me, and I was taken aback when I noticed his eyes were completely black. From afar they looked like fallen, but bigger. Close up, they looked like the worst possible demons imaginable. Looking into their eyes sent chills through every part of me. It was like looking into a black hole and feeling like the more I looked, the further I would fall into their world. I was petrified.

"We have more company!" Caleb shouted, with a look of fear.

"Meet the newest members of my family!" Aden declared.

Vivian, Caleb, and Davin held their swords up and congregated in a circle with their backs facing each other. I hid behind Michael. Slowly, the fallen started edging toward them.

"What are they?" Davin asked, rocking back and forth, ready to defend himself.

"They're not fallen. They are demons," Michael answered, his voice betraying the alarm he was feeling.

"They look repulsive. Their eyes are completely black," Caleb stated, grimacing.

"There are too many of them!" Davin shouted in panic.

"Not a problem. Come to mama, and I'll show you what hell is really like," Vivian taunted.

"Stay behind me," Michael instructed, as his wings extended. Though his wings were blocking my view, they were also protecting me as I stood behind them.

Suddenly, I heard the loud metallic clangs from the swords, and I knew the demons had attacked. I looked up, and I was surrounded by sparks. The clashing of the blades was so powerful, it created a shower of fire. I froze from fright. As I drew in deep breaths, I felt excruciating pain on the palms of my hands. I hadn't realized I had rolled my fingers into a ball, clenching so tightly that my fingernails dug into my skin. I released my fingers, knowing I would be safe as long as I was behind Michael, but that wasn't enough. I needed to know that Michael and his friends, my friends, were safe too. Inching away little by little from my safety zone, I backed away until I had a clear vision of the room and knew exactly where everyone stood.

Michael turned to his right, facing several demons head-on. Raising his sword over his head, he placed it in a horizontal position as he swung his weapon, cutting off the demons' heads. I gasped in horror at the sight of them being decapitated. Demons or not, it was repulsive to witness. Michael defended his own neck by swinging vertically. As the sword came down, he thrust it into the demon's chest. In that split second, the demon burst into black ashes. Some of the ashes landed on my shoulder, and I quickly brushed them off in disgust.

More demons leaped toward Michael. He leaned to the right. One demon barely missed him on the shoulder as he sliced through a monitor instead. Bright golden sparks were shooting in all different directions, like fireworks. At that moment, Michael's wings blocked the sparks from flying toward me. Swiftly Michael swirled his sword to his left and drove his weapon into the second demon's chest. With a snarl, a nearby demon lunged toward him, and the tip of his sword barely nicked Michael in the chest. Michael gave him a look that could kill, spun around, blocked an incoming blow from his right, and jumped into the air. As he landed, his sword swung around, eliminating the demons surrounding him.

Vivian was now positioned adjacent to Michael. As a demon charged toward her, with a flick of her wrist, the swords were caught up in a circular motion. The demon's sword went flying; slicing anything along its path, until it finally landed about twenty feet from them. His eyes wide with shock and full of fear, Vivian took the opportunity to drive the sword into his heart. Drawing the sword out, she pivoted to her right and blocked an attack by driving it straight up. She recoiled backward, barely missing a blow as her long hair fell across her face. She gracefully ducked, dodging a swing that came from behind. She flipped, positioned herself behind a demon, and thrust the sword into his back. Screeches of pain and defeat echoed all around.

Instantly, Davin was standing nearby, surrounded by demons. His sword swung from left to right, blocking, attacking, and slashing each of them. As more appeared, Davin dodged all the blows except for one small, unexpected swipe that cut him across his arm, knocking him down to land on top of a demon's feet. As the demon gave a menacing smile, he positioned his sword to plunge directly into Davin's chest, when Vivian knocked it out from behind.

"Take that, you worthless monster," Davin shouted and gave Vivian a thankful smile as he flipped back up. He somersaulted and landed behind more demons. I couldn't see what happened, but black ashes rained on the floor, and without a trace, they vanished.

"Ashes to ashes and dust to dust you shall become," I heard Caleb say as the demons were executed.

Suddenly, without warning, Michael was surrounded by ten of them. He gently pushed me to the side. "Stay here under the desk."

"Come and get me!" he shouted at them.

There were many of them swarming in full force. I was terrified, worried about Michael. My fingers dug deep into the floor as I took a peek. Michael's wings were opened slightly, and when they came close enough, he opened all the way. His wings were like blades. He spun around, slicing one after the other until all ten lives were taken, leaving Michael in a tunnel of ashes. I couldn't believe what I had just seen. As soft and delicate as his wings were, I would have never imagined that they could be used as a weapon. It was frightening and completely remarkable at the same time. Relief overcame me as I saw Michael standing there without a scratch.

Unexpectedly, the table that I was under disappeared. It was thrown at Michael from his blind spot, knocking him across the room. I stood alone, exposed and defenseless, as the demons edged toward me. Noticing a scalpel next to my feet, I quickly picked it up and waved it in front of them. Even though I knew I didn't have a fighting chance, I had a burst of adrenaline. I noticed Michael standing; ready to bolt across the room in my direction. Before Michael could reach me, the demons collapsed. I blinked in surprise, the scalpel shaking violently in my hands. Then I saw Caleb, Vivian, and Davin standing right before me. In that moment I realized three things — the three of them had killed the demons standing before me, all the demons were eliminated, and all of my friends were safe. Not to mention that what had started as a storage room had now become unrecognizable. It was unbelievable!

Knowing this wasn't completely over, I immediately turned to Aden. He was backing away with an intense glare in his eyes. All the demons had turned to ash, and he was left standing alone. Aden knew he was defeated; his eyes were boiling with anger.

Michael tenderly touched my cheeks, relieved that I was safe. He turned to Aden. "Can't find enough fallen to do your dirty work, so you had to play with fire? Went down to see the devil himself? Are you crazy?" Michael's voice was loud and angry. "You don't have that kind of power anymore. Who helped you open the gates of Hell? What happens if they turn their backs on you? You will leave the humans defenseless against these uncontrollable demons!"

"I am your superior. You do not ask such questions!" Aden commanded and narrowed his eyes at me. "And you…" He pointed to me. "Too bad Lucy got in the way. You should have been there to protect her. It was too bad I had to go through her to get to you." He smiled a cold, evil smile.

As he started talking about Gamma, I immediately reached for the bracelet she made me. It didn't hit me at first. I thought Gamma's stroke was due to her age, but it wasn't. Aden had killed my Gamma.

Michael gently placed his hand on my back and said, "He is trying to get to you through your emotions. Don't listen!" His touch and his words calmed me.

"Too bad she had to have a massive stroke. I enjoyed making her suffer."

My fists were clenched tight. I could only imagine feeling the satisfaction of punching him, because there was no way I could get close enough to do what I wanted.

"It's not true. They don't feel any pain when they have a stroke, Claudia," Davin spoke, walking toward me.

Under normal circumstances that might be true, but Gamma was an Earth angel. I couldn't hold back any longer. "What did you do to her?" I shouted.

"Nothing much, just the usual torture. She wouldn't give me the answer I wanted to hear, so I squeezed it out of her head. Such a pity. If only she had cooperated. She could have lived another twenty years," he said, giving me that evil smirk.

"You are the devil!" I shouted angrily. "How could you?"

"It wasn't difficult. She fought me with everything she had. She just didn't have much strength since she had aged."

While listening to him, my body burned with anger, like a wildfire blazing inside me. I felt like I was going to explode.

"Let it go, Claudia. His powers are weak, with the demons out of the way," Michael said as he rested his hand on my back.

Then he focused his attention to Aden. "Aden, now I know why you need the fallen and the demons. Besides having them fight your battles for you, you feed on their evilness. You draw from their energy. You are truly pathetic, and yet you call yourself a leader."

"Come with me, Michael," Aden's voice was deceptively sincere. "Better yet, why don't all of you come with me?"

"Don't waste your time. We're not mindless, like your puppets," Caleb said.

"Your time is up. Either you surrender, or I will kill you myself," Michael ordered, slowly closing in on him.

Without a word, Aden started to laugh hysterically, and just as Michael plunged into him, Aden disappeared. His laughter resonated, sending chills prickling down my back. His swift, sudden disappearance had startled me and all I could do was stare at the empty space where he had just stood. Where had he disappeared to? It didn't matter where, as long he was gone. I knew he would be back, and now I knew for sure the reason why. Even though I was extremely relieved that he was gone, my body started to shiver as my thoughts turned to Michael.

Michael was left standing where Aden had been, his shoulders slumped, empty-handed and anguished. The opportunity to eliminate Aden was in his hands, and just like that, it had vanished. Knowing he would blame Aden's escape on himself, I needed to reassure him that it was not his fault.

"Michael," I cried out softly with a raspy voice.

Immediately, he tilted his head and looked at me.

I was also debating whether or not to tell them what Gamma had said, when Michael grabbed me. "Are you all right?" he asked. He caught me as my knees buckled, and stopped me from falling to the floor.

"Yes, now that you are all safe," I said, feeling relieved. My heartbeat finally steadied, along with the shivers. His hold was all I needed to calm me. I placed my head on his chest and let out a heavy sigh.

"I'm sorry. We would have been here earlier, but we were detained by other demons," Michael said, apologetically.

"I know," I said, as he continued to embrace me. "That explains why the demons disappeared while I was running away. I thought they were fallen. These demons, where do they come from?" I asked Michael.

"Demons, also known as evil spirits, were angels, followers of Lucifer, and some are children of fallen angels. They are disembodied spirits. They were sent to a spiritual prison called "Abyss." Humans call it "Hell." When they enter your world, these demons must occupy bodies of unbelievers. Their eyes turn black so that we can distinguish them. The only way they could be released is by a gatekeeper or by the Royal Council. How they escaped is unclear, but the answer lies with Aden. I do not know how he did it. The only thing that I could think of is that he must have found a fallen gatekeeper to do his dirty work. What puzzles me is that I can't think of any fallen who was a gatekeeper."

"Oh." It was all I could say.

There was dead silence in the room until Davin spoke. "Well, we're always happy to get rid of them for you." Then he pulled me out of Michael's grip. "Share a little," he joked, giving me a tight squeeze.

I sucked in my breath from the tightness.

"Sorry," Davin said, chuckling while releasing me. Then he became serious. "I'm just glad Aden disappeared instead of making us disappear."

"Well, he didn't have a chance. It would have been four against one," Vivian answered back. "Since his powers were weakened, I think we could have taken him out. I believe he knew that as well, so he just disappeared."

"That's true. We were lucky that he was getting weaker with the demons out of the way. But what puzzles me is what he could possibly want with you, Claudia." Davin looked at me with curious eyes.

I didn't answer.

"There must be something else besides you crossing over to Halo City, because he wouldn't go to this much trouble bringing the demons to Earth," Vivian said. Then she turned her attention to Michael. "What do you think?"

"I don't know. Let me think about this," he said, brushing the question off as if it wasn't important. "No more questions," he demanded. "Claudia has had enough. We'll talk later."

The alkins didn't ask me any more questions after that. Everyone had something to say, except for Caleb. I could tell Caleb's thoughts were elsewhere. I ran to him and embraced him. He was as stiff as a board. "I...I...thanks," he said, surprised as he leaned away from me.

I didn't care, nor was I insulted by his action. He was here to help me, and I was grateful.

"Don't mind Caleb. He isn't used to it. I think physical affection was missing in his previous life on Earth," Vivian spoke as she patted Caleb on the back. Caleb quickly looked down, feeling uncomfortable with Vivian's words.

"You know nothing about my life on Earth, and none of us remember our past," Caleb said as he stared into the space where Aden had been. Caleb turned and looked at us. "What made him turn so evil? I could only imagine that he was once a good angel, don't you think? It must have been hard to avoid such temptations that were forbidden, only allowed for the humans. I think eventually, when you live among humans, you think and become like them. Look at us! We miss being here even though we can't remember our past, whether it was pleasant or not. It's the freedom to choose, to love, to live to the fullest, that we all hunger for."

"Wow, Caleb! That was the most you've ever said," Davin said jokingly, placing his hand on Caleb's shoulder.

Smiling, Caleb pushed Davin a few feet from where he stood. "Shut up!" he said playfully. "You talk too much. Sometimes I have important things to say. I may not share what I'm thinking, but I think about many things."

"We all think about "what ifs." We wonder about our lives on Earth that we have no memories of," Vivian responded.

Michael wasn't paying attention to our conversation. He suddenly wrapped his wings around me as he was deep in thought, staring into the same space where Aden had stood. He looked worried. "Aden will be coming back with more fallen and demons. He's just testing our limits. His army is growing," Michael said, looking extremely concerned. He tilted his head toward the door, grabbed my hand, and said, "We should get going."

About halfway out the door, I noticed Caleb standing in the middle of the room with his arms stretched out. The door behind us closed by itself, and Michael whispered into my ears, "He's putting everything back, cleaning. We call him the sweeper."

My eyes practically popped out. "I see," I said, looking behind my shoulders only to hear soft noises. It was incredible to witness their powers: Davin, the gatekeeper, Vivian, the locator, Caleb the sweeper, and Michael, with multiple powers and more I had yet to witness. Michael was amazing just the way he was, and it didn't matter if he had any powers at all.

Chapter 19

We stepped inside the elevator, and all the mixed emotions I stored so tightly inside began to unveil. The adrenaline that pumped through my body as I was running for my life had temporarily pushed aside the loss of Gamma. Now that I was safe, the reality of Gamma's death settled in. So many overwhelming circumstances had taken place within a short period of time. My body became weak, and I thought I was going to faint. I just had to hold myself together for a little while longer.

"Can we stop by Gamma's room?" I asked timidly.

"Yes, of course! I'm so sorry. We were so worried about your safety that we didn't even think about your Gamma. We didn't mean to be insensitive like that," Michael said apologetically.

"No. Not insensitive. Very thoughtful," I quickly replied.

I was just ecstatic that they were here with me again. Davin squeezed in between Michael and me and placed his arms around our shoulders. "Sorry about your Gamma. I don't know if I ever lost anyone in my human life, but I can only imagine. It must be extremely difficult," he said.

"Thank you," I replied.

"Room five twelve?" Davin asked.

"Yes," I said.

As we approached the room, there was a nurse that I recognized sitting behind her desk, smiling. As soon as she realized we were headed toward the room, she stopped us.

"Excuse me, but that room is off-limits," she said firmly, blocking the door.

"Nurse…" Michael quickly looked at her name tag. "Sara. Her grandmother just passed away about an hour ago. I would really appreciate it if you would allow us to have some peaceful moments to honor her grandmother's passing," Michael said persuasively, giving her his irresistible smile.

The nurse just stared at him. "I don't know. They have already taken her body." She smiled back flirtatiously.

"Would it be all right to step inside for a bit?" Michael asked.

The nurse was hesitant. Michael leaned in closer to her. A twinge of jealousy struck me, and I didn't like the feeling at all.

"Please," he said with hardly a gap between the two of them.

She whispered, "Okay, but please make it quick. I'm not supposed to let you in there."

"You won't even know we were here. We'll make it quick," Michael said and winked at her.

Flirting at such a somber moment was inappropriate, and I was jealous, though I knew he was doing it for me. I was grateful that I would be able to pay my last respects. Instead of putting her under a trance-like state, he was able to persuade her without using his angel power.

Nurse Sara motioned her head toward the door without a word and backed away. I walked in first, but I could see through the window that she was smiling and walking sideways back to her desk.

Michael cleared his throat as Caleb walked in. There was no evidence that Gamma had been in here. Her body had been taken away, and only memories and unanswered questions lingered. Feeling hopeless and confused by her final words, I was lost and heartbroken.

I couldn't stop the tears from falling. I didn't want to cry in their presence, but I could not control my emotions. Michael wiped my tears and kissed both of my hands. "That's all right, Claudia, let it all out," he said tenderly. "I know you'll miss her, but remember she will always be in your heart. More importantly, you will remember her love and the memories you have created together."

Immediately I was comforted by his words. I had no right to complain about memories when they couldn't remember anything. Then I remembered Gamma's words. She was an Earth angel. I couldn't wait any longer. "I have something to tell you. Gamma told me…she…" The words would not come out. What was I afraid of? I trusted them completely. "She told me that she was an Earth angel," I blurted out quickly so that I couldn't take it back.

Vivian, Caleb, and Davin stared at me in shock.

"Your Gamma was an Earth angel?" Vivian asked as she walked closer to the bed.

"She said many things to me. I don't remember everything, but yes," I replied and covered my eyes with my hands, feeling tormented by the fact that I had the Holy Spirit's soul. Should I tell them now or later? When I tell them, will they look at me differently? Many thoughts ran through my mind and I decided it was best to tell Michael first.

"It's all right. You don't have to tell us right now," Michael said, giving them a hard stare. "Claudia and I will talk after I take her home."

"Did you text her, Vivian?" Michael asked, changing the subject.

I knew Michael intentionally changed the subject so I wouldn't have to answer any more of their questions. Texting reminded me of my phone so I tapped my pockets, and sure enough, it was gone.

"Yes, I texted Claudia's mom to let her know that she was on her way home," Vivian said, handing me my phone.

"You texted my mom?" I asked in surprise.

"You dropped it upstairs, and Michael asked me to text your mom so she wouldn't worry. You had several missed calls from her."

"Thanks," I said and gave her a quick smile.

"Anytime, it's quite fun," she said.

"Thank you," Michael said quickly. "She's had enough for one day. Let's get her home safely."

They flew alongside Michael as he held me in his arms. When we reached my house, Michael waited for me in my bedroom while the alkins sat on the roof. I ran inside the front door. "Mom!" I called.

Without a word, she embraced me, and tears ran down her face. "Oh, Claudia, I can't believe she is really gone. Are you all right, honey? I was on my way back to see Gamma when I got a flat tire. I tried to call you. I would have been there with you. Since I couldn't reach you, I called the hospital, and they told me she'd passed away. I wanted to be there. I'm so sorry I wasn't there with you. Since you were no longer at the hospital, I came straight here."

"It's all right, Mom," I said, holding her tightly as tears ran down my face.

"Did she wake up at all? Did she say anything?"

"No," I lied. "She didn't say anything. She was sleeping peacefully."

I would have said anything to help ease her pain. Suddenly she had a blank look. "I can't believe she's gone. It's like a dream," she whispered.

I knew what she meant. Gently I placed my hands on her arms to guide her to the sofa. "Sit down, Mom. I can't believe it either, but I know she wouldn't want us to be like this. She would want us to rejoice in her life." I wasn't sure what I was saying, but it seemed to work.

"You're right, honey." She paused and stroked my hair. She looked at me tenderly.

It didn't matter whether she was my biological mom or not. She was my mom, the one who had raised me and took care of me when I was sick, the one who loved me, and the one who was here with me now. But knowing all that, a part of me couldn't help but look at her differently. I wanted this feeling to go away. So I told myself at that instant that even though my life seemed like a lie, it was real because I was living it. I had to put all the secrets aside and continue from where I had left off.

"I don't know what I would do without you. I can't believe how much you have grown. You know that she loved you as if you were her own grandchild. She would have done anything for you," she said.

I nodded, unable to speak, for fear of uncontrollable tears. Mom had no idea how right she was. Gamma had died to protect me.

She changed the subject. "Before I forget, I've called the principal, and you don't have to go to school this week."

"Oh," I said in surprise and absolute appreciation. "I can use the rest."

"Good, that's what I thought. I know you're exhausted. Get some rest. I almost forgot…Patty dropped off your duffel bag. I put it in your room."

"Thank you," I said and kissed her on the cheek. Then I anxiously headed toward my room. As I quickened my pace, so did my heartbeat, for I knew Michael was waiting for me in my bedroom. He was staring at the moon, head tilted, deep in thought. He turned to look at me, and at that moment all I could do was melt and let the troubles disappear. I didn't know what came over me. Without hesitation, I embraced him and then let out a heavy sigh.

"I don't blame you," he said. "You've been through so much!" Safe in his arms, I let my guard down as uncontainable tears ran down my face.

"Sorry," Michael said. "It must be hard for you. Let it all out. I'm right here."

"I can't believe she's gone," my voice choked, desperately trying to hold back the tears.

He held my face and gently wiped my tears. He was searching for words. "She'll always be with you."

"I know," I said, thinking that it was a good time as any to let him know what Gamma had said. "Michael, I need to tell you what Gamma told me."

"Okay, I'm listening." He looked concerned as he led me to the edge of my bed.

"She told me that my mother's death was not an accident."

"Claudia," he called my name with a perplexed look, knowing my mom was right outside the door.

"It sounds bizarre, but let me finish. Sophia, my birth mom, not my mom out there, had a relationship with an angel, but she didn't know he was an angel. She died to protect me...and...the soul of the Holy Spirit." I was rambling so fast out of confusion, and I didn't know if he understood anything I was trying to tell him.

"I'm trying to follow, but I'm not sure what you are trying to tell me." Michael looked confused.

Feeling nervous, I got up and paced back and forth, trying to find the right words. Why couldn't I just say it, plain and simple? I was afraid of what he might say or do because I knew it would change things for better or worse—mostly for worse. Telling him would make it all too real and I wished with everything I had that it wasn't true.

"To make a long story short, I think," I said and walked toward the window, "Michael, I have the soul of the Holy Spirit. It's in me."

He took a moment to respond. "Not that I don't believe you, but how could that be? Margaret sounded so sure that they had taken all of Isaiah's descendants."

"Gamma told me that my father was one of God's first angels."

Michael looked stunned at first, and then he looked terrified. "Royal Council," he said quietly. "How could that be?" He paused, thinking; his eyes flickered here and there as if he was putting missing pieces together. "Your mother asked Gamma to hide you from Aden. The Royal Council doesn't know a child exists." He looked straight at me. "Every hundred years, a group of Royal Council enters your world to determine the fate of humanity. They stay for a short time, living among humans, determining if apocalypse is needed. One of them had a forbidden affair. This is the only explanation. Aden knew all along. He had to have known. He was waiting for you to become an adult so that you could give your soul to him freely. This all started close to your birthday. Aden must have known before or after you were born," he said, sounding extremely troubled.

Then, without another word, he stood next to me and gently held me in his arms. His wings found their way around me; he seemed to do this when he was in protective mode. I didn't mind it at all. The warm, secure feeling I felt from it eased my fears; it seemed to have a hypnotic effect.

"Don't tell anyone. I need to figure out what we need to do. I don't want Phillip to know. I'm afraid he will do something I will not agree with, like tell the Royal Council. Your life is in great danger, more than I had anticipated. I need to leave for a little while. I'll ask Davin to watch over you."

"I don't want this. I don't want it to be true. I'm really scared." I pressed my head deeper into his chest.

"I knew there was something bothering you besides Gamma's death, but I waited for you to tell me when you were ready. It will be all right, Claudia. I'm here," he said softly and held me tighter. "Aden killed Gamma because Gamma was an Earth angel who was protecting you. It was Gamma who pulled you back from the Crossroads, wasn't it?"

"Yes," I confirmed. "She stopped monitoring my visits because she thought I had stopped going there, but something always pulled me there."

"Also, Aden wouldn't have done the things he had been doing for a mere human. Now that I have all the facts, I need to leave for a while. I hate to leave you, but I need answers. I'm asking you to find a way to stay home until I come back."

"My mom already arranged it so that I don't have to go to school this week," I said.

He stood tall, towering over me, looking down into my eyes. "Good! Just stay put. Do you think you can do that for me?" he asked sternly.

"Yes," I said, smiling into his dazzling eyes. I became lost again. Michael looked embarrassed; I had never seen him blush like that before. He laughed softly and brushed his hair back.

"You're doing it again," he said.

"What am I doing?"

"Making me crazy for you," he said, smiling.

"How crazy?" I asked, surprised by his words. I closed the gap between us as I caressed his hair.

"You know I won't be able to control myself," he whispered, his eyes closed.

"Claudia, are you all right?" My mom knocked softly at my door. "Are you talking to yourself, or are you on the phone?"

Startled by Mom's voice, Michael disappeared right in front of my eyes, and I fixed myself to look presentable just in case she walked in. I ran to the door. "I'm fine, Mom. I'm just talking on the phone," I said, hoping she wouldn't come in for a chat.

"Okay, honey. Get some rest," she said and walked away.

Feeling extremely relieved, I turned around and jumped, startled by his sudden reappearance. "You scared me," I whispered softly, placing my hand over my heart as it skipped a beat.

"Sorry, but I don't like being away from you," he said, placing his hands over my shoulders, trying to calm my nerves.

I smiled and put my arms around his neck. "Now, where were we?"

"Claudia, please keep my mind at ease and just stay home."

"Only if you give me a kiss," I said.

"That's not fair. You know I can't give you just one."

"I know," I said, giving him a sly smile.

His response was not what I had expected. "Claudia, I'm being serious. Your life is in grave danger, more than I feared. I'm going to send Davin to watch you for now."

"Will you be gone long?" I asked.

"However long I'm gone, it will be too long. I'll worry, but I know you will be in good hands. I trust Davin, Caleb, and Vivian with my own life. I need to tell them about you, but only if you are comfortable with it."

I had no choice. "Yes, of course. I completely trust you," I said.

He embraced me again. "One for the road," he said and kissed me intensely, leaving me standing in a daze, wanting more.

He disappeared into the cloudless night sky. As much as I hated to see him leave, I knew he felt the same way too. You're supposed to be floating in clouds when you're in love. How is it possible to love someone and yet feel such pain at the same time? As I tucked myself into bed, I thought about Gamma, Claudia, and Sophia, my real mom. I wondered what she had looked like. I also tried to picture how my dad would have looked, but I couldn't. He was a spiritual being; a being I could never imagine as my dad. So I just closed my eyes.

Chapter 20

"Hello, Claudia."

I was just about to fall asleep when I was startled by Davin's greeting. I groggily sat up on my bed. "Davin," I said, surprised to see him so soon, even though Michael had forewarned me that Davin would be watching over me.

"Sorry, I didn't mean to scare you like that," he said apologetically. "Michael asked me to look after you. He told us that your father was one of the Royal Council and that you have the Holy Spirit's soul. We were in shock."

"Oh," I said softly.

"Don't worry, we won't say anything."

"I know. I trust you."

"Something is bothering you. What's on your mind?"

"It's just that I have so many questions."

"We all do, and I know how difficult it must be for you," he said tenderly.

"It's hard to believe," I said, looking away, still unable to believe it myself. "I feel so useless."

"What do you mean?"

"Do all alkins have powers?" I asked.

"Depends on what you mean by power."

"I was just wondering why I'm still me. If I'm who I am supposed to be, why can't I do anything special?"

"Claudia, I don't know. Give it some time."

Davin sat next to me on my bed, trying to comfort me, but it didn't work.

"Did Vivian and Caleb leave with Michael?" I asked.

"Yes, but they'll be back."

"I should get some sleep," I mumbled quietly. I didn't even know if he heard what I said. "It's a good thing I don't have to go to school tomorrow."

"You must be exhausted. It's been a long day."

"A long week," I mumbled again, barely keeping my eyes open.

"If it's okay with you, I'll be sitting on that chair. I'm supposed to watch you like a hawk. Michael will have my throat if I leave you even for a minute."

"Sure. Wherever makes you comfortable," I said, my eyes still closed.

"I'll just read some of your books or try the computer. Google or something. There are so many things I need to learn about your world."

"Okay then. Good night, Davin. Do alkins sleep?" I thought the question was silly, but I had to ask.

"Let's just say I had to before, but since we were sent to Halo City, it has not been a necessity."

"What happens if an alkin kills an angel?" I asked.

"I think it's forgivable if it's done under self-defense, don't you think? Are you trying to find a way to get rid of Aden, like the rest of us?"

"It did cross my mind, although I wouldn't know how. I don't know how it could be done." Then anger boiled inside me. I didn't know where this energy was coming from. I sat up on my bed. "I hate him! I hate him so much that I wish I could kill him myself! I want to see him suffer as much as he has made me suffer!" I was full of rage.

"Whoaaa, Claudia. I've never seen you angry like this. Let's bring your heart rate down a notch. Don't give him the satisfaction of knowing that you're thinking of him."

"I'm just confused, frustrated, and angry."

"I understand. I guess I would feel the same if I were in your shoes. But for now, our focus is to keep you safe. At least now we know for sure why he is after you." Davin continued telling me stories that sounded like whispering voices as I drifted off to sleep.

Beep! Beep! Beep! My alarm clock went off. Davin frantically tried to turn the alarm off while juggling it like a hot potato. The alarm clock rang loudly, to the point that it was annoying, but I was too tired to get out of bed to turn it off. I motioned for him to come to me, my eyes half opened.

"Sorry, I was just playing with it, and —"

"Don't worry, I'm going back to bed," I said as I slammed the off button.

"I could have done that, but I think I would have broken it," I heard him say as I dozed off to sleep again.

When I opened my eyes with ease, I knew I had a restful night. It took a few seconds to bring me back to reality as I glanced over to my desk to see Davin posed in exactly the same position as before I fell asleep, his feet crossed on top of the desk with his arms resting behind his neck.

"Good morning, sleepyhead. I didn't know you could sleep that long."

"What time is it?"

"Time for dinner."

I didn't believe him. "No, seriously, what time is it?"

"I am serious. You slept for eighteen hours."

Shocked, I sat up so quickly that I felt a head rush. I placed my hands over my head to stop the room from spinning.

"You okay?" he asked.

"Yeah. Just a head rush," I murmured.

"It seems that I have that kind of effect on you." He grinned.

I smiled back, remembering the first time we met. He held me so I wouldn't fall. "Yeah, I guess," I replied with a small laugh. "Did my mom come to see me in the morning?" I asked, worried.

"Yes, but don't worry." He pointed upward. "The roof."

"Thanks, sorry."

"You owe me one or two, or more," he said jokingly.

"I know, someday," I said. I knew he was joking, but the truth was that I owed him for many things. "Did you leave? I mean, did you need to go back?" What I really wanted to know was if he had a chance to see Michael.

"Yes, I felt a bit weak so I had to go back. Caleb watched over you while you were sleeping. See, everything turned out fine." Then he smiled as if he knew what I really wanted to ask. "I'm sorry, I didn't see Michael. I don't know what he is up to, and he won't tell us. That's just the way he is, always looking after others before himself. All I know is that when he makes a promise, he's good for it. Don't worry; I'm sure he's fine. By the way, this thing keeps on shaking." He handed me my cell phone.

"Oh, you don't know what it is?"

"Of course I do. You think I'm that ancient?" He gave a teasing smile.

"No, I didn't mean it that way." I could have kicked myself because the last thing I wanted to do was offend him.

"I was just kidding. When I picked up the calls, this thing didn't answer back." He looked confused.

"Let's take a look. It's actually letting me know that I have text messages. I guess Vivian didn't show you?" I questioned.

"I don't pay attention to things we don't use. Vivian is fascinated by technology, unlike me," he said.

"See, I have two messages. The first one is from Patty. It says: Sorry about Gamma. How r u?" I texted her back: Thanx for dropping off my bag. Don't worry. Text u later.

The second one was from Kristina. How r u? Gotta talk about b-day on Fri. What should I wear. Lol!

"Human girls, why don't you just pick up the phone and talk? Why do you need to make things complicated?" he laughed, obviously amused.

Our conversation was interrupted by the vibration of my cell phone. I picked it up. "Hello."

"Hello, Claudia."

"Hey, Kristina."

"I just found out. I'm sooo sorry to hear about Gamma. How are you?" she asked caringly.

It had been only three days since I last saw her, but it seemed like I hadn't spoken to her in years. "I'm fine," I said softly.

"Maggie wanted to call, but I told her that I would."

"It's all right. Just let her know I'm fine," I said.

"Sure. I know it's not a good time, but Ryan's birthday is this Saturday, remember? Can you go?"

I wasn't up for a party, so I tried to think of an excuse. "I know I promised, but…but I didn't have time to buy a gift."

"Don't worry. I bought a big one. I could say it's from both of us," she said. "Usually I would beg you to come out, but I know you probably don't feel up to it. Maybe it will do you some good to see your friends."

"Well, I don't know." I was hesitant at first, but she was right, I did want to see my friends. "I did RSVP to the Evite. I'll need to ask my mom."

From the corner of my eyes, I could see Davin frowning and shaking his fingers back and forth. He was mouthing the words, "No, no, no."

"I gotta go, Kristina. Thanks for calling. I'll call you later."

"Are you crazy?" Davin blurted out as soon as I hung up. "You know I can't let you go. Michael will be furious with you and especially with me."

"Calm down, Davin. I didn't say I was going to go alone."

"Oh." He calmed down and then was deep in thought. He gave me a curious look knowing I was up to something.

"He said to stay put, but as long as you're with me…," I said, putting thoughts into his head.

His mouth dropped. Then he gave me a conniving smile. It didn't take much to convince Davin.

"So let me think about this." He was pacing back and forth, probably weighing the odds of Michael finding out. "Girls…dance…girls. Okay, if we go, we can't stay out too late."

"It ends at midnight," I said.

"What? What party ends at midnight?"

"My curfew."

"Oh, okay then. And you have to stay right next to me so I won't feel guilty for you talking me into this, which I will regret if Michael ever finds out. Is that a deal?"

"Don't worry, Davin, I won't leave your sight. I'm not going to party the night away. I made a promise, and I just want to see my friends. Who knows, it may be my last party."

"What? What do you mean?" he asked.

"What if something happens to me? What if Aden—"

Davin didn't let me finish. He had a serious look I'd never seen before. "Claudia, you can't think that way. You need to know that we will do everything to keep you safe. Our lives will be lost before yours. We are your guardians."

"I…I…okay," I said, looking down, feeling humbled. I didn't know what to say. His words, our lives will be lost before yours, echoed in my head. I was extremely touched, and I knew he meant it. With another question in mind, I looked up. "Davin, when this is all over, will I see any of you again?" My eyes were uncertain.

"I don't know what will happen. I just don't know, Claudia. I wish I could make things easier for you and give you the answers you want to hear. Let's not dwell on matters you cannot control. But one thing is for sure, knowing Michael; I don't know how he does it, but he always gets his way."

I gave him a smile because I knew he was trying to make me feel better. Then I changed the subject. "Hey! How are you going to get girls to dance with you dressed like that?" I pointed at what he was wearing, scanning his outfit up and down.

He looked at himself. "You're right. I look too plain in jeans and a T-shirt." He winked. "Don't you worry, I'll look my part."

I couldn't help but laugh. Our laughter was interrupted by Mom. "Claudia, dinner time."

"I'll be back," I said, feeling stomach pangs from hunger.

"Don't worry about me. I'll just surf the web on your computer. I've got a lot to learn. You humans are way more complicated than I thought."

Just as I was halfway out of my bedroom, Davin placed his hand on the screen, and the computer turned on. **Amazing**, I thought.

🦋

It had been about a week since Gamma passed away. A part of me didn't want to go to Ryan's birthday party because I was still grieving, but Mom thought it was a good idea since I would be surrounded by friends. Although I knew Gamma was gone forever, I was surprised at myself for not falling apart.

"Hurry up, you're gonna be late," Davin whispered.

"Haven't you heard of being fashionably late?" I whispered back through the door so Mom wouldn't think I was talking to myself.

"I didn't know you wanted to be late."

"Do you have a car? I told my mom that I had a date." I took a deep breath and walked out.

"You didn't say anything about a—" He stopped mid-sentence. Davin stood by the door staring at me. "Claudia, you look great. I mean, not that you didn't before, but—"

I interrupted. "Thank you. I know what you mean." I showed him two items that I held in my hands. "It's called makeup and a curling iron. They're two great inventions that can make any girl look good."

"Well, thank you to the inventors," he said, making a whistling sound.

He made me blush. "Well, you look great yourself. I don't think any girl will be able to resist you."

"Really?" He checked himself in front of my closet mirror. His black slacks and dark gray dress shirt made him look like a GQ model.

"Let me do something to your hair," I said, squeezing gel on my hand.

He backed away as soon as I held up my hands. "Wait a minute. What is that? Nobody messes with my hair." He lightly tapped his hair. "This is gold to me."

"Let me make it golden then." Without his permission, I ran my fingers through his hair to slick it back. He fussed and turned, but ultimately gave in. "See, much better."

"Really?" He looked at himself in the mirror again, amazed how a different hairstyle could change his appearance.

"This is gel," I said, amused that this simple thing was so new to him.

Suddenly, Davin looked out the window, startled.

"What is it?" I asked quickly and moved behind him as my heart thumped rapidly.

"I feel a presence," he said sharply and stood dead still.

I swallowed briskly and held my breath as I waited for Davin to tell me what to do.

"We can relax. It's Caleb and Vivian," he said.

When Caleb and Vivian appeared, I exhaled with relief as my premonition of fallen or demons flying through the window disappeared.

"Don't think you're going anywhere without us," Vivian said, smiling.

Davin and I were surprised to see them, but I was mostly overjoyed. "Vivian, you look great!" She had on a spaghetti strap V-neck dress that framed her thin body.

"It's fun dressing up, and I love your dress too," Vivian said, looking at me approvingly.

I wore the black chiffon dress that Patty had given me for my birthday. "Thanks," I said.

Then we both looked at each other and said at the same time, "Fashion Wear."

As we giggled, I gave her a tight squeeze to show her how happy I was to see her again. I quickly turned to Caleb, not wanting to leave him out. "You look nice too."

He gave me a big smile. He wore dark gray slacks and a black-buttoned down shirt, which looked great on him. They always looked beautiful, but dressed up, they were drop-dead gorgeous.

"Are we going to complement each other all night, or are we going to the party?" Davin interrupted.

"Do you have a car?" I asked.

He looked at me with a blank face. Then his face lit up with an idea. "I could go steal one. I mean, borrow one for the night."

I frowned, with my hands on my hips. "You don't have one?"

"I'm not supposed to leave you."

"I thought you could do some kind of magic thing, and poof, it's here," I said.

"I'm an alkin, not a magician, if you haven't noticed," he said sarcastically. "Yes, I could make one appear, but I didn't know which one. There are too many. And I thought I was driving your car."

"But you're my date. You're supposed to pick me up in your car."

"Now you tell me. How am I supposed to know? I haven't had a date in how many lifetimes, remember? I don't even know what you mean by dating. We learn by observing and that thing you call "Googling" on the computer. That's what I was doing while you were eating and sleeping, learning about your mannerisms. You humans are too complicated."

"Sorry, I should have explained it to you. I forget sometimes," I said, feeling guilty for getting mad at him.

"Don't worry. Caleb and I did some research. I have one parked right in front of your house," Vivian said proudly.

"Good thinking," Davin replied. "I hope you stole, I mean borrowed, a fast car."

"What do you mean?" Caleb said. "I get to drive it. After all, I borrowed the car that I want to drive."

"He has a point, Davin," Vivian spoke in Caleb's defense.

Davin frowned and said, "Fine! Let's go."

We parted ways, and Davin rang the doorbell. Caleb and Vivian waited for us by the car.

"I got it, Claudia. I can't wait to meet your date," Mom said, excitedly. I took a quick peek to see what she was doing while I pretended to be getting ready in my room. I observed her sneaking a peek in the mirror, straightening her dress, and brushing her hair with her fingers. As I walked out of my bedroom door, Mom's eyes grew big. She walked to me, placing her hands on my shoulders, smiling and staring.

"You look beautiful, honey! I hardly ever get to see you with makeup and your hair in curls. It makes me happy that you're out of your room and having fun."

"Thanks, Mom," I said while blushing. "Aren't you going to open the door?"

"Ahhh…I almost forgot," she said as she headed for the door, still staring at me.

"Hello," Davin said politely while extending his hand. He was acting like quite a gentleman, much more mature than the usual Davin.

Mom looked impressed and graciously shook his hand. "Hello," she said back.

"Mom, this is Davin." I introduced hastily. Mom could tell I was in a hurry as I walked out the door and gave her a look.

"Well, you better get going. It was nice meeting you, Davin." Then she turned to me. "Remember your curfew."

"Don't worry. I'll bring her home by midnight."

"Thank you," Mom said politely. "I would appreciate it if you kept your word." She smiled again and looked at me. "Tell Ryan happy birthday for me."

I nodded and placed my hands through Davin's arm and pulled him along. As I turned around to wave good-bye, she whispered something that sounded like, "He's very good-looking."

I thought to myself; if you think Davin is good-looking, wait till you see Michael. I just gave her a big grin and waved her back into the house so she wouldn't see Vivian and Caleb. Although I was very excited to go to the party with my alkin friends, I missed Michael madly. Where are you, Michael? What are you doing?

Chapter 21

"Cool car, Caleb!" Davin said, making a complete circle around the heavily tinted black Ferrari 612 Scaglietti. "I think I'm in love. So, who did you steal this car from?" Davin asked, placing his hand out in front of Caleb, waiting for the car keys.

Caleb stood his ground with his arms crossed, shaking his head.

"We didn't steal it. We borrowed it from the dealer. I'm sure they won't miss it just for one night," Vivian said, admiring the car too.

"It's called stealing," Davin challenged as he gave a big frown.

"So if you got it, it's called…"

"Borrowing," Davin said quickly.

"Great, you make it sound like a sin when I do it."

"Just messing with you. I'm just bitter 'cause I don't get to drive it."

"You two need to see each other more often, or is it that you two need to be away from each other more often? Either way, we need to get going," I said.

"Sorry, Claudia. Davin gets on my nerves sometimes. He's acting more like a human these days."

"Are these two like this all the time?" I asked Caleb.

"Only when we're down here. There must be something in the air. I'm almost positive they were brother and sister in human life," Caleb replied back.

Vivian let out a short laugh. "You're funny," she said lightly to Caleb.

Davin released a heavy sigh. I don't think he was paying attention to our conversation. He was admiring the car too intensely. "Sure you don't want me to drive it, Caleb?" Davin asked with a pleading look.

"Don't get your hopes up, Davin. Hop in the front, Vivian. Let's get going," Caleb said as he settled himself into the driver's seat.

Something about the car seemed to have given Caleb a sense of power. I'd never heard him speak in such a commanding voice before. Davin and I sat in the back, and I watched Caleb punch in the address of the hotel on the navigator. Realizing that I was actually sitting inside an ultra expensive luxury car, I observed every detail. The one most obvious was the black leather seat I was sitting on. I thought it would feel soft and plush, but it was actually really hard and tight.

Boom! Boom! Boom! went the music and I was startled by the sudden loudness.

I could feel the vibrations from the speakers underneath the seat. Davin rested his head back while tapping his fingers to the music. Caleb, with his window down, tapped his hand on the door, and Vivian nodded her head to the beat. It was amusing to watch the alkins enjoying themselves, as if they were ordinary teenagers.

"Here we are," Caleb said, turning the ignition off. Suddenly I felt nervous. How was I to explain who they were?

"Don't get out yet!" I yelled quickly. Stunned by my outburst, they froze and looked at me. "Well, my friends will wonder who you are. Sorry, I didn't mean to scare you," I said, shrugging my shoulders. We were all on edge. I didn't blame them for being shaken up by my sudden outburst.

"What would you like for us to say?" Vivian asked.

"Well, I thought I could say that you are my cousins from San Francisco."

"Okay," Caleb said like it was no big deal.

"Could we keep our names? Who knows? I may mess that up," Davin said with a chuckle.

"Sure, that would make it easier for me too. Let's go," I said.

We walked excitedly to the front entrance of the hotel. There was a huge sign: "Ryan's Birthday Party, Grand View Room, thirtieth floor." I suddenly felt a knot in the pit of my stomach, knowing we would be up so high, but I knew I would be fine since we were indoors.

"Thirtieth floor; it looks like the elevator is to the right," Vivian said, pointing to the direction.

We all followed behind her. The crystals from the chandelier caught my eyes first as they burst with unbelievable brilliance that sent sparkles throughout the room. The front lobby was decorated with beautiful arrangements of flowers placed in tall vases everywhere I looked. Not only did they make the room colorful, they certainly brightened up the dimly-lit lobby. As I continued to walk, I noticed the intricate designs of the marble floor that glistened from the candles nearby. Dark brown leather sofas and couches were arranged on antique rugs.

Suddenly I stopped in front of a huge, striking painting of an angel. She was painted standing with her golden wings expanded. Her long, dark hair accentuated her chocolate brown eyes. Her face stood out from the rest of the painting, and I couldn't peel my eyes off of her. On the corner of the painting read, "Katherine."

"Who is she?" I asked.

"No idea, but she is unbelievably breathtaking," Davin replied, mesmerized by the painting.

"That's strange," Caleb said. "That name sounds familiar. I believe Katherine was one of the Twelve Angels. I don't know if that is her for sure, but I do remember the name."

"Well, let's go. We need to be back by midnight, as Davin promised your mom," Vivian said, her brow furrowed.

"Claudia told me her curfew was midnight. I was only trying to be a gentleman," Davin explained.

I didn't want Vivian and Davin arguing over what time we should be home. "That's all right. I don't want to be home too late, and plus I don't know if we should be here without Michael." I was having doubts about our decision, but it was too late. We were here and might as well make the best of it.

As the elevator opened, I noticed that it was very elegant. Mirrors completely surrounded us, making the space look much bigger than it was. The elevator buttons and trimmings on the walls had gold borders. As we headed straight up, I felt my stomach drop to the floor. The ride seemed endless as I watched the numbers rise. The numbers lit up one by one as we passed each floor. The thirtieth floor couldn't come fast enough for me.

"Here's our floor," Caleb sounded so excited.

The mere sound of the music lifted our spirits as we anxiously walked through the Grand View Room. What a view! The back wall was completely covered in glass from floor to ceiling. You could see all the vibrant lights reflecting from buildings, streets, and moving objects below. I felt like I was inside a rainbow, admiring the beauty from afar. What was even more amazing was the height of the ceiling. I had to tilt my head way back to get the full view.

"Wow! Look at this place," Vivian said.

Before I had a chance to look for my friends, Kristina and Maggie rushed up to give me a hug. Then they eyed Caleb, Davin, and Vivian.

"These are my cousins." I lied. They couldn't stop staring. "Heelllooo," I said, waving my hand in front of their eyes.

"Oh…hi," Kristina finally spoke, her eyes still glued to their faces. Then she gave me a questioning look as to who they were and what they were doing here.

As I led the way across the dance floor, which was in the middle of the room, I turned to Kristina and whispered, "I thought they could just blend in. Let's hurry. I didn't ask Ryan."

"You never told me you had cousins," Kristina whispered.

"You never asked," I whispered back.

"You never told me you were bringing them," Kristina whispered again.

"I didn't have a chance. They showed up unexpectedly," I said.

"Oh," she said quickly.

Feeling bad for coming empty-handed, I asked, "How big is Ryan's gift?"

"I got him a gift card. Don't worry, I already signed your name on the card. I didn't think you would mind."

"Are you kidding? I appreciate it. I'll pay you back."

"Don't worry. I know where you live," she teased.

As I laughed, Maggie spoke, "Right here. Here's our table."

We found our seats and sat for a while, just enjoying the music and the ambiance, when a waitress walked by. "Would you like anything to drink?" she asked, smiling and batting her eyelashes at Davin.

"No, thanks," Davin replied. "Perhaps the ladies," he said, waiting for us to respond.

"We already have our drinks, thank you," Maggie replied.

"Some water, please," I said. Suddenly, my throat felt dry.

When I saw Ryan, he was surrounded by his basketball team friends, along with a bunch of girls. I decided to stay hidden as long as I could.

"So, which school do you go to?" Kristina asked my so-called cousins.

I nearly flipped. I hadn't anticipated my friends would ask questions. Davin, Caleb, and Vivian looked at me with uncertainty. I interjected quickly, "They go to a private school called The Guardian." As soon as I spoke, I could've kicked myself. Couldn't I have thought of a better name?

"Oh," Kristina said.

"Where is that school located?" Maggie asked.

Shoot! Why does Maggie have to be so nosey tonight? "Not too far from downtown. On a street called Crossroads," I replied quickly, not thinking about what I was saying. Knowing they would ask more questions, I had to think fast, or I would be caught in a tunnel of lies. As I was thinking of what to do or say, I saw Davin swaying to the music. "Ask Kristina to dance," I whispered in his ear.

He smiled, nodded, and turned his face toward her. "Kristina, would you like to dance?"

Kristina looked surprised. "Are you asking me?"

"Your name is Kristina, right?"

Still stunned, she replied, "Yeah…sorry…sure." She stood up, smiling.

Then Davin whispered to me, "Stay right here, and don't move." He turned to his friends. "Don't leave her sight."

Although I'd rather be sitting than dancing, I saw the look on Vivian and Caleb's faces. They looked like they wanted to join in the fun too. Hesitantly, I said, "Let's all dance together."

Davin took Kristina's hand. We walked to the dance floor and danced together in a circle. I spotted Ryan again and gave him a birthday hug. I was hoping to distract him from noticing my guests, but he was slightly buzzed and was unable to tell who was who. I wondered how he got an alcoholic drink. As I looked around, I saw that everybody was enjoying themselves. I could feel the vibrations from the bass of the music. I had forgotten who I was as we danced late into the night. It was so nice to see Caleb, Davin, and Vivian having such a great time along with my friends. What a perfect view. What a perfect place. What a perfect night. Although it would have been more perfect with Michael here.

Suddenly the loudness of the music dimmed as the DJ announced that it would be a couples' song. As we all headed toward our table, Kristina's eyes were locked to something or someone behind me.

"Kristina?" I questioned.

She didn't respond. Before I even had the chance to see who she was looking at, I saw Davin and Caleb take a few steps back. Suddenly, my heart stopped completely, out of fear, until I heard his voice.

"May I have this dance?" he asked gently.

I froze. "Michael," I whispered his name, while my back was still to him.

I was afraid to turn around to look him in the eyes. As I slowly turned, I was awestruck to see him looking so debonair, dressed in black slacks and a royal blue dress shirt. I had simply died and gone to Heaven. Still stunned to see him, I couldn't move or speak. Michael led me to the dance floor, guided my arms around his shoulders, and placed his arms around my waist as we swayed to the music. I placed my head on his chest, listening to the lyrics. "Are you really here tonight or are you just a dream? Out of nowhere you appeared and captured my heart. I surrender all my love to you. Give me forever. That's all I ask."

"This is surprising. You haven't asked me one question. Lost your words tonight?"

"I'm sorry," I said apologetically, waiting for him to lecture me.

"I should be extremely mad at you, but you look so beautiful that it is me who is lost for words."

He pulled me back and our eyes met. He gave me that killer smile as he spun me around. He made my heart flutter every time he smiled. He pulled me gently closer to him, and our eyes locked again. We couldn't keep our eyes off each other.

"Your eyes are twinkling," he said.

"They twinkle because they love what they see," I said, flirting and relieved at the thought that he wasn't mad.

He smiled again. "Promise me," he said, in a serious tone, as we still swayed to the music.

"It all depends on what you're asking me to promise," I answered.

"Promise me that next time you'll do as I ask. I'm only concerned about your safety."

I knew I was guilty, and he had every right to be mad at me. "Sorry, next time I'll do better. Please don't be mad at your friends, and especially at Davin. I'm the one who wanted to come, and they followed me to keep me safe as you instructed."

"For tonight," he said.

"How did you know I was here?" I asked apprehensively.

"Vivian told me before she left to join you."

"That's why you are dressed up. You knew I was going to a dance?"

"Yes," he confessed.

As I was thinking that I was worried about nothing, we were suddenly bumped by someone.

"Excuseese ve," he slurred.

It was Ryan.

"Wee seeee...you got new voyfriend," he slurred again, almost falling down. Effortlessly Michael held him up.

Ryan almost fell again as he shoved Michael, but Michael didn't even budge. Ryan tilted his head upward to meet Michael's eye's. Ryan's eyes were filled with anger, and then curiosity. "You suuupeman or...sommiving?" he asked, giving a dirty look. Ryan didn't wait for a response from Michael, and instead, turned to me. "Do I vet a bir-birday kiss?" He closed his eyes and puckered up.

"Ryan, you're drunk. Happy birthday," I said and started to walk away, when Ryan grabbed me and swung me around to face him. I wondered how he even got drunk since alcohol was prohibited at the party.

Michael grabbed Ryan's wrist to free me and commanded, "Don't you ever touch her again."

Ryan fell to his knees from the pain of Michael's grip, and that's when his friends huddled behind him.

I gave Michael a look to let him know I was fine, and he let go of Ryan's wrist. "He's drunk and won't remember a thing tomorrow morning," I said loud enough for his friends to hear.

"You stink like hell," Michael said angrily to Ryan.

"Let's go, Ryan," Jake said and pulled him away. Jake turned to me. "Sorry, Claudia. You know how he can get. He still cares for you."

"No, I vant...Clauvia," Ryan slurred again, rubbing his sore wrist.

"You're making a fool of yourself. Good thing your parents left early," Jake said, pulling him further away from us.

Ryan looked at me, with sorrow in his eyes. I knew I had hurt him, but I didn't realize how much until tonight. Michael continued to glare at him until he was out of sight. We walked toward the rest of our group. Michael held my hand, guiding me behind him in a protective mode, as usual.

Chapter 22

Michael didn't say a word to the alkins. In fact, he seemed to be content. He sat next to me with his arm around my shoulders. I couldn't believe we were here all together like everything was normal. With Michael here, the night was definitely perfect. Suddenly the ceiling started to open up. Everybody was admiring it, with their eyes glued to the starlight that gradually beamed into the room.

"Now we know why they call this the Grand View Room," Maggie said, as she continued to stare.

I could only imagine what others were saying as they pointed to the top. As the roof of the hotel completely disappeared, the DJ played the "Happy Birthday" song and we all sang together. Singing and staring out into the open space, I spotted Orion and immediately thought about Austin. I hadn't spoken to him in days. He was expecting my phone call after the hospital, but I didn't bother to call.

Suddenly, I became aware that I didn't know what time it was. "Is it late?" I asked, panicking.

"It's midnight," Kristina replied.

"What!" I couldn't believe it. "I'm supposed to be home." I sank down further into Michael's arm.

Vivian looked at Davin with a worried expression.

"I can take you home right now," Michael said looking at me, waiting for my response.

Then I remembered Mom was working the late shift tonight. Talking myself out of the guilt for missing my curfew, I told myself that it could happen just this once. After all, when would I ever get this chance again? "Actually, my mom is working late. She won't know. It will be okay," I said, hoping that it would be.

"Are you sure?" Michael asked, uncertain of my decision.

"Yes," I answered back confidently.

It was quiet at our table, and I hadn't realized all eyes were on me until Kristina broke the silence. "Should we dance again?" Kristina asked, swaying to the music.

Everyone stood up except Michael and me. "You all go ahead. Claudia and I need to talk," Michael said.

They all left for the dance floor and Michael turned to me. "I missed you every second," he whispered into my ear as he gently caressed my hair. Then he placed his hands on my cheeks. "I've tried so hard just being the guardian angel that I'm supposed to be, but I can't control the human emotions I feel. It drives me absolutely crazy when I'm not with you. Every thought of you awakens me. You've changed me in ways I can't explain. I don't know if you would call it fate that somehow our worlds have connected, but for whatever reason, our lives will never be the same."

All I could do was look at my guardian angel who loved me back. Many times I had to pinch myself to realize that this wasn't a dream. Yes, I did believe that things happened for a reason, but this was too good to be true. He was right. Our lives would never be the same.

"How were you able to come here when I'm not even in danger? Isn't Phillip expecting all of you back soon?"

"I told Phillip that we needed to be down here more often. He surprisingly agreed."

"That's wonderful," I said happily.

Tenderly he cupped my cheeks with his hands again. "I missed you madly," he said.

"I missed you too," I said back. "I know that our relationship isn't normal, but there's got to be a way we can be together, isn't there?" I asked with a hopeful look.

"Let's talk about it later. Let's enjoy tonight."

"About tonight, I just wanted to get away, and I thought coming to this dance would kind of take my mind off things."

"I'm glad you came. You could have danced with other guys if you wanted. Although if you had, it would have made me feel jealous."

"Seriously? You would be jealous?"

"As silly as it sounds, yes."

"Do you know what it means to feel jealous?" I knew this was a silly question to ask, but there were many feelings they were trained to put aside for so many years.

"I think so, like when I overheard Kristina tell Vivian something about Ryan being your boyfriend."

"Ex-boyfriend," I said quickly.

"I felt something strange in the pit of my stomach. It was hate and anger at the same time," he said calmly.

"Yeah, I know the feeling," I said, remembering the nurse who was flirting with him. Then I laughed softly, thinking how strong this feeling was that could get anyone all worked up.

He leaned closer. "Let's not talk about other people," he said, nuzzling my neck and then up to my cheek. Then he softly planted kisses on both my cheeks. "That one was for Monday and the other one was for Tuesday, when I wasn't with you." He kissed my forehead. "That one was for Wednesday." He kissed my nose. "That one was for Thursday. This one is for today."

He leaned over to kiss me on my lips when we heard Davin clear his throat. We looked up to see Davin and the others giggling and waving.

"Claudia, we have to go," Kristina said. "Maggie and I came together, and we didn't ask if we could stay out that late."

I stood up and gave Maggie and Kristina a hug. "Thanks," I said to Kristina. "Thanks for talking me into coming. I really had a great time."

"I'm glad, and I'm really sorry about Gamma," she said and gave me a tight squeeze. Then she looked at me with a huge grin. "When did you hook up with Michael?"

"Long story. Tell you later," I said. At that moment I thought about Patty. Somehow I had to tell her about Michael, although I couldn't tell her the whole truth. One way or another, she would find out that he was at Ryan's birthday party, and she would be devastated that I hadn't told her first. I just had to find the right time.

Maggie gave me a tight squeeze too and said her good-byes to my so-called cousins. I watched them walk across the dance floor until they were out of sight.

It was way past midnight, and all the guests had already left. The only ones left were the cleanup crew. Michael used his powers on them and they left. We had the room to ourselves.

"I had so much fun. I'll never forget tonight. This is one memory they can't take from me," Vivian said as she looked around the room. Then she said suddenly, "Michael, Claudia's necklace is made from the crystal of our home, correct?"

Michael didn't say a word, instead he just nodded.

I gently placed my hand on the crystal to confirm that it was still there.

"That crystal turns black when danger is nearby," Vivian stated.

"I've never seen one before," Caleb said.

"That's because we never needed one before, but this was Michael's idea. Phillip doesn't know. Pretty cool if you ask me," she said.

Caleb looked at Michael with a concerned look on his face. "Michael, where were you all this time? And were you able to find the answers you were searching for?"

Just as Michael was about to speak, he suddenly glued his eyes on me. Everyone was looking at me, and that's when I realized my crystal had turned black. The ceiling had almost completely closed when Aden and his followers slipped through the small opening.

Vivian and Caleb leaped out of their seats and pulled out their swords. Michael grabbed me so fast that I didn't realize I was standing next to him.

"We came to join the party." Aden smiled, pleased with himself for completely blindsiding us. "We can make this easy. Just hand her over to me."

"Over my dead body," Michael said angrily. He expanded his wings to protect and cover me entirely. "I will kill you if I have to, and I will do everything in my power to stop you."

"Michael, just listen to yourself. You would die over this one? How noble you have become. The Michael I knew would have done the killing for me."

Michael didn't say anything.

"I can't believe this. You are in love with this one. How could you allow this? You have broken one of the Divine Commandments. How many others have you broken?"

"You have no right to question me. How many have you broken? And what do you know about love?" Michael replied.

"Love is evil. It makes you weak. See what love made you do. You are lost!"

"You are absolutely wrong. It makes you stronger. Amor tussisque non celantur."

"Enough!" Aden shouted. "Come and join me, and you can be with her forever."

"Never! I followed you once before, and I promised myself that I would never do it again," Michael replied.

"Very well. Let's do this your way. Die!" he shouted with an evil laugh that sent chills to my bones.

Vivian and Caleb positioned their backs to each other.

"Stay close to me," Michael commanded.

Michael's feet were shoulder-width apart. He curled his fingers around the grip of his sword, and his right foot slid back, pulling his entire body into a fighting stance. The fallen and demons were creeping closer, and my heart pounded with anticipation. It seemed as though the number had tripled from the last encounter. My palms became damp, and the adrenaline ran through my veins so fast that I could feel my blood pressure skyrocketing.

"There are too many of them. Where's Davin?" Vivian asked, thrusting her sword forward and backward, trying to keep them at a distance.

"I saw him walking Claudia's friends to their car," Caleb replied, extending his arm, lunging forward as the fallen backed away.

"Right behind you! Always talking about me, how sweet!" Davin shouted, as he entered the room.

Michael swung his sword to his right, piercing a demon right in his ribs. With his free hand, he rammed his fist into a fallen's face to his left. The fallen flew across, only to tumble on top of more fallen, breaking the tables and chairs as they collided. Michael then dodged a swipe, lost his balance, and fell to his knees. I gasped in horror, but quickly calmed when I saw him back on his feet. As he swung vertically to block an attack, he yelled, "Down, Claudia!" The look of terror in his eyes made me move without hesitation. I ducked down as Michael lashed right above me, slicing through a demon's neck. Michael swiftly enclosed me behind him.

Across the room, I saw a demon grab Caleb by his neck and slam him against the table. His weapon slipped out of his hand, leaving him defenseless. Out of nowhere I saw a smaller sword dart across the room to pierce precisely into the demon's back, just as he was about to thrust his sword into Caleb. The demon bellowed out in pain, dropping to the floor. At that moment, I exhaled, not realizing I had held my breath the entire time.

Vivian was standing on top of a table when a fallen grabbed her from behind. Twisting with all her might, she tried to release from the hold. As the demons approached her, she extended her long legs, kicking them away from her. She then slammed her head against the fallen holding her hostage, pivoted, and drove her weapon into him. More demons surrounded her; she lunged lower, severing the heads of the demons around her with her sword.

While evading demons and fallen, Davin leaped from table to table. Finally he planted himself on the bar. He pulled his weapon out, ready for his enemies. As they attacked, Davin managed to avoid blows, but he barely saw the spinning kick coming at him in time to leap back, landing flat on his back. A demon standing close to him lashed out, slightly nicking him across his chest. Davin cursed out loud, and anger raged from his eyes. He managed to grab a bottle of wine, knocking it over the demon's head. When it shattered into pieces, the liquid poured down, leaving him blind. Davin turned him into ashes. Heaving, he flung out from where he stood, charging swiftly like a wild creature, killing whatever stood in his path until he reached the other side of the room.

Tables, chairs, and shattered glasses were everywhere. All were broken into unrecognizable objects, like a tornado had ripped through the room. I was exhausted from watching and holding my breath, praying that my friends had the strength and endurance to make it out alive. It seemed like an endless fight. Aden must have thought the same thing for he shouted, "Enough!"

All was at a standstill. I wondered what Aden had up his sleeve, because even I knew he wouldn't just walk away.

"Perhaps this may change your mind," he shouted.

Out from the ceiling appeared a demon with Alexa Rose. The demon lowered her as she dangled in fright. My heart sank to see her in the middle of all of this. Michael was right. Aden would do anything to get what he wanted.

"Michael!" she called desperately.

"Let her go, Aden, she's only a child!" Michael demanded.

"You heard Michael. Do it!" he yelled at the demon who was holding her.

"Michael!" Alexa Rose screamed as she was let go.

"No!" I screamed and immediately stopped when I saw Alexa Rose suspended in midair. I immediately turned to Michael and saw his hand raised to where Alexa Rose was floating.

"I learned how to use my hands to control things like you do," Michael said to Aden.

Aden looked furious. He raised his hand too, and Alexa Rose gravitated toward him. "I would have taught you everything I knew if you had stayed with me. Now give me what is mine!"

Aden was pulling Alexa Rose closer to him. He was stronger than Michael.

"Michael!" she yelled, as her delicate little hands reached out for him.

I couldn't take it any longer. It was too much to bear. Losing my common sense, I ran out of my protective area and toward Aden.

"Stop, Claudia," Davin yelled.

It was too late. Aden used his free hand to levitate Davin toward him. Then he pinned him against the wall, and the fallen nearby moved toward them. Vivian and Caleb dashed forward to help Davin defend from the attack. When they reached him, they were surrounded by fallen and demons. The tips of their enemies' blades were pointed at their chests. Aden released Davin, his eyes focused on me like a hawk preying on its next meal.

"No!" Michael yelled with anguish, knowing what Aden would do next.

Although my whole body felt light, I couldn't move. I could see myself rising off the ground toward Aden. No matter how hard I tried, I couldn't free myself from his control.

"Who to choose? Who to save? Did you know your precious Alexa Rose has a wonderful talent? She is a gatekeeper. She got out herself, looking for you," Aden said. "Don't you wonder who opened the gates of Hell for me? For her first time, she did pretty well. She would make a great addition to my collection."

"Noooo!" Michael cried with rage.

"I'm sorry, Michael. He told me he would hurt you if I didn't do it," Alexa Rose cried. "Please don't be mad at me! Please don't be mad," she begged over and over, as tears fell down her face.

"It's all right, Alexa Rose. I'm not mad at you. It's okay. Aden, please, don't do this," Michael pleaded.

"I'm done asking you to join me, and I'm done playing around. I choose both for myself. David!" Aden shouted to the demon up on the ceiling. "Catch!"

Alexa Rose was lifted up toward the open ceiling. "Michael!" Her painful shrieks echoed through the room.

"Nooo!" Michael yelled, as he attempted to save her one last time.

Alexa Rose ascended through the ceiling, and David grabbed her.

I was terrified for Alexa Rose. She was in the hands of a demon now, and there was nothing we could do. My heart shattered, and I felt like we were defeated. If I was in this much pain, I could only imagine how much it hurt Michael.

"Now what to do with this one? Say bye to your love."

"Aden, she is not the one. Don't do this. I'm the one you want. The Holy Spirit's soul is in me. You're looking for a son."

Aden suddenly stopped and listened intently. Michael continued to persuade him. "We've been leading you on so that you would think she is the one, but you've been fooled. You've been chasing the wrong alkin. You are looking for a son."

"I don't believe you. I've been tracking her for eighteen years. You think I'm a fool?"

"I'm not going to argue with that," Davin mumbled.

"I have proof. The one bears a birthmark, and I have one to prove it."

"What birthmark?" Aden asked, with anticipation in his voice.

I remembered Michael talking about a birthmark, but Michael didn't know what it was. He must have found out somehow. Davin, Caleb, and Vivian looked stunned. They knew he was only saying those words to save me.

"Show me," Aden demanded.

My eyes were glued to Michael as he flew toward Aden.

"You better be telling me the truth, or your friends below will die. You are outnumbered," Aden reminded Michael.

"It's the omega symbol," Michael said, as he carefully kept his distance.

I remembered seeing the symbol somewhere. It looked like an upside-down horseshoe. The birthmark didn't even cross my mind when Gamma told me I had the soul of the Holy Spirit. I wondered if she knew. Then I remembered Michael telling me that only the Royal Council, Phillip, Margaret, and Agnes knew. Gamma couldn't have known. I knew every scar and every freckle on my body, and I had never seen a birthmark like that. Could Gamma be wrong about me?

"Show me, Michael," Aden demanded.

Aden still held me captive, as Michael and Aden exchanged words in what appeared to be Latin. When Michael reached out his right arm to show the birthmark, Aden extended his arms and slashed Michael's wing. The sword came from nowhere. Michael yelled in agony, and my heart tore into a million pieces. Although his left wing was still intact, it looked broken. It wasn't strong and full like his right wing.

Then Michael's body started curling, and I thought he was going to fall. Just when I thought all hope was lost, Michael suddenly sprung forward into Aden and pushed him across the room. Michael broke Aden's hold on me and I began to fall. Michael used his powers to levitate my body toward where the alkins stood, and Davin deftly caught me.

Aden was furious as he charged toward Michael. Michael wrapped his hands around Aden's wrist that held the sword. Both of them struggled to retrieve the sword, twisting and turning in midair. Michael released his left hand and jammed his elbow into Aden's chest. When Aden lunged backward, he extended his leg and kicked Michael in the stomach. Michael was pushed back several yards, but he quickly charged forward and rotated over Aden's head. Catching Aden by surprise, Michael snatched the sword out of Aden's hand. They tumbled multiple times in midair until Aden's back slammed against the wall. Then Michael drove the sword into Aden's heart.

"Omega stands for the end for you," Michael said and drew the sword out.

Aden's face held a look of shock. Still floating, his wings folded halfway as his body weakened.

"Michael," Aden said weakly.

"You left me no choice," Michael said softly and sorrowfully. "May God have mercy on you."

Then Aden's eyes closed, his body arched, and his arms and legs grew limp as he started slowly spiraling downward like a lifeless feather. When he collapsed to the floor, his body flared up in flames. Quickly the flames died, and his body was gone. It was as if he had never existed.

Michael did not move as he floated there, but his face expressed a mixture of emotions. He lowered his head for a long second, then flew straight up. With Aden no longer there to lead them, the fallen and demons looked lost and confused. The alkins raised their swords while Davin pushed me behind him.

Suddenly Caleb dashed ahead just as Michael jabbed the sword into David's chest, causing him to release Alexa Rose. She fell straight down into Caleb's arms.

During the commotion, Davin grabbed me. Vivian and Caleb, with Alexa Rose still in his arms, rushed out of the room, while Michael flew behind us. The next thing I knew, we were somewhere near the hotel.

I turned to Michael and looked at him with worried eyes.

"Don't worry. I'll be fine," he said in a weak voice. Unexpectedly, he reached for me and held me in his arms.

"He's gone now. You're safe," Michael whispered in my ear, trying to console me.

I wanted to say something, but I could barely make out a word. I didn't realize that I was trembling until I heard my teeth chatter. Although I knew we were out of danger, the adrenaline was too much. I couldn't breathe, and a jumble of thoughts ran wildly through my head. I should be used to it by now. This wasn't the first time I was chased by fallen and demons. I could see Davin, Vivian, and Caleb watching me with concerned expressions on their faces. They were so calm, as if nothing had happened. Even Alexa Rose, now in the arms of Vivian, was just as composed.

I finally managed to say to them, a bit frantically, "Why…why aren't you scared out of your minds? Why aren't you shaking?"

"It's all right, Claudia," Michael whispered again, as I continued to tremble. "We're trained to control our fears. What kind of guardian angel would I be if I trembled like you?" He laughed softly, trying to make me laugh.

It didn't work. I nodded. I understood and felt bad for losing it like that.

"I can make it better," he said and held me tighter. Next thing I knew, there was a dim light glowing around us. Instantly I was calmer, and I knew it was from Michael. It was the same warm, secure feeling I had felt when Davin had held me at the Crossroads.

When he released his hold, my body no longer trembled, and I felt safe again. I looked up at Michael. His smile gave me comfort, and I found my words again. "Aden, is he really dead?"

"Yes," Michael said, lifting the sword to show me. It was absolutely stunning, about the length of my arm. The sword looked similar to the ones they used. "The Sword of the Divine," Michael said, looking at its tip and turning it left to right. "This sword was designed specifically for the Twelve Angels. Only by piercing this sword through an angel's heart can one truly kill an angel." There were no bloodstains. As if he could read my mind, he said, "Angels don't bleed."

There was an inscription on it. "What does it say?" I asked.

"Angele Dei…Angel of God," Michael replied, still captivated by the sword. "I wish I could keep this beauty, but I'll have to give it to Phillip."

We were all mesmerized by the sword when, suddenly, Alexa Rose hugged Michael. She patiently waited for Michael to let go of his hold on me. He didn't pick her up as usual because of his wound; instead, he knelt down to her level and gave her a long, warm embrace, as if it had been a lifetime since he had last seen her.

"Sorry, Michael," Alexa Rose said in her sweet angelic voice, as she placed her head on his shoulder. "Please don't be mad at me," she pleaded.

He placed his hands on her arms and pulled her back a bit, forcing her to look at him directly in his eyes. "I'm not mad. I was very worried. I almost lost you, you understand? Don't ever do that again. Don't ever look for me. You're not supposed to be here. If Phillip or the others find out, you will be punished."

"Okay, Michael," she answered back with tears streaming down her face.

"Promise me," he said.

"I promise," she replied, as Michael wiped her tears. "I was really scared. I thought I was never going to see you again." Her voice was shaky.

He embraced her tightly again. "Me too. I'm sorry too. I know how much you worry about me. I should have checked up on you. But you have to understand, I need to take care of things, and I can't worry about you too."

"Okay, Michael. Can we go home now? I want to go home," she said wearily, making small gasping sounds.

"Soon," Michael said and pulled her away to look at her. "You're a gatekeeper?"

"I don't even remember how I did it." Alexa Rose shrugged her shoulders.

"We'll have to discuss this later," Michael said.

"Michael, I hate to break up our little reunion, but we need to get you to Agnes," Davin said, with concern in his voice.

"Davin is right," Vivian interrupted. "We should get going. With Aden out of the picture, Claudia is safe. We need time to heal and rest. Caleb will clean up."

"Let's take Claudia home first," Michael replied. Michael looked at me lovingly, but sadness was written all over his face.

"I'll be okay. You need to go," I said, trying to be strong. "I…" Before I had a chance to say anything more, Davin grabbed me, and we were headed for home.

We arrived safely at my house, in my room, and all was quiet. "Here we are," I said sadly, knowing it may be the last time I saw them. I tried to blink the tears away, but one found its way down my cheek.

"See you soon," Vivian said, giving me a tight squeeze as her eyes swelled with tears.

As soon as Vivian released me, Caleb unexpectedly hugged me and gave me a kiss on the cheek. "I had a great time tonight…well…I meant the first half of the night. I almost felt like a human. I won't ever forget you." He smiled and backed away.

Caleb's affection touched me deeply. It was the first time he ever gave me a hug or a friendly kiss. Then Davin turned to me.

"Don't get into trouble, or we'll have to come down again. You know how much I dislike being here," Davin teased, nudging me on my shoulder as he took a few steps back. "See you when I see you." He winked and gave me a warm smile.

At that moment, I realized how much they cared for me. Maybe it was knowing that we might never see each other again. Whatever the reason, I knew they would miss me too, although maybe not as much as I would miss them.

They turned their backs to Michael and me to give us some privacy. As Michael came toward me, Alexa Rose unexpectedly rushed past him to give me a most heartfelt hug. She smiled warmly with her beautiful blue eyes, then ran toward Vivian. It was the first time she displayed any affection toward me. Surprised by Alexa Rose's action, Michael let out a huge grin. We locked eyes as he approached me. Then he gently guided both of my hands to his chest. I imagined putting my handprint on his heart and thinking, mine, forever. His look was worth a thousand words, and I knew exactly how he felt. I was afraid to let go for fear that I may never see him again.

"I'll be back. This isn't good-bye," Michael said, trying to sound cheerful.

Desperately holding back the tears, I nodded. I believed him. He then cupped my face and gave me a sweet tender kiss on my forehead. "My heart and soul are where you are. I am here," he spoke again, gently touching the crystal necklace.

All choked up and unable to say a word; I took a deep breath and nodded. I watched them disappear into the moonlight as I heard, from a distance, Caleb and Davin arguing over who was going to drive the Ferrari back to the dealer.

All the lights were off, and Mom was still at work. It was peaceful and late into the night. As I lay in bed, I tried not to think about the "what ifs" that could have happened at the Grand View Hotel. It was still hard to grasp the fact that Aden was really dead, but knowing that he was, I felt relief beyond words. At the same time, I worried that since I was out of danger, Michael and the alkins would not be coming to see me anymore. I was also worried about Michael. I knew he would be fine, but until I saw him whole again, I would worry. My eyes were getting heavier, and I couldn't control it any longer. "Good night, my guardian angel," I whispered as I dozed off to sleep.

Chapter 23

I was glad it was Veterans' weekend. Not only did we have a day off from school, but we had also prearranged a day off at Fashion Wear. Patty planned a hiking trip with some of our friends. As much as I disliked hiking, I had to make it up to her. Going hiking again was the only way to do that. She used my guilt as an opportunity to get me to do anything she wanted. I was pleased to do it.

I also promised Mom that I would help her pack Gamma's belongings this morning. I wasn't looking forward to it, knowing that it would make me emotional, but I needed to be there for her.

"Are you ready, honey?"

"I'll be right out, Mom," I said, mentally preparing myself, knowing how I would react at Gamma's house. I knew one thing for sure; I had to be strong for Mom.

"My car or yours?" I asked cheerfully, stepping out of my room.

"Why don't we both take our cars so you can just leave from Gamma's to meet up with Patty?"

"Okay, that sounds fine. I'll see you there."

After starting the engine, I noticed the bracelet Gamma had given me for my birthday. I smiled, recalling that day when she slipped one on my wrist and told me to put the other in the car. The smile quickly disappeared, and was replaced by grief at the thought of never being able to see her again. My body cringed from the heartache, and I forced myself to try to feel nothing. Since it would be my first time at her house since her passing, feeling numbness would be the only way I would make it through packing without falling apart.

It was a short ride, so I just waited in the car for my mom. I must have sped. I thought Mom would give me few words for speeding, but instead, she put her arm around my shoulders and we walked inside Gamma's house together. All was still. It felt strange to be inside the house without her. We both looked around the living room with aches in our hearts. Nothing was out of place. It was as if she was stilling living here, but the silence was a sure sign of her absence.

"I just need your help packing a few boxes, honey. I don't intend to pack everything in one day," she said, with tears in her eyes.

Seeing her eyes water up like that was just enough to make me almost lose it. I turned my head, trying to avoid eye contact. Don't look at her, and keep your thoughts on happy thoughts, I said to myself. My fist curled into a tight ball as I held my breath, desperately trying to control my emotions, trying to feel as little as possible.

As we both walked into her bedroom, the first thing I noticed was her bed, untouched. Besides the bed, her room was furnished with a mahogany dresser and a nightstand. It wasn't like I had never seen her bedroom before, but today I noted every little detail of her room. The room that used to make me feel warm and inviting now felt empty and cold.

"Honey, could you pack her stuff from the closet?" Mom asked finally.

"Sure, Mom," I said and took the box from her hand.

"I'm going to pack up in the other room," she said quietly, as one teardrop fell.

Hesitantly, I opened the closet door. Her clothes were hung neatly, organized by color. As I scanned through her clothes, a white cashmere sweater caught my eyes. I gently loosened the sweater off the hanger and held it close to my face. I could smell the sweetness of her favorite perfume. I imagined hugging her as if she was right here. Standing here, thoughts of Gamma and the happy times we'd had together danced in my head. She had made me feel like I was the most special person in the world. I could do no wrong in her eyes.

Guilt started to race through my mind as I was thinking that I should have visited her more often. Tears fell to the floor and I reached down to wipe them up as more found their way down my cheek. As I started to stand up, I noticed something behind the jackets. Sliding the hangers slightly to the left, I saw a small shelf. Curious, I picked up a small, wooden treasure box that was on top. A part of me thought I shouldn't open it because it was her private possession, but curiosity got the best of me. First, I looked behind me to see if Mom was in the room. Then I slowly opened the treasure box, like a little girl sneaking a peek at her hidden Christmas present.

Inside were a few letters, pictures, and a journal. I thumbed through the pictures of Gamma and me, and Gamma with Mom. I gently tucked the pictures back to pick up what looked like a journal, hoping to find some answers to my questions. I glimpsed through the journal and read a few pages about me. I knew that she cared about me and loved me like her own, but reading it was harder to take, and my eyes filled with tears again.

Focusing on why I was here in the first place, I pulled her clothes off the hangers, folded them, and neatly stacked them inside a box. After I finished my task, I sat down and placed my head between my knees trying to get a grip on all this. When I looked up, I noticed an envelope tucked inside her favorite blue jacket. It was addressed to me. Find my letter; Gamma's words suddenly came back to me. I was so furious at myself. How could I have forgotten? I knew it was from Gamma, so I tore it open, feeling excited and anxious.

Dearest Claudia,

If you are reading this letter, it means that I am too weak to speak or I have already passed on. I'm so sorry that I couldn't tell you sooner, but it was for your own protection. I wrote this letter just in case I didn't get a chance to tell you everything that you should know. Many things I'm about to tell you will be very difficult to believe, but I'm telling you the truth, and you must believe me.

God's first angels make up the Royal Council. They are the ones who make the decisions for humanity. The Royal Council is special because, not only are they powerful, they have the souls of the Holy Spirit. Your father was one of the Royal Council. I know this because your mother told me that she fell in love with an angel, one of God's first angels. She also told me that she had a visit from another angel. He told her that when the time was right, he would come for you, the child with the soul of the Holy Spirit. And because of this, I told her about me. I knew both of you were in danger because the angel that visited your mother was a fallen angel named Aden.

I had to make a decision; either to report you to the Royal Council or to protect you. Your mother begged me not to tell the Royal Council because you would be taken from her, so I couldn't refuse. I loved her as if she was my daughter, and I let my human emotions take me over.

Aden was one of the Twelve Angels. These Twelve Angels helped the Earth angels to guide the humans. But he rebelled. He wanted to create an army to fight the Royal Council. His soul was taken away, and his powers were weakened. He knew that the only possible way for him to enter the holy realms was by taking the Holy Spirit's soul. This would allow him to enter Halo City and regain his powers back to full strength. And because of this, he was after your soul.

Your mom and I hid from Aden as long as we could, but somehow he found us again right before you turned one. I would have been able to save both of you, but he had someone helping him; her name was Julia. Your mother tricked Aden and Julia. She led them to follow her while I ran away with you. I'm so sorry that I couldn't save your mother.

Later, Ava Emerson adopted you, and it wasn't by chance. I purposely made that happen because I knew in my heart that she would make a great mother for you. Unfortunately I had to instill in her mind that her husband had died in a freak car accident. I wanted to make sure that she wouldn't remarry so that all her energy would be on you. I know it sounds horrible for me to have done this to her, but you have to understand that everything I did was for your protection.

You see, honey, the only way for Aden to get the Holy Spirit's soul is if one who carries it gives it willingly. You will never be fully in danger from Aden because he can't kill you to get what he wants, but he can hurt the ones you love.

My powers were strong once; but now that I'm old, they have weakened, and I won't be able to fight him. Since I wouldn't help him by convincing you to give up your soul willingly, he has taken my life. Don't worry. I knew this time would come sooner or later, but it was my honor to watch over you. Because I knew I couldn't be with you forever, I've asked someone else to watch over you. You must be strong. Don't ever let him have your soul, even it means he will hurt the ones you love. You must not, or humanity will be lost forever.

I know this is a lot to take in, but I believe in you. You are strong, just like your mother. I know you are sad that I have passed on. I know you will miss me, but not as much as I will miss you. Some humans believe a myth that when they pass away, their souls become a star. Though I am not human, look for me up in the sky and know that you are not alone.

As I have mentioned before, you cannot fight destiny; humans search for the meaning of life when it's right in front of them. Everybody has a purpose, even Earth angels. We all need to live as we do, and our purpose will unfold naturally. Then it will be our time to pass on when it has been fulfilled. Be strong. Move forward and live your human life to the fullest, responsibly. I will miss you. I loved you as my own.

Exhaling and sitting there motionless, I took in Gamma's words. I was practically holding my breath the whole time. I couldn't believe what I was reading; had it been the first time learning about the existence of Earth angels, the Twelve, the Royal Council, and the soul of the Holy Spirit, I would have flipped. But the news didn't strike me hard because Phillip had already explained it all to me.

Regardless, she had just revealed everything I needed to know about my life. Tears rolled down my face. They were tears of frustration, tears of sadness, tears of anger, and tears of hope. I felt completely worn out. I didn't want to believe it, but the truth was written in her letter. Michael was right. Aden knew about me before I was born. He was waiting for this opportunity for 18 years. He was waiting for a member of the Royal Council to make a mistake. And who did Gamma ask to watch over me? It didn't matter. Aden was dead. I had my guardian angel, and he was all that mattered to me.

Startled by Mom's voice, I broke out of my thoughts. "Claudia, are you ready?"

"I'll be right out, Mom," I replied.

"Claudia," she called again.

I quickly placed the rest of Gamma's belongings in the box and placed the letter in my pocket. "Almost done, Mom." I was so distracted that I hadn't noticed leaving some things out. Just in the nick of time, I was done. Mom came through the door. I could tell she had been crying. Avoiding eye contact, she took the box from me. "Thanks, honey. I know this was hard for you too."

I placed my arms around her, and suddenly she lost control. Although my eyes were glossy, I had no tears to shed. My heart was aching not for Gamma this time, but for my mom. Knowing the life she could have had was taken from her made me feel extremely guilty. The husband and the children she could have had were gone, all because of me. When she finally got control of herself and her tears subsided, she slowly let go. We were interrupted by a soft knock at the door.

I quickly wiped away the evidence that my eyes were watery. When I opened the door, I was surprised to see Patty. I was sure I had asked her to meet me at church, but maybe I read the text wrong. Nevertheless, I was overjoyed to see her.

"Hello, Mrs. Emerson," Patty said politely.

Before Mom could say anything, I grabbed Patty and squeezed her so tightly that she lost her breath. It had been a while since I last saw her, and even though we texted every day, it wasn't the same. I was so happy to see her.

"Hello, Patty. It's good to see you again," Mom said, giving her a hug after I let go. "Someone missed you tremendously."

"Yeah, I have that kind of effect on her. Too bad I don't have the same effect on the guys," she said, laughing.

"Well, I'm just glad she has someone else to comfort her, besides me," Mom said to Patty.

"I'm so sorry for your loss," Patty said to Mom. Her tone changed from playful to serious.

"Thank you," she said.

As Patty and Mom were talking, I quickly walked out the door so Mom would get the hint that I wanted to leave.

"You girls be safe now. Don't come home too late," she said, smiling. "Is Davin going?"

"Who?" I asked. I practically choked. She had met Davin on the night of Ryan's birthday party. I didn't tell Patty any details about the party, only that I was going with Kristina and Maggie.

"How many Davin do you know?" Mom asked jokingly. "The friend who picked you up for Ryan's birthday party," she reminded me.

"Mom, no, no." I shook my head. "He's just a friend. He's not coming."

"Oh," she said, looking disappointed. "Too bad. He's pretty cute."

"Who's Davin?" Patty asked, unlocking the door to her car. Patty had gotten a used car like mine, only hers was silver.

"Just a friend," I said quickly, like it was no big deal. I opened the door and sat inside.

"Another guy? Who else is there?" she asked, raising a brow.

I could tell she was disappointed that I didn't tell her all about him. Since I didn't respond to her question, she didn't pursue the topic any further. Not drilling me with a whole bunch of questions was odd, and I wondered what she was up to.

"You okay?" Patty asked, gluing her eyes to the road.

"Yeah, I had to pack some of Gamma's things, and it was pretty hard on both of us. And, I...umm..." How could I ever explain to her that Gamma was an Earth angel?

Patty interrupted me as I continued to search for the right words. "I understand. You've been through a lot. But I just want you to know that you can tell me anything. I'm here for you." She placed her hand over mine.

"I know. You're my best friend," I said sincerely.

"Good, because, don't get mad," Patty said.

"What did you do now?" I asked softly with a frown. Knowing Patty, she had something up her sleeve, which was usually meant to do something nice for me.

"Well, I told you that there was a bunch of us going hiking..." She hesitated to say anything else and started twisting a strand of her hair with her left hand. She looked nervous.

"And?" I asked, wanting more explanations.

"Well, there's only going to be the four of us."

"Oh, that's fine," I said. "Who's going?" I was thinking that she was going to name some girls, but then I got a feeling that wasn't it, since she was acting weird again.

"You, me, Andrew and his friend," she spoke quickly.

"Who is his friend?" I asked, knowing she knew that I knew only one of Andrew's friends.

"Austin," she said quickly with a worried look. "I didn't think you would mind...you see...other people backed out. I swear, Claudia. There were supposed to be more people."

"Since you didn't do it on purpose, that's fine. I'll be fine with it. He's a little annoying, but I have no choice. It's too late to make you take me back home."

"What do you mean annoying?" she asked, looking offended. "He's not annoying. He's cute, and I think he's interested in you," Patty said enthusiastically.

"I didn't mean annoying," I said in a casual tone of voice, thinking I should pick my words carefully. "I don't want him to be interested in me."

"He's been asking about you." She smiled, ignoring what I had just said.

"Oh," I said. Great! Now it was going to feel like a double date. I would just have to be polite and endure today. "Does he know that there will be only four of us hiking?"

"I'm sure Andrew told him."

"I just don't want to give him the wrong idea," I said firmly so she would understand my point.

"Sure, don't worry. I'll make sure of it, but you two would make the perfect…"

I motioned my hand up. I knew what she was about to say, so I stopped her and quickly changed the subject. "So, what's going on between you and Andrew?"

Grinning from ear to ear, she said excitedly, "We're dating."

I'd never seen her so happy. I hoped things would work out for both of them, because finding your true love happened once in a lifetime if you were lucky. Two hours passed by quickly. We spent so much time catching up that, before I knew it, we were already at our destination.

Chapter 24

Austin and Andrew both opened the car doors for us, greeting us like gentlemen. We exchanged hugs, and they led us back into the same campground.

"I told you we would hike together someday," Austin said in a friendly tone.

"Yeah, I guess," I said with a smile. Deep down inside, I wanted to go home. I noticed his oversized bulky backpack, and I wondered what on Earth he had inside. He caught me staring at his backpack, and I quickly looked down.

"Here," he said, placing a backpack on my shoulders. "You have a flashlight, emergency kit, snacks, solar blanket, and a bottle of water."

"All this for one day?" I asked.

"Yep!"

"Thanks," I said, wondering if I should be thankful or upset.

"Not a problem. Need to be prepared, just in case."

"For?"

"Just in case I decide to keep you up here for a week."

"What!" I said, surprised.

"Just joking, Claudia. I don't think you would even survive past two days," he said with a smirk.

Feeling slightly offended, I was just about to retaliate with a good comeback when Andrew interrupted our conversation. "Ready to go?"

"You lead," Austin insisted.

Andrew led the way and Patty walked beside him. I started walking ahead of Austin, but he paced himself quickly and walked alongside me. I knew this would happen; it felt like a double date. I was just hoping that he didn't think it was.

He broke the silence. "Claudia, sorry about Gamma." He sounded sincere.

All of a sudden, I felt bad for not calling, but he did say to call if I needed to talk. Since I didn't, my guilt disappeared as quickly as it came. "I didn't call because I was just—"

He interrupted and didn't let me continue. "It's okay. I understand. Like I said before, I know what it is like to lose someone. Don't be sorry, it is me who is sorry."

I couldn't believe how sweet he was. He knew the right words to say, and I believed he was genuine. Now I felt bad for being rude. Little by little, I opened up to him. We started talking about school, and life in general. We were talking and laughing when we finally reached our destination.

It was just as breathtaking as I had seen it before. This was the same view I had seen with Michael, but we were on the opposite side. Thoughts of Michael and the alkins ran through my mind. I was missing Michael like crazy, but I didn't realize how much I missed Davin, Caleb, and Vivian too. I wondered what they were doing. Even in the company of my best friend, I wished to be with Michael and the alkins. I shook the thought out of my head and told myself to enjoy hiking with my friends.

"So what do you think?" Patty interrupted my thoughts.

"It's amazing," I said. How could I explain that I had seen this view before? I had to pretend that it was my first time. The view was so magnificent that I didn't even have to fake my reaction.

"I love hiking up here. This view helps me think and takes my troubles away," Andrew said, looking straight ahead.

"I agree," Austin said, patting his buddy on the back. He seemed mesmerized by the view.

"Is anyone hungry?" Patty asked.

"I don't know about anyone else, but I'm starving," I answered.

Before anyone else could respond, Austin laid a picnic blanket right in front of us.

I had a quick flashback of the day Michael and I had our first picnic together.

"Hungry, anyone?" Austin asked, invading my thoughts. "From my part-time job," he said, smiling.

He pulled turkey avocado sandwiches and several bags of chips out of his backpack. No wonder it looked so bulky. He had stuffed the picnic items in it.

"Thanks, Austin," Patty said as her eyes widened with delight. She sat down right beside Andrew.

Austin motioned me to sit down first, before he sat. When I sat down to pick up one of the sandwiches, Austin sat next to me. It was silent for a while as we devoured our lunches, admiring the view.

"What are you thinking about?" Austin asked.

If I told him, he would think I was crazy. "Just the clouds. What kind of shapes do you see in the clouds?" I asked.

"I see a happy face and over there...a bunny," Patty shouted with excitement.

"Let's see. I see a shape of a lion's head," Andrew said.

"How about you, Austin?" I asked.

"This one is hard to see, but I see Orion," he said, looking serious.

"How? Impossible," I said with a frown, knowing he was making it up.

"Okay, I can see a star," he said, pointing to five small clouds. "But it doesn't twinkle like your eyes," he said, his eyes looking into mine so intensely that I could feel the depth of his words.

I blushed and turned away, more from the embarrassment of Andrew and Patty listening. They turned their heads, trying to hide their huge grins, but it didn't work. While we were still munching on our chips, the white fluffy clouds disappeared and were replaced by dark gray clouds.

"What do you see?" Austin asked me, after silence had taken over our conversation.

I placed my hand out and felt a drop of rain fall on my palm. "I felt a raindrop," I said. Last time I was up here, it was hot, unlike the chilly weather today. I zipped up my light jacket and put the hood over my head as the cool breeze brushed against me. "Ummm...," I said as we all looked at each other, wondering if it would rain. Without hesitation, we got up quickly and cleared the picnic blanket.

The dark gray clouds were traveling faster, darkening the sky. Ominous clouds gathered in bunches, looking thick and fluffy. It was beautiful, but terrifying, as the cracking of thunder echoed around us.

"We better get going. Andrew and I have umbrellas with us, so don't worry," Austin said to Patty and me. I'm sure our faces looked concerned about getting drenched.

Andrew and Austin quickly pulled out umbrellas from their backpacks, and with a click of the buttons, they opened up. Andrew placed his arms around Patty, and they headed down the hiking trail. Although I felt uncomfortable sharing the same umbrella with Austin, I really didn't have a choice, since it started raining harder.

"You're very lucky today," Austin said. His voice was lost to the thunder and rain.

"What do you mean?" I asked, practically yelling, gluing my eyes on the trail. The path had become muddied and slippery from the rain, and I nearly fell a couple of times.

"No ugly bugs came out to scare you."

"It's a good thing because I would be the first one down, all drenched," I answered, watching in revulsion as my black-and-white tennis shoes were being splattered by Austin's steps.

"What are you doing tomorrow?" he asked.

"What? I can't hear you," I lied. The thunder cracked just as he had asked his question, and it was a good excuse to pretend that I didn't hear. I didn't know how to turn him down without hurting his feelings.

We were at the end of the trail when he stopped and spoke again, "It looks like someone is on your mind."

Still standing underneath the umbrella, my face flushed from walking, I felt hot all over from embarrassment. Was it that obvious? "What do you mean?" I tried to sound casual.

"You know what I mean. Anyway, don't say anything. Just listen." He lifted my chin up so I was forced to look him in the eyes. "What I want to say is that he is extremely lucky to even be in the same room with you. I'm the unlucky one who found you a little too late."

I didn't know what to say. I was stunned that he had such strong feelings for me.

"So if you need a friend to talk to, just call. I'd rather have you as a friend than not have you in my life at all." He chuckled. "I guess I'm Orion and you are Merope, the one who wouldn't love him back."

I didn't know what to say. I didn't even know if he wanted me to respond. As I was trying to think of something to say, he gave me a peck on the cheek and guided me quickly inside Patty's car.

"Follow behind us!" Andrew shouted through the open window from his car, as the rain showered his face.

As we headed slowly down the curvy road, I noticed Patty glancing my way several times before she spoke. "What was that all about?" she asked cautiously.

"Nothing," I said carefully. She understood that I didn't want to talk about it.

"Are you all right, Claudia?" she asked.

"I'm just tired, that's all."

Patty and I hardly exchanged any words as I continued to stare out the window. The thunder continued to roar with anger while the drops of rain pounded the ground. I smiled secretly, thinking of what Davin had said to me when we first met. When I had shed my tears in front of him, he wiped them and said he didn't want anyone down here to think it was sprinkling. As we continued to follow behind Andrew's car, we parted ways when we took a different highway.

"Did you have fun?" Patty broke the silence.

"I had a wonderful time. Thanks for bringing me up there."

"Wasn't the view magnificent?" Patty asked with excitement.

"Yes, it was," I said matter-of-factly.

"Wasn't it nice of Austin to pack us our lunch?" Patty continued with her questions.

"Yes, it was," I said.

"Wasn't it nice that you enjoyed Austin's company?" Patty asked quickly.

"Yes, it..." I stopped and rethought what Patty had just said. "You tricked me," I said and raised a brow.

She laughed. "Just checking to see if you're really listening," she said. "I know you want to deny it, but subconsciously you like his attention."

"What?" I said.

"I just don't get you. You have this well-educated, well-mannered hunk who practically throws rose petals for you to walk on, and you're not even remotely interested."

"He's not my type," I said softly, shrugging my shoulders. It was all I could say. "I'm just waiting for…"

She didn't let me finish. "Mr. Right, Mr. Perfect, Mr. Prince. There is no such thing, honey. There is no Mr. Angel out there, but if you want my opinion…" she paused and looked at me to see if I would stop her from speaking her peace. "I know you don't want to hear it, but I think Austin is good for you. And I'm only saying this because I love you like a sister, and I don't want to see you go out with another guy like Ryan."

I knew she was right. I just didn't realize it until recently. With Ryan, everything revolved around him; but with Austin, everything seemed to revolve around me. Perhaps if I wasn't in love with Michael, there could be something there for Austin. But it didn't matter because my heart belonged to someone else, and he was Mr. Perfect in every way. And he was an angel, all right. I just couldn't tell her.

After our conversation, all was quiet in the car except for the soft music. It was a difficult drive in the heavy rain, so Patty hardly spoke a word. Even the windshield wipers swishing back and forth on high couldn't give us a clear view of the road. Instead, it produced a hypnotic effect on me, and I didn't even notice that we had arrived at Gamma's house. We sat in the car, watching the rain drench everything around us. Then Patty finally spoke.

"I would go inside with you and hang out, but I'm exhausted." She looked at me worriedly. "I'm so sorry. You're mad at me, aren't you?"

"For what?" I asked, surprised by her words.

"Because it seemed like a double date. I honestly didn't plan it that way. I promise," she said, desperately wanting me to believe her.

"Patty, don't be silly. It's fine. I already told you. I believe you."

"Okay," she said, placing her hand on my shoulder. "Get some sleep then. I'll text you later." She gave me a long hug, and spoke solemnly, "I'll see you in a couple of days at Gamma's funeral. I'll be right there beside you." Then she squeezed my hand and looked at me with teary eyes. "You've been through a lot. I wish I could make the pain disappear. I know you miss her."

She was right. I had been through a lot; she had no idea to what extreme. I tried so hard to hold back the tears, but one found its way down my cheek after Patty's thoughtful words. "Thanks for everything. I'll text you later. Drive carefully," I said. I had to get out of the car. I knew if Patty or I said anything else, I would completely fall apart. After I got out of the car, she drove out of sight, and I got in my car and headed home.

Chapter 25

I was at the waterfall where Michael and I had been. Michael was standing at a distance, smiling. My heart raced excitedly. He came closer, and held me in his arms. He whispered my name, "Claudia." He kissed me tenderly, wrapping his wings around me. My dream couldn't have been any better.

Suddenly, the waterfall was pouring, making sounds like thunder. The peaceful water that surrounded us, falling gently, was now increasingly forming big waves. The boulders we were standing on started shaking and shifting, leaving gaps between them. It felt like an earthquake. Next thing I knew, I was pulled in by a rush of water. Michael and I had separated, and I couldn't see him anymore. I was shivering from the icy cold water that pierced through my body. It was difficult to swim. Trying to find a way out, I managed to grab onto what looked like roots protruding from a tree. As I struggled to hold on, I heard a voice.

"Claudia!"

I looked up to see Austin standing above me, reaching out for me. "Grab my hand. I'll help you."

He leaned in further. I was just about to give him my hand when he spoke again, "You don't belong with him."

I flashed my eyes at him angrily. Why did he say that? What did he mean by that? And why was he in my dream? "No!" I said, full of rage. I pushed the water with my hand to move away from him, accidently splashing water on his face.

"Kinda late for a water fight, don't you think?" he asked, wiping the water off his face with his sleeves.

"What are you doing here?" I yelled, as I was beyond irritated.

"That's a nice way to say hello to a friend who wants to help," Austin said calmly. "Let me help you. You're just barely hanging on."

He was right. I felt the roots start to detach from the strain of my weight and the powerful water pushing me forward. I changed my tone. "How did you find me?"

He didn't have a chance to reply. Our conversation was interrupted by Michael calling my name. "Claudia!"

"Where are you?" I yelled. I turned my back to Austin and looked for Michael in every direction. "Michael," I called, panicking. But all I heard were the echoes of my own voice.

"He can't find you," Austin said. "I can't help you if you don't want it."

I felt relieved when I saw a reflection on the water of what appeared to be wings expanding; Michael must be standing behind Austin.

"What do you mean he can't find me?" I turned to face Austin. But Austin was gone and Michael was nowhere to be seen. There was no one here but me. I was lost, alone.

I woke up with an uneasy feeling. Was Michael in danger? Why was Austin in my dream saying Michael couldn't find me? As I lay on my bed trying to analyze my dream, I was startled by my alarm clock going off. After I turned it off, I lay back down, and cuddled with Michael's shirt.

I didn't want to get up and face reality. It had been twice in just over a month that I had lost loved ones; first my friend, Claudia, and now Gamma. Remembering how difficult it was to say good-bye to Claudia, I didn't want to do it again. After I tucked Michael's shirt underneath the blanket, I slowly dragged myself out of bed. I started to reluctantly head toward the closet, but instead, I found myself walking in the direction of the window.

As I opened the blinds, I quickly looked away. Squinting and blinking from the brightness, my eyes finally adjusted to the light. The luminous rays from the sun spread warmth all over my body. I just stood there and closed my eyes, as if to melt the pain away; if only it were that simple. It had rained the past two days, and I was relieved to see the sun. I was glad that we didn't have to bury Gamma in the rain. It was a beautiful day, despite today's event. The funeral was already depressing enough, but I could imagine it being a hundred times worse in the rain.

After I changed my clothes and got ready, I sat on the edge of my bed, staring out the window. It felt good to just sit there and feel nothing. I didn't want to think about "what ifs" because there was nothing I could do to change anything that had happened. Gamma said everything had a purpose and a reason, and everything fell in its place at the right time. I only wished that some things that fell in place were different.

It had been days since I last saw Michael. I was beginning to wonder if I had dreamt him up, but the necklace I wore every day, his T-shirt, and the scar on my chest from Julia were sure signs that he was real.

Mom interrupted my thoughts when she spoke. "Claudia, you ready, honey?"

"I'm almost ready," I said, opening the door to look at her. We both looked dreadful dressed all in black, with pale skin, puffy eyes, and no makeup. We looked like we were burying ourselves. The truth was, I wasn't ready. I was dreading today, though there was no way out of this. Who said funerals were necessary? Why would you want to witness your loved one being buried underneath the ground? It was like shutting the door permanently, knowing they will never come back. At the same time, I understood why there was a need for a funeral; it was closure for the ones left behind. But at this point; a funeral wasn't going to ease the pain of losing Gamma.

I heard my mom's voice again. "Coming," I said, as I stepped outside into the bright sun.

After the funeral mass, we headed to the burial. We were waiting for Father Roy to get situated. As I looked around, I saw many of Gamma's friends, as well as many unfamiliar faces. I wondered if any of them could be Earth angels. Strangely, I thought I saw Austin by a tree, but when I looked again, he was nowhere to be seen. My mom stood in front of me, while my friends surrounded me. Kristina and Maggie stood to my left; Patty, Andrew, and John were on my right.

I was so preoccupied with my thoughts of Gamma and our happy times together that I didn't realize Father Roy was speaking. "There is an appointed time for everything, and a time for every affair under the heavens. A time to be born and a time to die."

My thoughts wandered again. It was hard to listen to the words when all I could think of was that Gamma was gone. Her existence had already become nothing but a memory. Father Roy continued. "We go to the same place. We were made from the dust, and to the dust we shall return."

My attention turned to Mom when I heard her weeping. Mom and I had shed so many tears that I was sure we had none left, but I was wrong. When I heard her soft sobs, it filled my eyes with tears yet again. Then, Kristina, Maggie, and Patty started sobbing too. Patty rummaged through her purse, took out a pack of Kleenex, and passed it along. She also gave me a quick squeeze to comfort me.

Watching Gamma's casket being lowered into the perfectly rectangular empty space that had been dug for her made me lose it. I felt like my heart was being ripped into pieces. My lungs forgot how to take in air. When my body became weak, too weak to stand, I knew I was falling apart. As my heart sunk to the ground, I wanted to collapse.

"Please...nooo," I cried softly, as my hand reached out for Gamma. "She won't be able to see. It'll be too dark down there. It will be too cold. I won't ever see her again. I'm sorry, Gamma. I'm sorry I didn't call enough. I'm sorry I didn't visit you enough. I'm sorry I went camping, and I wasn't there for you. I'm sorry that you gave up your life for me." My whole body was trembling. I was certain my knees would give out, but Kristina and Patty were holding me up, trying to comfort me, ready to catch me if I fell.

I didn't realize others heard my words until I saw them crying harder than before. Even Andrew and John were sobbing. They felt the depth of my pain, the pain that was hidden deep inside. The pain that I desperately tried to suppress was now pouring out uncontrollably. Tears streamed faster, and there weren't enough tissues to wipe them. Eventually I managed to somewhat compose myself, but short gasping sounds still lingered.

Feeling embarrassed by my emotional display, I gazed at the casket, knowing there was nothing I could do. As I tried to reorganize the wet tissues, I was startled by a voice. "Claudia," he called to me.

It was Michael, but I continued to stare at the casket. Was I being delusional? I missed him so much that I heard his voice. I looked up and blinked several times. Michael, Davin, Vivian, and Caleb were standing at a distance, dressed in black. Were they a figment of my imagination? A clear vision of them was just enough for me to smile on this dreadful day.

"Claudia." I heard his voice in my head again as I gazed back at the casket. "We're here." He felt so close. I could almost feel the warmth of his whisper in my ear. Then I repeated his words in my mind, *We're here.*

Suddenly it hit me that what I saw was real. I was ecstatic, and tears rolled down my face. But this time, they were tears of joy. My heart was lifted and happy again. They had come back. They came back to comfort me and pay their last respects to Gamma. When I looked up again to see them, I was disappointed. They were no longer there. Where did they go? I looked to the left, right, and behind me, but nothing. Patty nudged me and asked, "What's wrong?"

"Don't worry, I'm fine," I replied softly and didn't bother to look again. I wanted to see them so desperately that my mind was definitely playing tricks on me.

After Father Roy said his last words, one by one everyone gently tossed a red rose onto her casket. Then they headed to their cars.

"You go first," I told my friends. "I'll catch up with you in a second."

Mom and I stayed behind to say our final goodbyes to Gamma. We were standing there quietly, when I felt a soft, warm breeze. It felt as though a hand had brushed against my cheek, but there was no one around.

Something inside my pants pocket was crinkling. I pulled it out. It was a note from Michael. It read,

We're here. See you at home.
In my heart, in my soul – M

I read it again. My mind was not playing tricks on me. They were really here. I was overwhelmed with happiness, but at the same time, felt slightly guilty for feeling happy at Gamma's burial.

"Everything all right, honey?" Mom asked, glancing over my shoulder to see what I was looking at.

"It's nothing," I said, smiling and placing the note back in my pocket.

"Ready to go, honey?"

I let out a heavy sigh. "I'm ready," I said. I was ready to close this chapter. I know that time heals all wounds, but it was easier said than done. It had been an honor to have Gamma in my life. Happy memories of her were what I would always cherish and remember. Memories were what would keep her alive, Michael had told me once, and that was exactly what I planned to cherish. No more tears and no more sulking, just happy thoughts.

"I love you, Gamma," I said. "See you in my dreams, or when I look up at the stars."

Chapter 26

After the funeral, Mom took our grieving guests out to a late lunch. When we got home, I told Mom that I was tired, and that I desperately needed a nap. As I headed to my bedroom, the anticipation of finding them there was beating out of my chest. When I opened the door, my heart sunk deeply when I didn't see them. Maybe they had to do something first, I thought and decided to wait for them. After all, Michael did say, 'We're here. See you at home.'

After I changed into my comfortable clothing, I decided to take a nap. When I woke up, I didn't realize how long I had slept, until I opened the blinds. The sun was setting, with hues of violet that spread across the horizon. While I was marveling at its beauty, I took a deep breath, disappointed that they weren't here yet. Had I misread the letter? When I went to my desk to reread the letter, I saw a new letter.

I miss you more. See you at The Cliff.
In my heart, in my soul – M

My spirits lifted, and my frown turned into a smile. I placed the letter back on the desk. I nearly flew across the room, startled by Davin's appearance.

"Hello, there," he said, cheerful as always.

"Davin!" I shouted and hugged him tightly. I was so happy to see him.

"Claudia, I'm not Michael," he teased and returned the hug.

"I'm sorry. I'm just so happy to see you. Is everybody all right? I haven't seen you or heard from any of you in a while. I just can't believe you're here." I couldn't stop talking. He just stood there and let me say my peace.

"We're fine, and Michael is better. I told you the next time I saw you would be when you were in danger, but..."

"I'm in danger?" I asked frantically.

"Calm down, Claudia. Everything is fine. I guess I should have picked my words better. Sorry, I didn't mean to scare you like that," Davin said, as he placed one hand behind my back. "What I meant to say was...the next time I saw you would be when you were in danger, but you're not, and here I am."

"Oh," I said, relieved. "I guess I overreact sometimes. I should have known better and let you finish. Where are Vivian and Caleb?"

"They were sent back before the funeral ended. Phillip found out about Gamma and gave us permission to pay our last respects to her. Vivian and Caleb wanted to stay, but Michael thought it was best for them to leave."

"Oh." I felt disappointed that I didn't get to hug and thank them for going to the funeral.

Davin sensed my sadness. "Don't worry, they'll come back. I'm actually here to take you to Michael."

My face lit up. "You are?" Then I wondered why he asked Davin to take me to him. Why wasn't he here himself? Maybe he was still weak from the injury? After all, Davin said he was better, but didn't say he was completely better. "Where is Michael? Is he all right?"

"Don't worry. He's fine," he said quickly, and changed the subject.

"If he is better, why isn't he here?" I asked again, wondering what he was up to.

"You'll see. I'm not supposed to say. You'll just have to see. Do you want to go or stay here all night?"

Just as Davin asked the last question, I jumped up and stood right in front of him.

"Not fashionably late this time?" he teased.

"You didn't steal a car, did you?" I asked, teasing him back. He gave me a sly look.

"Borrowed," he said and gave me the biggest grin I had ever seen on his face.

"No, you didn't," I was trying not to laugh.

"Same car, 540 horsepower," he exclaimed.

Before I knew it, Davin grabbed me, and we were headed to the car.

He was driving slightly over the speed limit, but when we got on the freeway, he started driving faster – faster.

"Ahhh! Slow down!" I yelled. "You're giving me a heart attack!"

"Don't worry, I'm a really good driver," he said, driving over a hundred miles per hour, weaving in and out of lanes. "Isn't this great? It's like flying, but on the ground."

"No!" I yelled, covering my eyes as I continued to hang on to my seatbelt for my life.

"You've been flying with Michael too much," he teased.

"Not enough," I mumbled.

He was thoroughly enjoying himself, and I enjoyed watching him get so much pleasure out of something so simple. I knew that his vision and coordination were more than perfect, so I let him be. After all, when would he have this opportunity again? And if I could, I would do it too.

When we finally reached our destination, my body was plastered to the seat. We were at the same campground. With my knees still shaking, I managed to get out of the car. I was about to fall flat on my bottom when I felt a pair of strong arms around me.

"Michael," I turned and threw myself at him. His embrace felt so warm, and I felt complete.

"Davin," Michael said, in a scolding tone.

"I was trying to get here as fast as she wanted to get here," he said innocently.

"You know you can travel faster than a car," Michael reminded Davin.

"But it's not as much fun," Davin said lightly.

"Leave the fun part to yourself," Michael said seriously.

Davin shrugged his shoulder. "Sorry, Claudia, I thought it would be fun for you too. I forget that you don't feel the same rush as me."

I turned to Michael and shook my head, so he wouldn't be mad at Davin anymore.

"Next time I get to drive," I winked.

He smiled, pouted, and gave me a hug. "See you when I see you."

Unexpectedly he placed his fist out, and I looked at him with a questioning expression. He took my hand and banged it on top of his fist like a hammer. And then he took his fist and banged it on top of mine. "You know the handshake people do to say hi and bye?"

I got the idea, but I didn't know he knew it. "Oh, now I know what you were trying to do."

"Get a clue, Claudia, you're acting more like an alkin than a human," he teased.

Then he turned to Michael. "See you later, Mr. Ruin the Fun. Don't be too late." Then he flew straight up and disappeared.

Alone at last, and I was suddenly struck with shyness. "Fly with me, Claudia, I'll show you 540 wing power." Michael winked and we were already up in the air.

We didn't fly high like last time; instead, we flew up to The Cliff. As we drew closer, he told me to close my eyes. Closing my eyes meant he was up to something, and I did so without hesitation. I couldn't wait to see what he had planned. When I opened my eyes, my body stiffened, fixating on the same space where Aden had floated. I knew with every fiber of my being that Aden was dead and that he couldn't hurt me any longer, but just the thought of him brought back horrifying feelings that coursed through me.

Suddenly, Michael's wings enclosed me, and my fear subsided. My body was relaxed and at ease. I knew this warmth, this place I wanted to be for all eternity. Slowly I turned, and I was lost in his eyes. I glided my hands up to feel his soft wings. The wounds had healed completely; no evidence of his injury could be seen. No matter how many times I had witnessed the strength that it exerted, it still amazed me.

"Claudia, look." He lowered his wings. Then he turned me around.

My eyes opened wide in surprise to see many white lights strung above the trees, sparkling brilliantly. The lights intertwined from the tops of the branches and dangled as they reached the bottom. Hundreds of lit candles were placed throughout the surrounding woods. We walked further in, and the whole place was glowing. It was like we were in some enchanted forest, and he was my prince. It was the most romantic scene I could ever have imagined. I was deeply touched by all of his efforts that had gone into planning such a perfect reunion. This was the reason he had asked Davin to bring me to The Cliff. I continued to stare in awe, and my eyes glistened with tears of happiness.

"What do you think?" he asked, wiping my tears.

"I can't believe you did this for me."

"You're worth all this trouble and much more," he said, still wiping my tears.

"Sorry. I'm just way too emotional these days."

"I don't blame you. It's been overwhelming for you. I wish I could make it go away."

Wanting not to spoil this beautiful ambiance, I stopped the tears from falling, wiped the last tear myself, and lightened up. "A good-looking alkin told me things happen for a reason." I ran my fingers down his shoulders.

"Who's this good-looking alkin? Are you cheating on me?" he asked, nuzzling my neck, knowing I was referring to him.

"I didn't know we were dating. Would you feel jealous?" I asked, enjoying his nuzzling.

"Extremely."

"You're un…unbelievable," I said, barely making out the words, lost in his arms.

Suddenly he stopped, and I had to catch my breath.

"I know," he said, trying to hold back a laugh. "You told me that the first day we met. You remember? I wanted to prove it."

I giggled, recalling the first day we met when I was extremely mad at him. "Of course I remember. But this time, I mean it in a good way."

"I know you do." Then he changed the subject. "I'm sorry I was away, but I asked Davin to keep an eye on you."

"You did?" I asked in surprise and pulled away to look at him. "But I never saw him."

Since you were not in immediate danger, I asked him to keep an eye on you from a distance."

"Aden is dead. Why would I be in danger?"

"It's nothing. I'm only trying to be cautious." Then he brushed off my question.

"Michael, you didn't answer my question."

"It's really nothing. I shouldn't have said anything," he replied, not able to look at me.

"Please tell me," I begged. "You know I won't stop asking."

He gave a short laugh. "That's true. I don't want to worry you, but I'm just being cautious. There are many fallen who might have the same ideas as Aden. Not that I was suspicious of anyone. Please don't trouble yourself and put a lot of thought into what I just said. When it comes to your safety, I'm overly protective, that's all. Promise me you won't worry?"

"Okay," I said with hesitation. Although I just promised him that I wouldn't worry, I knew a part of me would. But I was more curious to know where he was and what he had been doing. "Where were you?" I asked, changing the subject.

"I needed to think about what we are going to do with you."

"I think you should just whisk me away to where no one can find us. Fly with me, Michael," I said, giving him my most puppy-eyed look, even though I knew it was impossible.

"If only it were that simple. I would take you anywhere you pleased."

I knew he meant it. "If only," I whispered. "What are you going to do with me?"

"Honestly, I don't know. I don't want to tell Phillip that you have the Holy Spirit's soul because he will take you to the Royal Council. It's possible they would make you stay with them. It may be a place without me. And I can't be without you." He then placed his head gently against mine. "They know Aden is dead, and I'm going to have to explain why he was after you. Unless I can come up with a good explanation, it will be out of my hands."

My heart sunk.

He lifted my chin, and my eyes met his. "If they do find out somehow, I will do everything I can to stop them from telling the Royal Council. I honestly don't know what the Royal Council will do, but I'm not willing to take any chances of them separating us."

"What do we do in the meantime?"

"The plan is that you go back to your normal life, whatever normal is for you now." He cocked his brow. "Since Davin, Caleb, Vivian, and I got permission from Phillip to see you more often, I'll get to visit you, even if you're not in danger."

"Did you ask or tell Phillip anything else?"

"I told him about us."

"You told him about us?" I repeated his answer, unsure of what he had just said.

"Yes, and he also knows I kissed you!"

I was in shock. "What! He knows?" Suddenly I flushed with embarrassment.

"And I told him that I am in love with you."

"What?"

"I also told him that you make me absolutely crazy."

I finally caught on to his playfulness. "Did you tell him that you're making things up?" Then I pushed him gently across his muscular arms, frowning. His fingers tickled the sides of my ribs and I arched my back from the tingling sensation. Without warning, he scooped me off my feet, and I was wrapped like a cocoon inside his wings. I could tell we were floating off the ground. I traced my hands along his face to memorize every turn and every angle. "Can I ask you a question?"

"I was waiting for you to ask me that," he laughed.

"How did you make Alexa Rose float? And I heard your voice the day of Gamma's funeral. How did you do that?"

"I reached out to Margaret when I was away. She taught me how to make people float, and how to transfer my thoughts to you on the day of your grandmother's funeral," he said excitedly. "I'm not good at it. And it takes a great deal of energy, but with practice, I can do better."

"Can all angels learn special skills like that?"

"No, I'm the unlucky one who has the ability to learn. It's what makes me different from the other alkins, besides my wings and the fact that my father is, or was, one of the Twelve," he said humbly.

"Unlucky?" I asked, remembering when Aden said he would have taught Michael everything he knew.

"It's the only reason why Aden was interested in me," he said with shame written all over his face.

"I'm so sorry, Michael," I said, feeling so much compassion for him. "I think you have a wonderful gift, and you can use it to do good things."

He let out a huge smile, "For you, I will learn to do anything."

I didn't know what to say; instead, I placed my hands on his cheeks and asked him another question. "Do you wish to be human still?"

"No."

"I don't understand. I thought you wanted to be human. When did this all change?"

"After I became your guardian angel, I never wanted to leave your sight. I wanted to protect you and keep you safe. If I were a mere human, I couldn't do that. I found my purpose." He paused, setting his eyes deeply into mine. "If I had to die to save you, I would. I would do it in a heartbeat. Life isn't worth living, unless you have someone worth dying for."

I knew what he meant. "I would do the same for you," I said as I traced the outline of his lips with my finger.

"I know you would. But if you died and I lived, I might as well be dead. You are my breath of life. Without you, there is no purpose. You are my reason. I need you for my life to make sense."

"I need you too."

"But I need you more," he said softly.

I closed my eyes, letting his words sink in, and repeating them inside my head.

"What are you thinking?" he asked.

"Just that I can't believe you're here. I can't believe you're real." I ran my hands along his face, memorizing every curve, every line, every crinkle when he smiled, knowing that we would be apart again. "Where will I be when I wake up?" I already knew the answer to my question, but I asked anyway.

"I want to be able to tell you that you'll still be here with me, but I have to go soon. You'll be safe in your bed," he said, gently stroking my hair with his hands. It was a sure way of making me fall asleep. I didn't want him to, but his caress was so soothing.

I closed my eyes, spellbound by his touch. Then he spoke again.

"Penny for your thoughts?" he asked.

"That's my line, and I could use all the pennies you give me. You'll go broke if you want to know what's on my mind."

He chuckled. "That many? Ask away. We've got all night."

"When did you first start to have feelings for me?" I asked shyly.

"When you first looked at me with those eyes that said I want you."

Flushed with redness, I asked, "That obvious?"

"It's when you first looked at me, speechless, and fought back with your words. You looked so cute when you were mad at me. And when you smile, it makes me absolutely crazy for you."

"Then why were you so mean, rude, obnoxious, arrogant, and—"

He interrupted before I could finish. "I get the point. Let me explain. I had feelings for you before you even crossed over to Halo City. I'd already fallen for you. I had loved you…even before we met. I would wait for you to come, and it was always for a short period of time. After you crossed over, I didn't know what to do with the feelings that appeared stronger than I was, feelings I was told not to feel. They were feelings I've been suppressing for so many years. And when you came along, it was as if you had taken me over. I didn't like it. I thought that if I tried to be rude to you, the feelings would go away. But it just grew stronger every time I saw you, so I just decided to do what Phillip told me to do."

"What did he tell you to do?" I asked, overwhelmed by his words.

"Follow my heart."

I gave a huge grin. "I'm glad you did."

"I know you are," he said arrogantly with a smile. "Following my heart would be like following you. For you are the reason I want to be who I am."

My eyes peered into his beautiful eyes. It didn't matter how many times I looked into them, I got those same quivering butterflies dancing in my stomach, feeling just like the first time. And without a word, he stole a soft kiss. I closed my eyes and let him steal more. When he stopped, I opened my eyes to see his eyes gazing lovingly into mine.

"Ask me," he said. "I can tell you have more questions."

I started laughing. He was right, I did. "You know me so well."

"More than you know."

I refocused and rethought the question I wanted to ask. "Before I forget to ask, do you think that Gamma may have been wrong about me?"

"Why would you say that?"

"I don't have a single birthmark on my body."

"It's because you don't know where to look."

"I don't know where to look?" I repeated his words, remembering when he lifted his right arm to show Aden his fake birthmark.

As if he could hear my thoughts, he said, "I made a fake birthmark on my arm, so I wouldn't have to turn my back to Aden. Also, I had the advantage because he didn't know about it—what it looks like or where to find it." Then he turned me on my side and lifted the back of my hair. Lightly, he traced a small area on the back of my hairline. What was he tracing? He went up, curving around and then back down. It was the upside-down horseshoe—the omega sign. "There it is. Now we know for sure. It's small and hardly noticeable."

"Oh," I frowned. There was a part of me that was still having a difficult time accepting who I was. Michael noticed my mixed emotions. Apparently I was not good at hiding them.

"I'll be there for you. Don't worry. Don't fight what you cannot control. Fight for what you can."

He was right. Like Gamma said, I couldn't fight destiny.

He continued, "I've been here for you, haven't I?"

I nodded solemnly.

"Then we do this together, okay?" He cupped my face.

I nodded. "I love you," I whispered.

"Decorde totaliter et ex mente tota, sum presentialiter, absens in remota," he whispered back.

I had no idea what it meant. "Say it in simple language," I said, remembering the time when he had been rude to me. He had spoken his first Latin words to me, and then told me that he would say it in simple language.

He looked at me in surprise and started to laugh hard. "You remember that?"

"I remember everything. Mr. Rude, Mr. Arrogant, Mr. Mean…"

"I get the point. I guess I was all that, but it was for your own good," he teased.

"No, no, no. It was for your own good," I reminded him.

"True." He nodded. "What do I get if I tell you what I said in simple language?"

"You get a kiss," I said proudly.

"Nope, not good enough."

"A long kiss?" I questioned.

"Nope, not good enough."

"My shirt?" I giggled. My eyes widened to ask if I was on the right path.

He smiled and said, "You know I could see right through it if I wanted to."

I gave him a "you wouldn't dare" look. "You promised," I said, reminding him.

He laughed softly. "Yes, you're right. Now where were we?"

"My shirt, I think."

He laughed again. "Nope."

"Okay, I give up."

"A smile."

"That's it? You just want a smile?" But I couldn't produce one, knowing that he wanted to see me smile.

"That's all it took for me to fall madly in love with you," he said sincerely.

I flushed with redness, and the joy in my heart erupted into a huge smile, no effort needed.

"There. Now it's my turn." He planted tender kisses up and down my neck and finally said, "In simple language…with all my heart and all my soul, I am with you even though I am far away."

I couldn't fight it any longer. His touch, his words, his kisses drove me absolutely wild. I pulled him closer and showed him how much I cared for him, giving him long, passionate kisses. We were lost in our own little world, just Michael and me. It was perfect.

After a while, Michael stood up. The candlelight framed his silhouette with a glowing radiance. He looked like an angel appearing out of my dream, and my heart was overflowing beyond anything I could possibly describe. He pulled out a blue blanket and a picnic basket from behind a tree. "Time to eat," he said, gently laying the blanket on the grass, and pulled out a container from inside the basket. "Compliments from Italy this time. Seafood linguini." Then he opened up the huge container.

I grinned steadily the whole time as I watched him. "My favorite," I said softly. The aroma that escaped as he opened the container made my stomach ache with hunger. He laid out everything in front of us and set the place for two instead of one. He must have seen the look on my face. "I'm eating with you this time. Can't have my date eating by herself." He winked and sat across from me.

"I would love that. Thank you for everything," I said, gazing deeply into his eyes, hoping he would know how grateful I felt.

"I wouldn't have it any other way. Don't worry. You'll make it up to me." His brow lifted, giving me a flirty smile.

After dinner, we lay side by side on the blanket and fed each other strawberries. I didn't know what time it was, but I knew it was late. Not only was I getting tired, but the lights that shone millions of miles above us were clear evidence. I hadn't noticed the stars until now. In Michael's presence it was hard to focus on anything but him.

Looking at the stars reminded me of my friend, Claudia, my real mom, Sofia, and especially Gamma. I thought about how Gamma touched my life. My Gamma was an Earth angel. I was one of the few lucky ones who had been blessed to have known and be loved by her. My Gamma was up there looking down on me, I thought, as I searched for the brightest star. Then I turned to Michael, "Beautiful, isn't it?"

"Yes, they are. But I'd rather stare at you." He turned toward me, gently stroked my hair and slowly traced his fingers up and down my side. "It's getting late."

"No," I said, not wanting tonight to end. "Can you freeze time so we can stay like this forever?" I asked, with my eyes closed.

"I wish I could. I'm just your guardian angel, not God."

"Some guardian angel," I joked.

"Hey…," he said and scooped me closer to him.

I rested my head against his chest, breathed him in and listened to his heart beat. I tried to hold on to every part of this moment, not knowing when I would see him again.

His supple wings gave me warmth and comfort. It was extremely difficult to stay awake. Before I fell asleep, I needed to tell him once more. "I love you as high as the sky and as deep as the sea," thinking no words could beat the depth of my love for him.

Slowly all the senses in my body lost control as I was succumbing to sleep. Tender kisses were planted on my forehead and gentle touches on my cheeks. Before I was completely lost to darkness, I heard Michael whisper, "Multiply my love by infinity and take it to the depths of forever, and you still have only a glimpse of how I feel for you. I love you more."

I felt full, full with this feeling I could not describe, bursting with warmth in every part of my being. He always said he loved me more, but it was me who loved him more. It was the reason I felt complete.

Epilogue

Effortlessly he held Claudia close to his chest and flew. His wings were wrapped gently around her, blocking the wind from disturbing her sleep. Safe in her room was where she would be, he told her, and that was where he took her. Her long auburn hair rippled down along her face like a waterfall, as he cradled her in his arms, not wanting to let go.

Gently he laid her down, and as he pulled the blanket to tuck her in, he spotted the T-shirt he had given her to wear when they went hiking. He smiled; surprised that she had kept it.

He backed away, giving her the space she needed as she rolled onto her side. Her hand reached for something, and when it found the T-shirt, she drew it close to her, hugging it like a teddy bear. Her chest rose up and down and she let out a soft sigh of relief. Michael stood there watching, smiling, envious of his own T-shirt, wishing it was him instead. He could have easily switched positions, but he knew better. He was running out of time and would be late for a debriefing in regards to Aden's death.

He lovingly looked at her and realized how proud he was of her. This delicate half human, half angel with no powers to defend herself was strong enough to endure all that she had. She didn't ask to have the Holy Spirit's soul; it was her destiny, one she could not erase. Regardless, she was brave and accepting of this out-of-the-ordinary circumstance. How he wished he could take all the craziness away for her, but then, he would not be a part of her life. Undeniably, he needed her. He wanted her in ways he knew he couldn't; it was forbidden, but he couldn't control the human emotions he felt for her. He loved her too much, and it didn't matter if he would be punished for loving her. Knowing her was all that mattered to him.

"Dream of me," he whispered into her ear, and then kissed her cheek, barely touching her skin so he wouldn't disturb her.

Standing up, he took a step back and watched her sleep. He took in a long deep breath, let out a heavy sigh, and as always, felt tormented and empty knowing he had to leave her. As he turned his back toward her, he noticed the silver moonlight seeping through the cracks of the half-drawn blinds. She had called him Superman once, but she had no idea of the powers he possessed.

He was always worried about what she would think when he did things that weren't normal by human standards. As he reminisced about the things she said to him, he chuckled lightly to himself. She was everything to him. To him, she was his guardian angel. With these thoughts in mind, he faced her, memorizing her face one more time, as his back made contact with the wall.

"Te Amo," he said in Latin. He slowly opened up his wings and disappeared. Out in the crisp, cool air, the beating of his wings was too soft for human ears to hear. He flew upward and then disappeared before he could blink. The light was his guide as he traveled through a tunnel of different hues. Soon after, the light faded and he stepped onto the dirt road where he had first seen Claudia. But this time he was on the other side. He was about to enter, crossing over to Halo City, when Davin stepped out.

"Hey," Davin said.

Michael returned the greeting with a smile.

"You okay?" Davin asked.

"I don't know. But don't worry, I can figure it out myself," Michael grumbled as he kicked a pebble far into the clearing.

"Let me help you, Michael," Davin said sincerely.

"No! I mean…" His tone of voice was softer. "I can't ask you to lie for me."

Davin started laughing lightly. "What do you think we've been doing? We're keeping your secret a secret."

Michael nodded, realizing what he had allowed his friends to do, and it broke his heart. "I'm sorry," Michael apologized, unable to look Davin in the eye.

"No need to apologize. Don't feel bad, Michael, you would have done the same for me if the roles were reversed. Anyway, she's quite adorable...funny...nice." Davin's brows arched thinking of other words to say.

Suddenly Caleb and Vivian stepped out.

"Were you eavesdropping?" Michael asked.

"Yeah, something I learned from Davin," Caleb teased.

"Hey! Sometimes I do," Davin said with a sly smile. "Not all the time."

"Did you clean up the lights and the candles for me?" Michael asked Caleb.

"Yes, but seriously, you needed all those lights and candles?"

Michael chuckled. "Sorry, but yes. It wouldn't have had the same effect without them. Anyway, thank you for taking care of it for me."

"Anytime. They don't call me the sweeper for nothing," Caleb said lightly.

"Claudia, is she okay?" Vivian asked changing the subject.

"Yes. Safe for now, but I'm afraid there may be more fallen, demons, and who knows what after her," Michael replied.

"What are you going to say at the meeting?" Vivian asked. "If I tell them the truth, I may never see her again. She would be safe, and our world would be safe, but who is to say there aren't any more like her?" Michael said, torn and confused.

"Whatever you decide, we will be on your side," Davin reassured him.

"I know, but I'm asking too much from all of you," Michael replied.

"Don't worry about us," Caleb said, surprising Michael with his words.

"I appreciate your honesty. We better get going," Michael said hesitantly, not wanting to cross over to Halo City. He was torn between what he wanted and the right thing for a guardian angel to do. Could he give up Claudia? It was the right thing to do, but he would feel like he had betrayed her. In the end, he had to do what was best for her.

"After you," Davin said to Michael, waiting for him to open the field and cross over.

As Michael parted the field, they walked through one after the other. Before closing the field, Michael took one last look to where Claudia had stood the last time he had seen her there all grown up. He never expected her to ever cross over, nor did he expect to fall so completely in love with her. He couldn't help the way he felt. It was so natural and easy because of the way she made him feel, the way she made him laugh, the way his heart felt full when she was around. His thoughts were quickly interrupted by the sound of his name.

"Right behind you," Michael said. "Let's get this over with," he muttered under his breath.

Michael, Davin, Vivian, and Caleb entered the meeting room. Phillip, Margaret, and Agnes were already seated along with the two other alkin officers, Ruth and Paul. After they exchanged greetings, they found their seats at the round table. It was silent until Phillip spoke.

"Michael, why don't you start by debriefing us about Aden's death? And then we will ask questions if needed."

"Yes," Michael said, clearing his throat. His words had to be precise and clear, to the point. He couldn't lead Phillip to think he might not be telling the truth, for Claudia's sake or for his own. "To make a long story short, Aden thought Claudia had the soul of the Holy Spirit."

There was a hushed commotion among them, until Margaret cleared her throat and spoke. "That cannot be. All of Isaiah's descendants are with the Royal Council. We do not make mistakes," she said proudly.

Michael continued. "I think Aden was so caught up with revenge that after Claudia entered our world, he thought she had the soul of the Holy Spirit. He first sent Julia, and since Julia couldn't help him, he gathered the fallen. Not only that, he killed Lucy Reed, one of the Earth angels. So we had no choice but to take his life when he tried to take ours."

"It must have been difficult for you," Margaret consoled. "Even though he was lost in his ways, you did care for him a great deal once."

"Yes, but I had to do it to keep us safe. I only feel bad that I had to kill our own, someone who was once my superior," Michael replied.

"Then Claudia is safe?" Phillip asked.

"For now. But I'm afraid that the other fallen or the demons may be after her," Michael said carefully.

"Demons?" Phillip raised his voice. "What do you mean?"

"Somehow the demons escaped by Aden's doing. We were not successful at eliminating all of them. I don't know how he got them out," Michael said, thinking of Alexa Rose. He couldn't let her take this fall. He could blame it on Aden. "I'm afraid that there may be fallen and demons seeking revenge for Aden's death. She may still be in grave danger."

"Maybe you're right," Phillip said. "But what puzzles me is what possessed Aden to think that she had the soul of the Holy Spirit, besides her crossing over? He must have other explanations. Do we need to investigate this further? Do I need to bring this up with the Royal Council?"

"I think revenge was all that was on Aden's mind," Michael answered.

"I see," Phillip said. "Let me know if you need more assistance. If you are outnumbered by too many fallen and demons, you need to let us know. We may have to take matters into our own hands. When this is all over, we need to erase Claudia's memory of all this so she may go back to her normal life."

"Yes," Michael said. Whether or not he would follow Phillip's order, the decision would be made when the time came.

"Is there anything else you need to tell me?" Phillip asked.

"No," Michael replied. "I've told you everything I know."

"Very well. This meeting is adjourned. We are sad to see one of our brothers leave our world without a soul. It will be as if he never existed, but you had to do what was in the best interest for all. I know how hard it must have been for all of you. Be safe. Hopefully this will be the end of it."

They all stood up. As soon as they left, Davin grinned hugely. "Glad that was short."

Michael felt relieved beyond words. The tension in his muscles relaxed, and his heart beat steadily now. He knew this was the right thing to do. He felt it in every part of him. But he had withheld information, and for this, guilt set in. The Royal Council didn't know, so he too, would pretend he didn't know that Claudia had the soul of the Holy Spirit.

"Do you think Phillip was convinced?" Davin asked Michael.

"I hope so," Michael replied, hoping he had said enough to satisfy Phillip and the others.

"Speaking of unprotected, Claudia doesn't have any powers," Davin reminded them. "Are you sure she has the soul of the Holy Spirit?"

"Yes," Michael said. "I saw her birthmark, and Gamma wouldn't have protected her the way she did if she wasn't sure."

"But she can't do anything," Caleb said quickly.

Michael shot him a "don't say anything negative about her" look.

"I meant, she doesn't have any powers like us."

"I don't know. We'll have to wait and see. Her powers will come when she is ready. Don't discuss this with her. She's gone through enough. She doesn't need to worry about not having powers."

"When do we get to see Claudia?" Vivian asked.

"She needs some time to grieve. She needs some time to be with her mom, her friends, and to leave all this behind her. We'll give her some space for now. I'll let you know when the time is right," Michael said. "I need to check up on Alexa Rose."

"As you wish," Davin said. "We'll go with you."

They headed out the door side by side. Their friendship was not just bonded by who they were, but also by having the need to protect Claudia. In their eyes, Claudia was just human because she had no powers to defend herself. Until her powers emerged, whatever they might be, she was still vulnerable. She was also a friend they had grown fond of. After all, they could relate; she was half human and half angel.

Peeks to the next book

I closed my eyes and took in deep breaths. It was so peaceful just doing nothing and relaxing in the tub. All I wanted to do was think of nothing. Suddenly…

I reached my right hand for it, catching it before it fell. I felt a tingling sensation on my hand that I had never felt before…

He wrapped his muscular arms around me. I smiled, thinking it was Michael. "It's okay. It's me," he said quickly. It wasn't Michael. It was…

"But before I go," he said, cupping my cheeks, "One to remember me by, until we meet again." His lips were warm and soft. They molded perfectly with mine. I could tell he wanted more. His kisses ran down my neck. As he tugged my nightgown, he slowly…

Mary Ting resides in Southern California with her husband and two children. She enjoys oil painting and making jewelry. Writing Crossroads was a way to grieve the death of her beloved grandmother. It was inspired by a dream she once had as a young girl.

Visit her website www.marytingcrossroads.com

Facebook. http://www.facebook.com/CrossroadsBook

Twitter maryting

Follow Mary on Goodreads.

CPSIA information can be obtained at www.ICGtesting.com
Printed in the USA
270262BV00016B/1/P

9 781937 085759